Purchase
Multnomah County Library
Title Wave Used Bookstore
216 NE Knott St. Portland, OR
503-988-5021

D0056408

More Praise for *The Rabbit Back Literature Society*

"Were you hooked on *Twin Peaks*? A secret fan of *Northern Exposure*? Obsessed with *Fargo* (the movie, not the TV series, naturally)? Then *The Rabbit Back Literature Society* has got your name written all over it."   —*Harper's Bazaar* (UK)

"An exquisite balance of suspense, precision-engineered structure, and darkly playful humour . . . fascinating. And fun."
—*SFX* (UK)

"Charming and intriguing, switching from playful to creepy to heartfelt and back again . . . Good fun."   —*The Bookbag* (UK)

"A novel about big questions . . . wonderful characters . . . Amazing."   —*TQR Stories* (UK)

"Sly wit also characterizes *The Rabbit Back Literature Society*, a genre-defying Finnish novel."   —*Metro* (UK)

"Charming, chilling, and gripping from its very first page."
—*Bizarre* (UK)

THE
RABBIT BACK
LITERATURE
SOCIETY

PASI ILMARI JÄÄSKELÄINEN

THE
RABBIT BACK
LITERATURE
SOCIETY

Translated from the Finnish by
Lola M. Rogers

THOMAS DUNNE BOOKS
St. Martin's Press
New York

This is a work of fiction. All of the characters, organizations, and events portrayed in this novel are either products of the author's imagination or are used fictitiously.

THOMAS DUNNE BOOKS.
An imprint of St. Martin's Press.

THE RABBIT BACK LITERATURE SOCIETY. Original text copyright © 2006 by Pasi Ilmari Jääskeläinen. English translation copyright © 2013 by Lola M. Rogers. All rights reserved. Printed in the United States of America. For information, address St. Martin's Press, 175 Fifth Avenue, New York, N.Y. 10010.

www.thomasdunnebooks.com
www.stmartins.com

Library of Congress Cataloging-in-Publication Data

Jääskeläinen, Pasi Ilmari.
    [Lumikko ja yhdeksän muuta. English]
    The Rabbit Back Literature Society / Pasi Ilmari Jääskeläinen ; translated from the Finnish by Lola M. Rogers. — First U.S. edition.
        p. cm.
    ISBN 978-1-250-06192-8 (hardcover)
    ISBN 978-1-4668-6798-7 (e-book)
    1. Authors—Societies, etc.—Fiction. 2. Fantasy fiction. I. Rogers, Lola, translator. II. Title.
    PH356.J328L8613 2015
    894'.54134—dc23

                                                                    2014032370

St. Martin's Press books may be purchased for educational, business, or promotional use. For information on bulk purchases, please contact the Macmillan Corporate and Premium Sales Department at 1-800-221-7945, extension 5442, or write to specialmarkets@macmillan.com.

First published in Finland under the title *Lumikko ja yhdeksän muuta* by Atena Kustannus, a division of Atena Publishing Ltd

Previously published in Great Britain by Pushkin Press

First U.S. Edition: January 2015

10 9 8 7 6 5 4 3 2 1

THE
RABBIT BACK
LITERATURE
SOCIETY

PART ONE

1

THE READER was at first surprised, then shocked, as the criminal Raskolnikov was abruptly slain in the middle of the street, right before her eyes. Sonya, the hooker with the heart of gold, shot him through the heart. It happened midway through an essay on the Dostoevsky classic.

The reader's name was Ella Amanda Milana. She was twenty-six years old and the possessor of a pair of beautifully curving lips and a pair of defective ovaries, among other parts.

The assessment of her lips had been given to her that same Thursday, five minutes before the end of the lunch hour, by the biology teacher. She'd been told about the faulty ovary by a doctor fourteen months earlier. She'd left the doctor's office a woman with something cold and defective at her core, though the day outside was still warm and sunny.

Three months after the diagnosis and a couple of days after Ella's engagement was broken off, events had taken a turn for the better.

She'd made a mental inventory.

First off, she had good lips. Her fingers were said to be delicate and beautiful. Her face couldn't be called beautiful, as she had sometimes been reminded, but it was a pleasant face, sensitive, even appealing. She could see that for herself in the mirror. And a lover had once detected something artistic in the colour of her nipples—he'd gone at once to gather up his oil paints from somewhere in his apartment

9

and mixed the pigments for three hours before he'd got the hue just right.

Ella Amanda Milana stared at the page of notebook paper.

There were thirty-seven high school students sitting in front of her whose essays she was supposed to correct, and she was thinking about the colour of her nipples. The unexpected literary murder had taken away her focus. She could no longer maintain her abstract role as reader—not today, not in this class.

She looked up from the essay as if she'd seen a bug crawling across it and looked at the class, but the class didn't look back. The students were writing, bent over their papers, pens scratching like busy little rodents.

The essay was written by the boy sitting in the third row near the windows.

Ella was a touch offended, but she couldn't be angry with him. She wondered if a substitute teacher was expected to take such attempts at cheating seriously.

She had been a little bit angry for a long time, and she was angry now, but not at the boy. She was angry at her ovaries. The boy's literature essay was a temporary side issue. Her ovaries, on the other hand, were attached to her permanently, and she to them. She would have preferred them not to be a part of what made up the person known as Ella Amanda Milana, who was sitting in front of that class holding the spurious essay in her hands.

When she had introduced the classics list to the students, she'd claimed that she had read *Crime and Punishment* for the first time in high school and again in college.

She realized now that she had been thinking of a different book.

She had never read Dostoevsky's famous work in its entirety. She'd read the first twenty pages in high school, and got up to page fifty-two in college, but she hadn't finished it. Someone had borrowed it from her and then sold it at the used book store.

Nevertheless, she was reasonably sure that Sonya, the hooker with the heart of gold, had not shot Raskolnikov in the heart at the end of the novel. And she would be willing to bet that Raskolnikov, contrary to what the essay claimed, had not killed the old woman who ran the pawn shop by strangling her with a piano wire. She'd been to lectures on Dostoevsky at the university and she'd seen the movie and the television show, so she did know something about the book, even if her own copy had gone to the used book store four years ago.

She ended the class and called the boy out from the flood of students. She made a sarcastic reference to his reading skills, and his morals.

He fished the book out of his bag and handed it to her.

"Check it yourself, ma'am," he said. "That's how the story goes."

Ella let him leave, since he clearly had no desire to discuss it with her. She would deal with the matter later.

After she'd looked at the book for a moment, her cheeks began to burn. On the next to last page of the novel, Sonya shot two bullets into Raskolnikov's heart. And at the beginning of the book, Raskolnikov really did strangle the pawn broker with a piece of piano wire.

Ella dug her cell phone out of her bag and called her literature professor.

She'd written her thesis on the mythological aspects of Laura White's books for children. Professor Eljas Korpimäki had been her advisor, and had made no attempt to hide his pleasure: "An excellent choice. If you're interested in further study of the subject, get in touch with me and I'll see what I can do. There's a lot to investigate in White's work, and even I haven't managed to take a look at all of her output."

"Hello," the professor said. "Korpimäki here."

Ella identified herself and immediately asked him, breathing hard, "Does Sonya shoot Raskolnikov at the end?"

Her professor laughed.

Ella realized how peculiar her question sounded.

"Are you in literature class right now? You're in Joensuu, right?"

"That was just a four-month stint," she said with practised nonchalance. She tried to sound a bit more rational than she had a moment earlier. "I'm in Rabbit Back now. At the high school. And I just wanted to confirm this as fast as possible, since students will be students, and I've never... I mean, I don't have the book in my hands at the moment, and I can't seem to recall exactly how the story goes, but I need to check this plot point."

"I understand," the professor said. "Nobody shoots Raskolnikov, least of all Sonya."

Ella stared at the book in her hands for a moment and then said, "What if I were to insist that I've seen a version of *Crime and Punishment* where Raskolnikov gets shot? Sonya shoots him because she believes the world would be a better place without him."

The professor didn't say anything.

Ella knew she was sounding irrational again. Whenever she spoke with certain people, of whom the professor was just one, she lost her usual firm feeling of control. At the university she and a friend had developed a two-part theory to explain the phenomenon.

According to the first part of the theory, she became nervous in the presence of strangers if she sensed that they had a genuine interest in her and her ideas. But she rarely got nervous, although she interacted with numerous people on a daily basis, some of whom were, in fact, attempting to form a relationship with her. This was explained by the second part of the theory, which held that all people have an inborn need to make their ideas and personality known to the world, but as a rule no one is interested in what is going on in anyone else's head.

That also explained God. People need an interested listener. They thirst for the undivided attention of someone once they've left childhood, so they invented God, someone to watch them and listen to them all the time.

"Could it be from some new, postmodern version of the book?" the professor suggested. "Are you sure it was the work by Dostoevsky? I think you must have been looking at some other book that used the same characters as in the original novel, or something like that. Hey, Ella, do you happen to remember what exact book we're talking about? I could use something like that in my Dostoevsky lectures. It sounds quite interesting. Could you maybe write a short piece on the subject? I'm editing a collection of articles, and a point of view like that would work quite well in it."

He sounded excited. Ella regretted calling him.

Dostoevsky's name was on the book, in its entirety. The title of the book seemed to be the standard—*Crime and Punishment*. It was published by Karisto in 1986, translated into Finnish by

M. Vuori, and examined for complete linguistic accuracy by Lea Pyykkö. Ella stared at the cover.

"I guess it could be some sort of new version," she said.

The Rabbit Back library was a red, three-storey fortress at the top of the hill above the school. Its main entrance was framed by two white marble columns.

The columns had been a gift to local cultural life from Mr Lindgren, the late owner of the stone works. Ella had seen a 1975 clipping about the donation of the columns in her mother's scrapbook. The newspaper article included a black and white photo, with a crane in the background and a group of locals in the foreground—quite a large crowd, including Lindgren himself, and next to him a young Laura White. It was said that Lindgren had been trying to impress the authoress. Behind Laura White stood a group of children—the Rabbit Back Literature Society, a collection of gifted children who would, with White's guidance, grow up to be writers.

Ella's grandmother, when she was alive, had referred to the library as "a lousy mausoleum that sullies the whole centre of town". She wasn't the only one who thought the building was grim, cold, and much too large. Some locals had learned to hate the place as children. The children of Rabbit Back had to walk by the library every morning panting and sweaty, since the long, steep road to the school passed the building.

Ella thought the place radiated nobility. There were oaks growing around it, which gave it a formal look, like a painting, and in the summer the twittering of birds washed among the limbs of the trees and could be heard inside the library when the windows were open.

Some way from the library there was a small wooded area, and hidden among the trees was Mother Snow's Book Café. When she was little, Ella would ride her bike there to buy ice cream on Sundays, and every time she went, she would stop at the library to try the locked doors and peek through the windows.

Ella found it difficult to stay away from papery dust of the library for any length of time. Even now, as she approached the place with the problematic Dostoevsky in her bag, she was overcome with the same veneration she'd felt as a child. She had been the kind of child you find in every library, lugging around stacks of books. Once, when she was sick in bed with pneumonia for two weeks, the librarian had called her house to ask if everything was all right. All the old ladies and gents in town used to greet her among the shelves: *Hello, Ella! Find anything good today?*

She'd read more than was healthy, hundreds of books every year. Some of them she read twice, or even three times, before returning them. Some of them she would check out again after letting them sink in a while. She'd thought at the time that books were at their best when you'd read them two or three times.

She walked between the massive pillars. She always felt a little tickle when she did it. A dog lying on the steps started awake and stared at her, then made a gruff noise and ran off. There was a sign on the door. Ella read it without stopping, opened the door, and went inside.

It was a cool, open space. She walked across the foyer towards the check-out desk through the familiar aroma of paper, dust, and old ink.

"I'd like to make a complaint," she said to the librarian, whose brown eyes looked at her through horn-rimmed glasses.

The woman at the desk wore a name tag: Ingrid Katz.

"Excuse me, but are you Ingrid Katz, the author?" Ella asked in a friendly tone.

"No, I'm Ingrid Katz, the librarian," the woman answered, just as friendly. A smoky smell wafted from her clothing. "You say you have a complaint?"

"Perhaps more of a notification," Ella said. "I recently found myself in a strange situation with one of my students. He wrote an essay which seemed to me to be a bit… questionable."

The librarian smiled. "Was it improper? They often are at that age. But it will pass. The age, and the impropriety. Luckily, everything does."

Ella took the book out of her bag. "Let me explain. It turned out that it wasn't the essay that was the problem, it was the book he was writing about. This book. *Crime and Punishment*, by Dostoevsky. It looks completely authentic, but strangely enough, it's written wrong. It's been changed. And he checked it out here. It has your stamp on it."

She slid the book across the counter. Ingrid Katz didn't seem particularly interested. She just smiled, got up from her chair, and turned around to the reference shelf behind her. The book lay on the the desk between them.

"Typographical errors sometimes happen," she said, her back to Ella. "Sometimes whole pages are missing. Or sometimes there are even superfluous pages added. After all, they're made by people, and when people make things, they always make mistakes. To err is human, and the whole history of humankind is a litany of various errors. I'm sure you've heard about the Christmas calendars."

"What Christmas calendars?"

Ingrid Katz shook her head. Her swinging hair momentarily revealed her thin, graceful neck.

"Heavens. It was quite a while ago, but it seems there was an Advent calendar, the kind that has little doors with pictures behind, and somehow the pictures were anything but Christmassy. They were downright pornographic, in fact. There was an article about it in the paper."

"I see," Ella said. "But anyway, in this book, Sonya shoots Raskolnikov. And Raskolnikov strangles the pawn broker with a piano wire. That's not how the story goes. I'm sure you're familiar with it. I was thinking that it might be some sort of censored version, but it seems to be an ordinary edition." She thought for a moment, made a restless movement, and smiled again. "It's a bit odd, I suppose, to complain about such a small matter, but I think we ought to get to the bottom of it. Where would we be if anything at all could turn up in books?"

Ingrid Katz came back to the counter and looked Ella in the eye.

"I can assure you that the book in question will not be returned to circulation. These things happen sometimes. It's not commonly spoken of, but there are quite a few pranksters working in publishing. Thank you for calling it to our attention."

"Don't mention it. Actually, I'd like to take it with me," Ella said, reaching for the book. "I know a literature professor who would like to make copies of the inaccurate passages."

Ingrid Katz's eyes flashed and she snapped up the book before Ella could get hold of it.

"That would certainly be fine, normally," she said, sliding the book under the counter, "within the restrictions of copyright, of course. But the book has been returned now, and I can't allow it to return to circulation due to these discrepancies. It's a matter of principle. We at the library must adhere to certain standards. I'm sorry, and thank you again for bringing this to our attention."

She turned back to her work behind the counter. Ella looked at her profile, her neck and the crown of her head, thought for a moment, then nodded and headed towards the reading lounge.

The reading lounge was on the third floor, along with the poetry and plays. As she climbed the stairs, Ella could see all three floors at once. There was a cove in the centre of the building that the stairs wound around in a spiral. At the highest point of the cove was a skylight made up of nine panes of glass. On sunny days it lit up the books below with a cathedral-like light, but at the moment all that peeped through were the crows and jackdaws on the roof.

The first floor held the children's books and adult literature. As Ella looked down she saw a group of statues standing in the first-floor lobby. According to the sign on the door it was the annual exhibition of the Rabbit Back Sculptors' Association, which this year was titled "From Nixies to Water Sprites—Mythic Representations from the Works of Laura White".

The second floor was non-fiction. Ella noticed that the dog book section, nearest the stairway, was marked with a yellow sign that read DOG LITERATURE. There were only a few books on the shelf.

When she got to the third floor, Ella picked up a copy of *Rabbit Tracks* from the rack and chose a table with a view of Ingrid Katz, who was still sitting behind the counter two floors below.

They called this area the reading lounge—at least there was a sign that exhorted her to PLEASE BE QUIET IN THE READING

LOUNGE. The "lounge" consisted of six worn tables next to the stair railing.

Ella leafed through *Rabbit Tracks*, glancing now and then at the librarian. According to the newspaper, the harvest in Rabbit Back was going well, and young Virmasalo, a local running hopeful, had won the silver in a national competition. There were demands for stricter dog control. The regular column by dog psychologist A. Louniala was titled "Man's Best and Oldest Friend", and was filled with care and training advice. The town council was considering a remodel of the council building. The literary supplement presented new and up-and-coming authors.

Ella knew her short story hadn't yet been printed. Perhaps later in the fall, the editor had told her. She shuddered as if someone had walked over her grave, and decided to call the editor and ask for the story back. She wasn't ready to show it in public yet after all. It had been a bad idea from the beginning; she realized that now.

There was a small news item on page four about a farmer named P. Lahtinen who had found a potato in his field shaped like Mother Snow. He had promised the unusual potato to Laura White, should she want it for her collection, and his wife had promised to make coffee and sweet rolls if the authoress came to pick it up in person.

Ella lost interest in the newspaper. The yellow sign kept drawing her attention. DOG LITERATURE, in black capital letters, every time she looked at it. Eventually she started to ask herself why she didn't leave.

She had finished all her classes for the day, but she had a large pile of papers to grade in the evening. And her mother was expecting her to bring home food and medicine. There was no way of knowing how confused her father had been that day. She had also been looking forward to a little afternoon nap.

But still she sat there, on the third floor of the library, leafing through the local paper and keeping the librarian under surveillance.

What she was doing was crazy, she understood that. On the other hand, Ingrid Katz was behaving suspiciously. She hadn't taken the discovery of the inaccuracies in the book as lightly as she had pretended. She also hadn't seemed surprised that the library might contain books with significant discrepancies in their contents.

Of course, Ella had run across a wide range of translations and outright translation errors, she'd read abridged versions of books, and books with missing pages, even one book with a missing ending. And sometimes official new versions of books were published when times changed and there was no longer a need to shelter readers from indecent language or dubious passages.

But she had never seen the very plot of a book consciously or unconsciously altered as it was in this version of *Crime and Punishment*. A prank like that would take a very unusual saboteur and it was hard to imagine what the motive would be. And how could such a book remain in circulation for nearly twenty years without anyone noticing anything strange about it?

Ella might have been behaving contrary to habit and to her own common sense that evening, but the existence of the irregular Dostoevsky deeply offended her, and when she was offended she could sometimes do impulsive, purely intuitive things.

*

The students' papers in her bag were waiting to be graded, and her mother was waiting at home for groceries and her father's medicine. People came and went.

Two hours went by. Ella Amanda Milana, substitute teacher of Finnish Language and Literature, sat in the library watching Ingrid Katz, librarian. She was starting to feel foolish, but she couldn't give up, not yet.

Finally, the librarian left her desk and walked through the crowd of stone nixies and pixies to the book stacks.

Ella shifted on her perch to see better. Ingrid Katz was standing at the D shelves piling books onto a cart. She emptied at least a metre of shelf and pushed the cart into the back room.

The back room was where the librarians went to eat lunch and change clothes. The only entrance was behind the check-out desk. The door to the room was hung with a poster of C.S. Lewis's *The Lion, the Witch and the Wardrobe*. It had a picture of the magic wardrobe with its door opened invitingly.

Ingrid Katz came out of the back room and sat at the counter for a long time. Finally she went to the second floor to help a man in a hat with something.

Ella had already left her previous position and descended to the lower level. She approached the check-out desk. She browsed the shelf of honour set aside for Laura White's books and their numerous translations.

Then she sprang into action.

She walked behind the counter, unhurried and nonchalant. She glanced around, touched her front teeth with her tongue, and slipped into the back room.

She formed a cover story in her mind in case Ingrid Katz found her there. She would say she was looking for Ingrid herself because she wanted to ask her a question and was in a hurry.

In any case, what could the librarian do to her, even if she did find her there? Kill her? Knock her unconscious?

Probably not, but she might very well call the police and file a criminal report on her.

What a hubbub that would cause. It would make headlines in *Rabbit Tracks*. SUBSTITUTE LANGUAGE AND LITERATURE TEACHER NABBED STEALING BOOKS. She would lose her reputation, and her job with it. She would have a criminal record that would follow her for the rest of her life.

Ella was getting scared. She realized now that she had better leave while she had the chance. She thanked herself for coming to her senses in time, before she'd done something really stupid.

Then she noticed the books on the table.

They were in three stacks. There was a bottle of Jaffa soda, a mandarin orange, and a bag of liquorice next to them. Ingrid Katz's lunch. Dostoevsky's *Crime and Punishment* was at the bottom of one stack. Ella's heart started to race as she picked up the book. She took five other books, too—the first few she could find that were thin enough to fit in her bag.

Her fingers were as cold as magpies' feet.

At the bottom of her bag was a comic book she'd confiscated during her morning class. Ella laid the comic over the stack of books and closed the bag.

Then she walked out of the library.

2

PAAVO EMIL MILANA was named after two historic runners: Paavo Nurmi and Emil Zápotek. When he was in his twenties he had been a runner almost comparable to his namesakes, just as his late father had wished—if not in performance, then certainly in spirit. He had the heart of a runner, as light and quick as a dragonfly.

For thirty years he had run ten kilometres every day. He would go for a run in the morning before leaving for the office and then again as soon as he finished work, even on the windy night when his daughter was born. He wore out six pairs of running shoes every year, and was given a new tracksuit every Christmas. His family fondly called him the Rabbit Back Rocket, and the custom had spread to the rest of the town.

Now, at fifty-five, Paavo Emil Milana spent his days sitting in the back garden among the grass and daisies and nettles, the currants and apple trees, the frogs, hedgehogs, bugs and butterflies. His garden season started as soon as the snow melted and didn't end until the first frost.

The change had come over the past six years.

It was no use offering him a book to read. It was no use trying to get him to go swimming, boating or visiting. He just wanted to look at the garden, to watch it grow—that's how he explained it to his wife, Marjatta, who had begun to think of herself as a widow and sometimes suffered from a terrible feeling of guilt because of it. Old age doesn't always wait till you're old, was her way of answering him.

Every day seemed to break off another little piece of Paavo Emil Milana's personality, and piece by piece he was less and less the Paavo Emil Milana she had married.

At the moment, Paavo Emil Milana was looking at his daughter over a wet pair of spectacles. "Can't a person decide for himself where he wants to sit?" he said angrily. "Have we turned communist? Is that what you're telling me? A communist country, where a man can't sit where he wants to? *Et tu?* Show me your party card. You must have it in a pocket somewhere."

Ella looked at his tense bearing. His grey, too-long hair flowed under the brim of his hat. Her mother would no doubt be tiptoeing into the garden with the scissors in her hand sometime soon. A tangle of chest hair lay under his plaid shirt.

"Anybody can sit wherever they like," Ella said. "That's your prerogative. It's just that it's raining out here."

He looked at the sky in surprise.

"And Mum says to come inside," Ella added.

Paavo Emil Milana tore his hat off his head. "If your mother says to come inside, then by all means do so. Children should obey their parents, contrary to what the Reds seem to think. Who exactly is your mother?"

"I mean she wants you to come inside."

"Aha. Are you that teacher, then? My daughter?"

Ella admitted she was, for the third time that day.

He peered at her over his glasses, a flash of bewilderment in his eyes. Then he smiled slyly. "I'll be right in. You go on ahead. I just have to listen for a moment."

"I already went on ahead twice," Ella said, "and you're still sitting here. You're not trying to trick me, are you?"

"I have some things to do here," he explained vaguely. "I won't be long. You go ahead, sweetheart."

"You're getting wet."

He looked indignant. "Wet? Let's think about the rain, shall we? Little spheres of water falling from the sky. They're harmless. Do you think that water only belongs in lakes and ponds and rivers, in pipes and bathtubs? What troubles we go to, building ourselves waterproof roofs, clothes, umbrellas, all to keep from having anything to do with water. We try so hard to separate ourselves from it."

He lifted his arms as if to embrace the rain.

"But we are made from water. You are, and so am I. Water is flowing through us all the time. The same water everywhere. Is water God? It is certainly life, at least. Life has its source in water. Just think about that."

Ella stood for a moment longer with her father in the rain as he sank back into solitary silence. They looked in the same direction for a little while.

There was a meadow on the other side of the garden fence. In the middle was a gazebo, a picturesque but dilapidated structure surrounded by thistles and nettles. A dark figure stood inside it looking out.

Years ago, a party for the whole neighbourhood had been held there. The hosts were a family who had recently moved to town and wanted to make a good impression. As was the custom in Rabbit Back, they had been showered with gifts of mythological statuary—elves, forest nymphs, gnomes, and one life-sized goblin, as big as a man, a crystallization of the artist's darkest impulses. The ecstatic party-givers had placed the statues around their house and garden, but the grim expression on the face of the goblin had so frightened their children that they had quietly carried it off to the gazebo. Ever since, it had made the gazebo a favoured place for the children of the town to test their bravery.

Now the goblin seemed to have company. Three dogs had gone under the gazebo roof to get out of the rain. Soon they, too, grew uneasy and trotted away.

Ella's father rubbed the side of his nose. Ella's gaze floated through the rain and fixed itself on her father's unshaven cheek, and the scar visible under the stubble.

The garden was the only place where her father felt at peace anymore. He was almost happy there. Soon winter would force him to sit indoors for months.

Ella fetched an umbrella, placed it in his hand, and went back into the house.

A curved stairway led to Ella's old room. The fifth and fourteenth steps squeaked when you stepped on them. Ella hadn't stepped on those steps since the age of five.

A lot of her old things had been taken out of the room. Her mother had made it into a sewing room. Ella Milana didn't remember her mother ever sewing anything but the flowered curtains that hung in the sewing room's open window, wet with rain.

Her substitute job would soon end and she would be transferred to another district. Until then, she would sit at her old writing desk and grade literature papers. Her legs didn't quite fit under the desk anymore.

There was a bag of sweets at a corner of the desktop. She

paid herself one for each graded paper. After every fifth paper she went downstairs to clear her mind. Once she'd finished all twenty-five, her work for the evening would be done. Then she would take a look at those books.

Taking a break from the grading, she glanced at the Dostoevsky, which lay on the bed, waiting. She had read through Raskolnikov's death as soon as she got home. She'd decided to save the rest for later.

She tried to forget about Dostoevsky and his companions and immerse herself in the literature assignments.

The essays blared through her consciousness with their insights, opinions, attitudes, misconstructions, confessions and justifications. Jokes, banalities and metaphors assaulted her sensibilities, and the floodgates of language standards creaked as dubious sentence structures and hyphenation errors dribbled through their cracks.

Every imperfect essay left a dent in Ella's mind. Sometimes their incorrect formulations would stick in her mind for days, swirling and blocking her thoughts. A couple of weeks earlier she had made a count and discovered that during her lifetime she would read approximately 74,148 such essays. Then she would retire, her head permanently dented by these odd sentences.

When she had only seven papers left to her evening's work, Ella stopped to admire one about the works of Agatha Christie. It struck her as above average, even exceptional. It was fresh, clear, and well organized. It wasn't about any Dostoevsky or Kundera, but for a high school student it showed some rather mature thinking.

She gave the essay a perfect ten and drew a little parrot next to the number.

Then she started to wonder if she should submit the paper for the Laura White file. The principal had made it very clear that all work earning a perfect ten should be copied for Laura White's file. But he had also urged caution in awarding perfect tens.

We enjoy a long and glorious tradition in our writing, so declaring a student's linguistic creation perfect should not be taken lightly. As a young teacher, Ella, you would be wise to keep in mind that a text can be very good without being commendable, and that even a commendable text is not the same thing as an exceptional one. It's terribly kind of Ms White to take notice of our school in her search for the new members she desires, and we should under no circumstances inflict any mediocrity on her.

The Laura White file was a brown leather portfolio that was kept behind the principal's desk. Ella had heard that Laura White sometimes appeared at the school, drank coffee with the principal in the school office, and took the papers from the file with her to read. She wanted to see the work of any good new writers in order to consider them for membership in the Rabbit Back Literature Society.

But the Society hadn't accepted any new members in three decades.

Ella read the Agatha Christie essay again, saw a hint of mediocrity in it, and wrote a minus after the ten.

Later that evening Ella was looking out her bedroom window and saw her mother leading her reluctant husband away from the garden. The wind was increasing, the stalks of grass and the limbs of the trees bending towards the glistening, wet earth.

"Library police. Good evening," a voice said behind her.

Ella spun around.

Ingrid Katz, librarian, gestured towards the books lying on the bed and smiled.

"I just came to tell you that you forgot to fill out an official check-out form for those books. And all of them are, unfortunately, out of circulation. So I can't loan them out anymore. It's odd that they should have ended up being taken out. I thought I had taken them off the shelves. But it's so easy to make mistakes, isn't it?"

Ingrid Katz was standing in the middle of the floor in her socks with her head at a questioning tilt. Ella swallowed her excuse. She felt belligerent.

She managed to sound like the injured party as she asked how it was that the Rabbit Back library had happened to collect such a large number of defective works of literature.

Ella had spent half an hour looking through the books she'd stolen. There were many books in the pile that were unknown to her, so she couldn't tell if they had any errors in them. But two of them were books she knew well, and she had found flagrant, bizarre, scandalous errors in them that would have had to be the work of an entire conspiracy of rogue printers.

Mersault, the main character in Albert Camus's *The Stranger*, wasn't convicted of murder, as he was in the official version of the novel. Instead, Josef K. broke into the prison, helped Mersault escape, and remained behind in his place. And while Aslan, the lion god in C.S. Lewis's Narnia, had sacrificed himself for the human children, this Aslan made short work of the White Witch by taking her head between his teeth.

"This is ridiculous," Ella said. "How in the world can something like this happen and not be in all the papers!"

Ingrid Katz shrugged.

"These things happen sometimes. What else can I say? There's nothing in it to make a splash in the tabloids. Literature doesn't interest a large audience. These are almost all old books. Somebody working at a printer's just decided to have a little joke at the reader's expense and did it to amuse himself."

Ingrid paused for a moment and leaned down to pick the books up from the bed.

"Well," she said. "I guess I'll take these with me. I understand that you're interested in them, and they would no doubt be collector's items on the open market, but I'm sure you understand that I can't let anyone have them."

"Why not?"

"Oh, no. It's against the rules. Any faulty copies must be destroyed."

"There must be a lot of these pranksters at the printing houses," Ella said. "All of these books were printed in different places. I checked. Unless there's one malicious individual moving from one printer to the next."

Ingrid Katz thought for a moment.

"Yes. It could be a conspiracy of printers' employees, or one individual saboteur. In any case, it's my job as a librarian to remove the offending copies from circulation. And I hope you won't talk about this in public. I really wouldn't want book collectors to descend on our libraries and try to steal these irregular books. I'm sure you understand."

Ella didn't say anything.

"What I mean to say," Ingrid continued patiently, "is that if you can keep quiet about this, I won't go blabbing about your behaviour today. I may not actually be the library police, but stealing books is indeed stealing, and it might be of as much interest to the authorities as the theft of an outboard motor, were they to hear of it."

There was a moment of silence. The librarian's threat was embarrassing to both of them.

"Were they to hear of it. Nice use of the subjunctive," Ella said drily.

"It is, isn't it?" Ingrid said.

They smiled at each other, ever so slightly charmed. Then the librarian went down the stairs with Ella behind her, pulled on her shoes, stepped out the door, and opened her umbrella, which was waiting on the porch.

Ella noticed her mother walking around in the garden, bent double. She looked up and waved. "He lost his glasses. Apparently the garden gnomes took them. Now I'm stuck looking for the silly things."

"I'd stay and help," Ingrid Katz said, "but I have to go and close up the library. We close at seven, and the new intern is there by herself."

She walked to her bicycle, put the pile of books on the rack, and pedalled away, one hand holding the umbrella, which the wind tried to wrest away from her.

Ella looked up Ingrid Katz when she got back to her room. The librarian and the author were the same person.

It made her smile.

She contented herself with Ingrid's explanation for the irregular books. Later she came to realize that under one reality there's always another. And another one under that.

3

Ella was watching her mother look at old slides. The hum of the projector filled the living room. It smelled like old times. Colour photos of a happy family glowed on the white wall.

Click. A mother, young and thin, smiling shyly. *Click.* A father posing as a runner with a false French moustache under his nose and a little girl clinging to his leg. *Click.* The father with his arm around the mother, who looks small and happy. *Click.* The mother standing in the garden naked, young, the father spraying her with the hose. *Click.* The little girl sitting in the garden swing with a book in her hands, *click*, in the hammock, *click*, in a boat. The backgrounds changed, but the book remained. The lawns were pristine, no bugs creeping through them, the sky a deep blue, and although there were red sunsets, night never came.

Ella sat in the corner with her chin on her knees and tried to send her mind back to the living, original memories behind the slides. She breathed in the scent of the projector and tried to follow its trail to the traces of memory in her mind.

She remembered the smell of the grass when she lay on the lawn reading a book of fairy tales. She went back in her mind to how her father's sweat smelled when he would sit down next to her on the sofa after a long run. She also found the scent of coffee and fresh cardamom rolls on Sunday afternoons, and the smell of the blue salve her mother spread on her back and chest when she was achy.

Ella Milana followed her memories as closely as she could. She tried to build these scents into a three-dimensional image around her and make it move. She pounded on her memory like a coffee machine on the blink, but her past returned only in small fragments. If all of her remembered images from birth to confirmation were laid end to end, they would have formed at most a short film of ten minutes, grainy, fuzzy and confused.

Ella couldn't remember things that she knew about on her own. She had memories of memories, or of things she'd been told.

Her dwindling memories were copies of the originals, copies that she regularly made new copies from, blurrier than the previous ones, fading to invisibility. Maybe she herself was blurry, a partially altered copy of the Ella Amanda she had been yesterday.

She had always trusted that she would have some kind of past she could return to, re-examine. But lately her mother grew nervous whenever Ella tried to ask her about the good old days. Her mother didn't want to waste her time dwelling on the past. All she was interested in were television shows and entering raffle drawings in the hope of winning a prize. It was no use asking her father about anything. Disease had nibbled Paavo Emil Milana's memories to pieces.

It was horrible, the swathe decay could cut through a person's memory. Swallowing up even the present moment. It was absolutely unbearable.

Paavo Emil Milana's glasses were found in the end. The frames were broken into four pieces lying in different parts of the garden.

The left lens was in the potato patch, the right one in the middle of the rose bushes. There were deep scratches on the left one.

"Paavo, honey, do you know how expensive glasses are? And you break your only pair and toss them around like a little child."

Paavo Milana squinted at his wife.

"I didn't break anything. The damned gnomes ambushed me. They didn't like me looking at them."

Marjatta Milana looked at her daughter.

"Old age doesn't always wait till you're old," she said, stroking her husband's hair. "Your hair needs a cut. It's as ratty as a forest troll's. People would hardly know you were a person if I didn't look after you."

When Ella Milana, substitute language and literature teacher, finished the last lesson of the day, one of the boys came up to her with a briefcase in his hand.

"May I have my comic book back?" he asked. When he saw the expression on her face he thought it best to swear that he would never bring a comic book to school again.

Ella dug through her bag and handed him the comic. He thanked him and started to leave, but then didn't.

"Well, what is it?" Ella asked impatiently. "It may be a little torn, since it's been lying in my bag for two weeks, but nobody told you to read it during the lesson."

The boy shook his head. "Yeah, but... it's not that. This isn't my comic."

Ella raised her eyebrows.

"Of course it is. I'm a literature teacher. I don't carry comic books around in my bag. I have placed exactly one comic book in this bag in my entire life—the one I confiscated from you."

The boy flipped through the comic book's pages with his brow furrowed, then tossed it on the desk and pushed his hair back. "Interesting comic, but it's not mine."

Ella sighed.

"Well then you've caught me. I admit it. That comic is part of the secret comics stash that I carry with me at all times. Forgive me. I'll give back your comic as soon as I can find it among my comics collection."

She stared at the boy until he gave up and left the classroom. Once he had left, Ella put the comic back in her bag. As she turned her phone back on she noticed that she had two messages.

The first was from Ingrid Katz. She said that Laura White had seen Ella's short story in the *Rabbit Tracks* literary supplement and liked it. Ingrid also added, in a peculiar tone, that she needed to meet with Ella sometime soon to talk to her about an important matter.

The other message was from Ella's mother and was more howled than spoken.

Ella's father had been taken to the hospital in an ambulance after some sort of accident in the garden. "Call me as soon as you get this message," her mother's keening voice pleaded. Then, remembering her phone manners, she added, "Thanks. I'll talk to you later."

4

PAAVO EMIL MILANA WAS IN Room 4 of the overnight ward. He was covered in cuts, scratches, scrapes and bruises. Ella and Marjatta Milana sat next to his bed. There were old people in the other three beds, staring at the ceiling, their mouths black holes.

He'll live, the doctor had assured them. He hadn't lost as much blood as they'd thought when he arrived, and his abrasions looked worse than they were. The old fellow had been quite confused when they brought him in, there was no denying that. They still didn't have a cure for Alzheimer's, at least not here at the health clinic, heh, and whatever shock he'd had would pass sooner or later. He might eventually be able to tell them what happened, or then again he might not. That was how it was. Sometimes you just had to accept that you would never know for sure—it could be one thing, could be another. But the sedative they'd given him ought to let him sleep through his injuries for a few hours.

The doctor said he didn't want to speculate about the nature of his injuries, but he speculated anyway.

His wounds seemed to be partly gashes and partly animal bites. They could very well be self-inflicted. He could have hurt himself with sticks or stones. Maybe he had stumbled in the garden and panicked and hurt himself on the sticks and thorns. Did he, by chance, have any suicidal tendencies? A garden is a lovely thing, but it's also full of sharp sticks. It was possible, too, that some small animal, a rat perhaps, had attacked him. In any case, he'd been given a tetanus shot.

"I don't know what happened," Marjatta Milana told her daughter. "I was washing the dishes. I had just been cutting out *Reader's Digest* car sweepstakes coupons and your father had been sitting in the garden all morning. Then I had the idea to go out and cut his hair at last, make him look a little more human. I fetched the scissors and went outside, but he wasn't in his chair.

"I was afraid that he might have got lost in the woods, although he's always stayed in the garden before. I had sometimes wondered if he might take it into his head to go into the park and through there into the big woods, which go on for who knows how far. I was about to call the emergency number, and then I heard a voice from the raspberry patch. And there he was, covered in blood. Oh my Lord, my heart just leaped from my chest. I was afraid I'd have some kind of attack and both of us would be left lying there in the garden to rot.

"But he was still alive. He was lying in the bushes on his back and making this weak sound. I said, 'Don't worry, Paavo, help is coming,' and then I ran inside and called the emergency number and then I guess I called you... I don't remember what I did... and your sister, too—I'm embarrassed to say it, but I think I did call her, sputtered something..."

Ella thought her mother was going to start sniffling, but she just cast a weary glance at her husband.

"This is all just too much somehow. And the kitchen's such a mess. The dishes just left to lie there... oh blast, I think I must have ruined my new porridge pan. I left it on the stove. If you could manage it at all, could you go to the house and clean up

37

a little? There's no reason we both have to stay here, and I'm sure you have your work to do."

Ella had been scrubbing the pan for an hour and a half when her mother called. Ella's father had woken up and recognized her, but he wasn't saying anything sensible. "What am I going to do with him?" her mother sighed.

Ella wondered whether her mother wanted some kind of blessing from her to send him to a nursing home.

"Keep trying," she said.

After several nights spent thinking about her father's case, she had developed a theory that the problem was a mathematical rather than a moral one. It wasn't right to drive your own husband or father from his home and put him in an institution unless it happened to be unavoidable. As time went on, however, the individual by the name of Paavo Emil Milana was less and less the Paavo Emil Milana that she and her mother knew, and more and more some other person that Ella wasn't particularly eager to get to know. Once her father's share dropped below a certain percentage, it would, according to Ella's theory, be time for him to part with the rest of the family and move away.

It was already late in the evening. Light poured in through the west window and filled the room with the reddish brown colour of the curtains. Ella left the pan to soak and spread the local newspaper on the kitchen table.

Next to the paper sat a clay gnome that Ella glanced at now and then. Her mother had made it in the art club a couple of years earlier.

The sculpture wasn't bad, but when you looked at it up close and turned it in the light, you could see its features in detail. At first Ella had found it hard to believe that it had been made by her mother, a woman who, like most people, normally made mashed potatoes, socks and lingonberry jam, not art.

The local ceramicists for the most part produced water sprites, pixies, elves, and gnomes. Laura White had made these creatures popular all over the world through her children's books, but in Rabbit Back in particular you ran into them everywhere you looked. They were presented as prizes in raffles, given as presents, brought to dinner as hostess gifts. There was only one florist in Rabbit Back, but there were seven shops that sold mostly mythological figurines.

Ella thought the statues were tasteless and depressing. She had asked her mother what had possessed her to go to the art club and why her first and last project there would have been a gnome, of all things. Her mother had said something about how the idea had just popped into her head in the garden while she was digging the carrot bed.

She'd had her hands in the dirt up to the wrists and had gradually found herself falling into a kind of stupor. She completely forgot what she was doing and noticed that she was thinking about a gnome. She started to feel faint and dizzy, and had some difficulty getting back to the house to lie down.

"It made me worry that I was going to turn out like your father," she said. "That there was something wrong with my head. Some brain malfunction. That gnome stayed in my mind, haunting me, and I had to get it out somehow. So I thought I'd try art, since I had a couple of friends in the club."

Page three of *Rabbit Tracks* advertised a "mythological mapper". It was the newest fad. ORDER NOW! MYTHOLOGICAL MAPPING FOR YOU OR A FRIEND! The service included an explanation of all the mythological creatures occupying your property. According to the ad, it cost eighty euros, and could be ordered through the Rabbit Back Mythological Heritage Society.

Every fourth issue of *Rabbit Tracks* included a pull-out literary supplement, with the pithy name *Ten*. Ella read the current supplement. She hadn't called the editor to withdraw her submission. Her story had been published on page five.

The supplement published local amateur writers. Rabbit Back boasted not only Laura White and her protégés but also a large contingent of amateur authors. The town was known to have no less than six writers' associations, and that was without counting the most noteworthy writers' association, the Rabbit Back Literature Society, which accepted members only at Laura White's invitation. The possibility of joining the Society was practically theoretical, since the entire present membership— nine lifetime member authors—had all joined in the first three years after the Society was established in 1968.

It was said that Laura White had been asked how many writers she imagined she would find in a place like Rabbit Back. At the time, the Society had only been in existence for four years, and none of its members had yet been published.

Laura White had held up the fingers of both hands. So the answer *might* be "ten", which was the preferred interpretation—that the authoress intended to discover and train ten new Rabbit Back writers in total. Of course she may have just been raising her hands to fend off the question. In any case, the literary supplement had taken its name from the incident.

The story was Ella Milana's first published work of fiction. It had a complicated, lovely title: "The Skeleton Sat in the

Cave Silently Smoking Cigarettes". She'd found the theme for the story close by. It was about a young woman with faulty reproductive organs.

Ella had once met Anna-Maija Seläntö, a member of the Rabbit Back Literature Society who now lived in Sweden. Seläntö had given a lecture at the university, and after the lecture Ella had asked the writer how it felt to see her own works published. Seläntö had smiled sweetly at her and whispered, "You know what? It makes you understand why a dog eats its own vomit."

Ella stared at her story and remembered the essays waiting in her bag. She'd set herself a strict schedule. She was supposed to have graded a third of the papers today, fifteen altogether, to keep the backlog from growing as new essays came in every couple of days.

She decided to leave them in her bag for now. No one expected a substitute language and literature teacher to grade papers every single night of her life, did they? It was a heretical thought, but it made her smile. In her mind, she gave the finger to all the powers of the universe that were trying to make her feel guilty about the uncorrected essays.

That was the day Ella saw Ingrid Katz, who told her an important piece of news.

But she was so preoccupied with the vestiges of Paavo Emil Milana that were still in her father, and a mother whose husband was rapidly becoming a stranger to her, that all she had to say at the time was "Oh, you don't say".

Paavo Emil Milana spent four more days in the hospital. Then they brought him home.

Ella drove the Triumph, her father sat beside her and her mother was in the back seat. It felt strange. Her natural place in this car with these people was in the back on the right, where she could see the scar on her father's cheek.

She had asked him the same question almost every time they rode in the car. "Dad, where did you get that scar?"

Her father rarely told bedtime stories or stories of any kind. Made-up stories weren't his thing. Ella couldn't remember ever seeing him read a novel. But every time she asked him this question, he gave her a different answer.

A drunken sailor tried to stab me in the throat and I dodged his knife and got cut on the cheek, he said once. *I fell out of a tree as a boy when I was trying to climb up to a magpie's nest and a limb tore a scratch in my cheek*, he said the next time.

Another time she asked, the answer was *I was cutting across a meadow with my aunt when I was little and there was an angry bull in the field. It almost caught us, and when we jumped over the fence, it just barely scraped my cheek with its horn.*

One of the answers he gave made Ella's mother scream. *You see, Ella, I once bought your mother a kitchen knife as a birthday present, and she had wanted a nightgown, and your mother was so upset that she took a swipe at me with the present I'd given her, and she would've killed me if I hadn't escaped to the bathroom.*

Ella didn't remember much about her childhood, but she remembered the smell of the inside of the Triumph. It gave her a headache, but she loved it. Sometimes she thought that if she could just sit in that car long enough she would get all her old memories back.

The car didn't belong to her father anymore, although the name on the registration was still Paavo Emil Milana. He would have been shocked at the state of the car. Before he got sick he worked on the car every week—checked everything out, cleaned the motor, washed it and rubbed it with Turtle Wax. One time when he was waxing the car he declared, "Show me a man who doesn't take care of his car, and I'll show you a man who's lost his soul."

Since she'd returned to Rabbit Back, Ella had occasionally driven the Triumph to work, but she preferred to ride her bicycle if the weather permitted.

When she left the house to pedal to the school, the first two kilometres were slightly downhill. The breeze was sweetly cool against her skin in the warm air of August. It was wonderful just to sit on her bicycle seat and let her speed build up by itself.

There were old wooden houses along the dirt road and gardens with their scrubby old apple trees and stone guardians, and here and there newer brick buildings. Along the way she could also get a glimpse of two old playgrounds, a tiny beauty parlour, the beach, dogs, fields, horses and trees—oak, maple, lime and birch.

Halfway to the school the road plunged into a grove of spruce trees where it was always nearly dark. In the summer the air was thick with hungry gnats and she pedalled as fast as she could.

Then the road merged with a paved road and that's when she had to start pedalling just to keep moving. The road passed more houses, a headstone carver's, and two workshops—one of which made wooden statues of Laura White characters that were sold all over the world.

The road was as hilly as a child's drawing; first down, then up, phew! then down, and up again to the highest point, from which she could see the roofs of central Rabbit Back and all the surrounding areas, and even farther on a clear day, all the way to the shimmering horizon. After a few of these hills and valleys she had to slow down, because there was a path between two spruces and a large stone that she always took as a shortcut. It took her straight to the school yard, provided the ground wasn't too swampy.

Halfway down the path there was a pond that looked like a puddle but was said to be bottomlessly deep. Henrik, the Johansson's boy, had once pushed a long pole into the pond without touching bottom, and then it felt like something tugged on the pole and the boys all ran away.

Ella had never taken that story seriously, but she passed the pond as fast as she could. She'd had foreboding dreams about the place. She heard strange noises and saw weird reflections on the surface of the pond.

She had walked this same route thousands of times, the first time when she was six years old, when she first started going to the library. When she returned to Rabbit Back to be a substitute teacher, she had ridden her bike to the school one Monday morning and before she knew it the breeze had wiped away thirteen years of her life.

She felt herself worrying whether she'd got her mathematics homework done and whether Johanna Rantakumpu would like her today and wondering if they would have P.E. inside and she would have to listen to Salli Mäkinen's taunts about her too small breasts and too fat thighs, and wondered whether she and the other girls would go after school to walk up and down in front of Laura White's house again, hoping that the miracle would happen and the authoress would see them and open her office window and invite them in for juice like she'd done with Aliisan Niemennokka two years ago, and maybe she would read to them like she had to her, from the Creatureville book she was writing, and who knows, maybe she would invite one of them to be the tenth member of the Society.

Then the uphill climb had eaten up her speed and the passing years had returned and she remembered that she was just a dreamy substitute teacher with defective ovaries and gracefully curved lips.

For a few seconds she was deeply sad. Then she felt relieved, and laughed so hard that she ran into the ditch.

Ella stopped the Triumph in front of the pharmacy. Her mother got out of the car and ran to fetch her father's prescription. Ella glanced at his profile.

He was still quiet. The day was bleak and rainy, the bank and the shops were looming grey bulks in the drizzling wet. Umbrellas glided back and forth.

Ella looked at her father, who seemed to be waking from a dream. She noticed a figure opening a jammed umbrella in front of the car.

The woman in the rain looked small and slim, which slightly surprised Ella—she had imagined Laura White to be bigger, more imposing somehow.

The raindrops dampened and darkened White's pale summer dress, but she finally got the umbrella open and walked away.

It crossed Ella's mind that she could have offered the greatest children's author she would ever know a ride. But the moment passed and White disappeared into the rain.

Her father breathed heavily.

Her mother appeared in the rearview mirror and dived into the car. "Well, how is everything?" she said.

Then Paavo Emil Milana opened his mouth and spoke the first of two poems that gave his wife a terrible shock.

How long have we been this way, lover, you and I?
The grass is growing through us, as hand in hand we lie,
and drink the songs of butterflies.
I've forgotten your name. Am I made of earth now?
So many skies have circled over us. There's nothing that I miss.

Ella's mother poured some coffee into her cup. There was a plate of cinnamon rolls on the table that she'd baked to celebrate her husband's homecoming. No one felt like eating them.

Ella's father sat in his office looking out the window. Ella and her mother had led him there, and he sat in his chair like an obedient son. His cuts and bruises were healing quickly, but his skin still looked messy, like mischievous, heartless children had drawn on it, scribbled and smudged all over it.

"What's got into him?" Ella's mother said. "He's never been much interested in reciting poetry. And now he decides to start."

She pressed a slip of paper into Ella's hand. "I wrote it down. You're a language and literature teacher. Tell me who the author is."

Ella shook her head. "It doesn't sound familiar. But I can call someone and ask."

And she did call, but Professor Korpimäki didn't recognize the poem, either. "Where did you say you found it?" he asked in a friendly tone.

"My father recited it," Ella said. "And since neither of us knew who the author was, I thought I would call you. Thanks anyway."

The next night her father sat up in bed and recited another one. Ella's mother handed her the paper at the breakfast table. It read:

At last I have a happy tune
a song that I can tell
of mayflies dashing and sparkling
and madness most beautiful,
sparrows plunging into clouds,
the sun on its rattling rails,
creatures of a land of frost
that stir a longing in my breast.
But I tell no tales
of how there lurks beneath the fields of hay
that thing into whose arms
we each will one day sink away.

5

I T WASN'T UNTIL many weeks later, when Paavo Emil Milana was dead and buried, that Ella Milana started to think about what Ingrid Katz had told her.

It was the author Ingrid Katz. You could tell because the author Ingrid Katz was more relaxed than the librarian Ingrid Katz, although she still had that something predatory about her.

"Laura White liked your story," Ingrid had said.

They had been chatting politely for five minutes, talking about anything but the tainted books, or the theft, or why Ingrid had asked Ella to come back to the library. Ella nodded and tried to look interested, as she had been doing. She'd actually been thinking about Paavo Emil Milana's current state.

She was also thinking that she had never been in the library after closing hours. It felt like she was up to something a bit perverse.

Ella's right eye started to twitch.

They were sitting in the children's section drinking coffee and eating yellow cake. The table was much too low and there were plush toy versions of Bobo Clickclack, the Odd Critter and the other Creatureville characters between them. Ella felt strange eating and drinking in the library. After all, there was a sign that said ABSOLUTELY NO EATING OR DRINKING IN THE LIBRARY!

Ingrid Katz had a peculiar smile on her face. Ella looked past her. A short distance away, an exhibit of mythological sculptures was gathered as if for a night-time council.

"As you can guess, this caused a bit of a stir in the Rabbit Back Literature Society. Something like this, after such a long silence. Ms White first told Martti Winter and Martti told me. Martti should have been the one to tell you, but these days Martti is what he is. He doesn't appear in public very often. It couldn't have been more than ten years ago that you couldn't go anywhere without running into him. But nowadays, *poof*, you never see or hear from him." She shook her head sadly. "Except maybe at the Rabbit Market bakery. They have the best pastries in town, and do you know why? Because Martti Winter is a regular customer there! They make custom pastries for him, if you can believe that."

Ella felt awkward. She wondered if Ingrid might be drunk, tried to smell it on her breath. All she could smell was liquorice and coffee.

Ingrid Katz wasn't the most brilliant author in the Society, but Martti Winter was its undisputed star. His works had been translated into dozens of languages. He was one of those rare Finnish writers who had become rich from his writing. His works were popular with both critics and a large reading audience.

Unlike Martti Winter, Ingrid Katz wrote small books. Critics liked them well enough, but they never got much publicity. As far as Ella could remember, all of her books were young adult novels filled with people committing suicide and having abortions and losing their virginity and suffering alcohol poisoning while living with parents who fought constantly and were in all ways unbearable.

"So, since Martti wasn't able to get in touch with you, the task fell to me," Ingrid said with a sigh. "But that's all right. You and I know each other, after all, because of that incident the other day."

She smiled jovially. "Well, what do you say?" she asked.

"About what?" Ella said. She was finding it hard to concentrate.

"About what we've been talking about!" Katz said. "About being the next to receive an honour that hasn't been bestowed on anyone in a very long time. And not because Ms White wasn't looking for new talent. I haven't seen her terribly recently, but I know that she reads the *Rabbit Tracks* literary supplement regularly. And she has her own portfolio there at your school."

"The Laura White file," Ella said.

Ingrid Katz nodded. "To be honest, I found your story... what was it called?"

"'The Skeleton Sat in the Cave Silently Smoking Cigarettes'," Ella said.

"Yes. Well, I didn't see anything remarkable in it when I read it in the paper. It seemed to me like a typical bit of slick lang-and-lit-teacher's prose. Very good, no doubt, for someone at your level of training, but not at all extraordinary. I just thought: Uh-huh. Next. But then I'm not the one who took nine tentatively promising children and trained them to be nine more or less successful authors, so what's my opinion worth? If Laura White sees something in your story, then there's something in it. And something in you. I can't see it, but I believe in it."

Ella was flustered. "This is all a little... I'm sorry, but could you spell out exactly what it is that you mean?" she said, smiling apologetically.

Ingrid Katz looked more serious and put her coffee cup back on the table.

"I'm talking about an offer," she said. Her expression was inscrutable. "Laura White promises to make a writer out of you, if you wish to join the Rabbit Back Literature Society."

6

S ITTING IN THE BATHROOM after the funeral, Ella Milana
remembered how her father had once read aloud to her
from a Creatureville book when she was a child. It was a book
Santa Claus had brought a couple of days before.

She remembered her father's weight on the edge of her bed,
his soft voice painting pictures in her mind. She remembered
how she had kept her eyes closed. She had a vivid memory of
the going-to-sleep passage in the book:

> *Mother Snow tucked Bobo Clickclack, the Odd Critter, Dampish,*
> *Crusty Bark and all the others into bed. She kissed them gently and*
> *called them her "own little creatures", which always made them*
> *smile under the blanket with pure contentment, and for a moment*
> *they all forgot that Emperor Rat stalked the night, whispering dark*
> *secrets that no living creature could hear without being badly broken.*
>
> *Then Mother Snow went into the kitchen and made herself a*
> *cup of hot cocoa.*
>
> CREATUREVILLE FOLK,
> BY LAURA WHITE, END OF CHAPTER TWO

She remembered interrupting her father and asking him what
the part about Emperor Rat meant and how they would keep
him away, since everyone in Creatureville was so afraid of him.

Her question was followed by such a long silence that
she thought he must have tiptoed out of the room. But he

hadn't—when she opened her eyes, he was still sitting there. He was pondering her question seriously—with such fierce concentration, in fact, that she started to feel afraid and regretted that she'd asked it.

"It seems to me," her father finally said with a sigh, "that Emperor Rat is one of those things that we're supposed to forget about. He'll come if he's going to come, but we shouldn't start dwelling on it, and we certainly can't start actively expecting it to happen."

Autumn seeped into the grass, plants and trees and gushed from the treetops up into the sky to cover the landscape.

Ella and her mother hunkered indoors out of the rain. The house felt grey and huddled tight. It was colder than usual for this time of year. Neither of them felt like lighting the old tile stove that they used to supplement the electric heat.

Ella told her mother about the memory that had come to her so suddenly. Her mother was watching a television show called *The Last Sixty Years of Our Lives*. Without turning her head, she told Ella she had remembered it wrong: "As far as I know your father never read aloud to you. It must have been me."

When the show was over, her mother started writing a shopping list for the next day, which was a Monday. Monday had always been the family shopping day. Her mother always said that writing shopping and to-do lists made it possible to keep things under control that would otherwise have weighed on her mind.

Ella sat next to her. There were crumbs and coffee stains on the kitchen table. Ella was tired. She had been up late trying to grade papers, but nothing had come of it. She was tired. Two hours earlier she had started to listen to her own breathing, and then her mother's breathing, and now she couldn't stop no matter how she tried.

The air rasped in through her mother's nostrils and flowed through her windpipes into her lungs, then came back out again with a weary puff and a drawn-out wheeze that had a faint rattle in it. Now and then she sort of wolfed all the air in at once and snorted it out so quickly that there was no way her lungs had any time to absorb the oxygen into her bloodstream.

Breathing was somewhat complicated when you really thought about it. Ella wondered whether people die sometimes from starting to think too much about things that you're not supposed to pay any attention to, like breathing.

She looked at her mother's shopping list and forgot her ponderings for a moment.

POTATOES

CARROTS

TISSUES

SOME KIND OF MEAT (CHICKEN STRIPS?)

WHEAT FLOUR

POTATO FLOUR

TOMATOES

FUNERAL (COFFIN FOR PAAVO, ETC.)

LAUNDRY SOAP (FOR COLOURS)

HEADSTONE

COFFEE

Her mother looked at her intently, her eyes dry.

"Might as well get everything taken care of," she said, and rapped her knuckles on the table. She was sitting up very straight in her chair, but her neck was bent backward somewhat, her head tilted feebly to one side. "Let's go to the florist, too. I'm sure Kuutti knows how to handle these cemetery sorts of things. You'll never hear a word of complaint about Kuutti's Flowers. Satisfied customers, living or dead. By the way, do you want to be next to your father and me at the cemetery? I need to know so I can order the right size headstone."

Ella didn't answer.

"I'm not trying to force you into the same grave," her mother said soothingly. "I was just thinking that if we're going to be taking care of these sorts of things I might as well ask you about it so that you wouldn't complain about it later—tell people you hadn't even been invited to share a plot with your family. I'm trying to take everything into account, including you, now that you've moved back home and everything."

"Thanks, Mum," Ella said. "That's very thoughtful."

"And there are money matters to think about," her mother said in a hurt voice. "You'll save a pretty penny if we put you under the same stone as the rest of your family. It may not feel like a pressing issue to you now, but you ought to plan ahead."

"What would you think if I wasn't buried in the same plot as you and Dad?"

Her mother looked at her sharply, then nodded, hers eyes wet now. "That's that, then," she said, and scribbled something on her shopping list. "We'll just buy a headstone for two. You can look for your own plot and choose all the features you want to buy."

The next night Ella Milana dreamed about the library.

The library floor was covered with grass. Ella was hurrying

between the stacks looking for something. She stopped at the M shelf. There wasn't a single book with her name on it.

She burst into tears. She'd never felt so terribly sad.

"Look on the E shelf," someone whispered from above. "But if you see Dostoevsky, please don't tell him I'm here. I had a ritual burning of his clothes, because they were cancerous, and he's quite cross with me. He also accused me of lying, and what's more, he's right."

Ella looked up and saw a long-necked cat sitting on top of the shelf. Much higher up there were bright-winged fairies hovering, guarding the library.

"Be careful not to step on those," the cat said, looking down at something. "You don't want to make them angry."

Ella looked down at her feet and saw small, shadowy shapes scuttling here and there.

She walked forward carefully so she wouldn't step on anyone and, following the cat's advice, found a row of books under E written by Ella Amanda Milana.

She ran her fingers excitedly along the spines of the books, greedily reading the titles of the novels. They were enigmatic, fascinating, brilliant titles. Some were just one word, others were extremely long. She sobbed with happiness.

The cat appeared on the top shelf again.

"Hurry!" it hissed. "The gates are open. Listen! Oh, listen! Listen to that rumble, that thundering clatter. They're coming. And everything, everything's still left undone!"

Ella plucked one of the books from the shelf and wondered at its weight. The cat laughed.

"Heavy as a stone, isn't it? But they make the pages out of crushed stones, of course. Hey, why don't you open it?"

Ella opened the book and was horrified to see that the pages were empty. She took down another book, and another.

"They're all empty," the cat said tauntingly. "You'd better hurry up. I'd start writing if I were you. Do you want to know how to write novels? I'll tell you the secret: start on page one and keep going, in order, until you come to the last page. Then stop."

"Just write! What will I write with?" Ella shouted. "I don't have a pen! All my pens are in my pocket and I'm not wearing any clothes!"

It was true—she wasn't wearing anything but socks, and even they were mismatched.

The cat scoffed. "Everybody comes to the library naked. That's why they come here—to dress themselves in books. And if you don't have a pen, maybe you can ask him."

The cat cast a dread glance over Ella's shoulder. Ella realized that there was someone standing behind her. Breathing down her neck. The breather was having difficulty staying in rhythm.

Ella noticed a book on the shelf titled *A Guide to Smooth Breathing*. It looked as if she had written it.

She picked up the book and tried to turn around, but she couldn't move. It was too cold. Someone or something had put its cold hand against her skin. The stinging cold on her back seeped through to her internal organs. It hurt.

The cat meowed and leaped out of sight. Snow started to fall.

Torrential rain began on the first of October and lasted for three and a half weeks. The school parking lot turned into a little lake where frogs splashed. Children flocked around the parking lot shrieking something about a water sprite and a long-lost boot and ran around splashing in the water.

Ella Milana didn't want to take time off from work. She drove to the school every morning in her late father's borrowed Triumph, walked into the teacher's lounge in her father's boots, changed into her own shoes, taught her classes, and went home, which was now partly hers, apparently—that's what she'd been told.

Her mother focused on small daily chores and melted into tears now and then.

Ella didn't cry, but her thoughts tortured her. She was constantly aware that while the rest of the world went about its business, her father, Paavo Emil Milana, was lying in a hole in the ground not half a kilometre from the school. There must be beetles and millipedes wriggling into his ears and mouth and nostrils all the time. She was particularly tortured by the thought that basically anyone at all could dig him up and drag him someplace, prop him in his seat in the coffee shop.

How strange to leave a member of your family lying in a shallow hole and go on with your daily activities!

One morning in the middle of a grammar lesson, in the middle of a sentence, Ella started thinking: if a person has a soul, was her father's soul gradually escaping, like air out of a leaky tire? She didn't particularly believe in the soul or in God, but the thought kept coming back to worry her.

She was offered condolences in the teachers' lounge. Her students didn't offer condolences; they were just still, silent, and troubled. When Ella tried to lighten the mood, it only made the situation worse.

"What's the matter?" she shouted, unable to resist. "Did somebody die?"

The principal asked her to come and talk to him.

"Listen, students are afraid to come to your class. And it's understandable. Death is a serious thing for young people, and when their teacher starts using gallows humour about her own father's death, it's going to upset some of them. I think it would be best for you to be more frank with them in your next class, and tell them you're sorry. That way we can keep this unfortunate complaint off your record."

The next day Ella Milana taught a class the nature of which became clear to her only as she picked up the chalk and started writing on the blackboard. Afterwards she admitted that it might have been an overreaction, but she never did regret it.

She wrote a sentence, turned back towards the class, smiled, and said:

"Let's have a surprise quiz. Please diagram this sentence and identify the parts of speech. You have ten minutes."

The sentence was: OUR TEACHER'S FATHER LIES DEAD IN A HOLE THAT WAS DUG IN THE GRAVEYARD HALF A KILOMETRE FROM THE SCHOOL AND THERE ARE BEETLES LIVING IN HIS EARS.

After class Ella went to tell the principal that she was going to the doctor because she wasn't feeling well. She mentioned in passing that she'd been invited to join the Rabbit Back Literature Society as a full member.

The principal glanced blankly at the "Laura White File" and nodded to indicate that he'd understood.

Ella Milana's substitute position was supposed to last until December. She explained to the doctor that she was suffering from depression, forgetfulness, and bouts of crying. The doctor wrote a prescription and gave her a sick leave slip for the rest of her contract.

She wadded up the prescription and shoved it in the Triumph's ashtray.

PART TWO

7

On the second Saturday in December a party held at the home of
Laura White ended with a tragedy of great import for Finnish
literature. It all happened in front of dozens of witnesses, as
world-famous children's author Laura White was descending from
the second floor to join her guests, and yet, following the incident no
one was able to report precisely what had happened.

Usually when something shocking occurs, people start to report
having had premonitions or dreams of the event. They speak in low
voices with furtive eyes of how they knew all along, knew in their
bones that something bad was about to happen. That winter evening
at Laura White's house, however, all seemed cheerfully optimistic,
blissfully unaware. It was one of those evenings that ends as you
whistle your way homeward to fall asleep with a smile on your face.
There was a lot of laughter. People talked, made jokes, touched each
other the way children do, innocent and uninhibited. Kisses were
even exchanged. Joy and expectation sparkled through the crowd.

Look at that woman! She hasn't danced in ages, but she's danc-
ing now, beaming at her partner with a big, bright smile! And what
is he doing? He's glowing like a lantern. He can't remember when
he's felt such a flush of happiness!

And that woman over there. A reserved bureaucrat by day, you
can usually find her in the back office at Rabbit Back Pensioners'
Services. Now she's nibbling at the tea biscuits on the buffet, happy
as a child.

And who are those two? They've been dating half-heartedly for
a couple of months but it's only here that they've seen each other in

*their best clothes, in the most flattering light, and it's given a whole
new shape to their relationship.*

*Go mingle, talk with people. They'll smile at you, you'll feel
welcomed, accepted! Tell a joke, and they'll laugh. Chat with them
jovially and they'll love you! This is the kind of party that lasts
forever because no one wants to be the first person to leave! No one
wants to abandon this sweet, light-hearted, intoxicating merriment!*

*Thinking back, no one could call to mind a single bad omen.
The sky didn't turn blood-red, comets shone absent, not one bird
flew into the window. Even the dogs, so ubiquitous in Rabbit Back,
failed to howl.*

*Everyone thought the party would continue happy, exciting,
delightful until morning, perhaps even longer.*

*There was a well-known theatre critic among the guests. Two
months later she commented on the incident in the Now section of
the Helsinki newspaper, in an article that asked critics to describe
their most startling real-life experiences. According to this critic,
the unfortunate incident at Laura White's party was "an utterly
abrupt, crass, unbelievable ending to the whole thing—an absolutely
inappropriate, laughably overdramatic plot twist!"*

EXCERPT FROM ESKO HARTAVALA'S ARTICLE
"THE LAURA WHITE INCIDENT",
FINLAND ILLUSTRATED WEEKLY, JUNE 2005

The Rabbit Back Literature Society celebratory gathering had
attracted cultural types from far and wide, the farthest flung, it
was said, coming all the way from Japan.

Nearly all of them were unknown to author Martti Winter,
and he didn't want to know them.

The Rabbit Back Popular Orchestra was playing in a corner

of the drawing-room—the pensive bass flirting with the dreamy saxophone and piano. Caterers wandered about offering wine, cognac, and hors d'oeuvres.

In addition to the drawing-room there were other downstairs rooms full of guests. Some stood in groups, laughing loudly, others stood in corners gossiping. The ones who had never been to Laura White's house before admired the paintings gleaming on the walls and the dark-hued furnishings.

No one ventured upstairs. It was understood to be the private quarters of the lady of the house. Some of the downstairs rooms were locked as well.

"Where is Ms White, anyway?" someone behind Martti Winter asked.

He turned and saw that it was Ella Milana speaking. She was fiddling with the straps of her gown, which were clearly too thin and too tight.

Winter knew very well that everyone was there because Ella Milana, the petite young teacher who stood before him, had been made a member of the Rabbit Back Literature Society. The place was swarming with envious amateur authors, their envy barely checked by their instinctive deference. She was the long-awaited Tenth Member.

These amateur authors were themselves envied, for of the hundreds of amateur authors in the district, they were the ones who'd been honoured with an invitation to the party. The majority had received prizes in writing competitions within the last few years or had stories in the literary supplement that were considered above average.

Martti Winter touched Ella Milana's arm with his fingertips. Her arm was thin, her skin dry and hot.

"She must still be upstairs, in her room, probably," he said. "Don't worry, you'll get to meet her when the time comes. Then you'll be officially introduced and so on."

People crowded around them. Three loud-voiced women stood closest. Winter had learned and forgotten their names. A youngish man bounced around among them, a writer for *Rabbit Tracks*. Or was he from some Helsinki paper? Winter had heard that there would be someone from *Finland Illustrated* at the party.

Winter was about to move aside when someone tapped him on the shoulder. He remembered the journalist's name now: Esko Hartavala.

Hartavala said he had read Winter's most recent novel, *Mr Butterfly*. He enquired whether Winter had ever felt the same temptation as the novel's main character to dress in women's clothes. "I don't mean to offend. I only ask because the inner thoughts of the main character are described so incredibly intensely, in such an achingly personal voice, that it's hard to believe anyone could have invented him entirely out of whole cloth."

The journalist rested one hand on Winter's shoulder and waved the other excitedly in the air. The waving hand held a cigarette, the ash of which dropped onto the front of Winter's jacket.

"I would be happy to take credit for all of the wonderful experiences I describe in my novels, but my life isn't quite that rich. Unfortunately we authors are sometimes forced to use other people's lives, too."

"Sounds rather beastly," the journalist laughed. "Or maybe writers are like vultures. Some people feel we journalists are." He mimicked a bird of prey and grinned.

Winter wondered whether they were having a conversation or conducting an interview. He stretched his lips in an expression reminiscent of a hungry crocodile and lifted the journalist's hand from his shoulder.

He then flicked the ashes from his jacket one by one.

"I confess that gathering material can sometimes have the flavour of a hunt," he said. "Even the best cook can't make chicken soup out of his own feet. There aren't so terribly many ingredients in anyone's life, less meat than there is on a sparrow. The average person could come up with at most two good novels. Many who think very highly of themselves can't manage more than a couple of anecdotes."

The journalist made a sound. Winter patted his arm, smiled warmly, and said, "It is sad, I know. In any case, if you want to write a bit more than that, your own experiences aren't enough. By the time you get to the third novel you're going to have to throw in a few pinches of someone else's life."

The journalist nodded and moved away, looking for an easier conversation.

"Why do I feel like I was a great disappointment to that poor fellow?" Winter wondered aloud, causing a burst of laughter around him.

One of the women laughed particularly loudly, shuffled a few steps towards him and touched his lips with her fingertips. "Maybe you frightened him. Tell me, am I in any danger of being used if I come too close, oh great and terrifying author?"

A dense cloud of perfume wafted around her.

"Go ahead and try," Winter said, somewhat wearily. "Open up to me. Reveal something interesting about yourself, and I'll use it when I need it. If I need it. Altered for my own purposes."

65

"How will you alter me?"

"Well… I might turn those curls of yours black and make you fatter or thinner by ten kilos or so, whatever comes to me. And maybe, just maybe, I'll change one of your eyes, perhaps this left one, into a glass eye."

The woman's mouth dropped open. "Huh?"

Winter smiled.

"Or I might give you a wooden leg, or some kind of disease. How does syphilitic brain damage sound? Or maybe I'll have you broken in two in an auto accident."

She gave a shrill laugh. "You are truly awful!" she said. "I'm not telling you anything now, or I might end up in your next novel."

Winter gave a slight bow.

"That is your right. It would no doubt put you in much less danger of being used. But I may nevertheless steal your way of moving, the expressions on your face! Perhaps I'll even take that way you have of smiling with your mouth open, your little tongue peeking out now and then between your teeth to see what's happening in the world. And those freckles that start on the bridge of your nose and continue all the way down between your breasts, that's a detail that might come in handy in a piece I'm writing at the moment."

The woman smiled, frightened. "You'll eat me alive."

She grabbed a companion by the arm and started lisping like a little girl. "Oh, won't you please be a nice man-eating lion and let me go if I tell you a juicy story about my friend here?"

Winter looked at her apologetically. "I'm sorry, but I don't bargain with my material."

*

Martti Winter had recently had a birthday. He'd turned forty-three. For his birthday celebration, he'd ordered a large chocolate cake covered in marzipan roses. He hadn't told anyone about his birthday. He ate the cake himself.

The baker said that it was a cake for twenty. It had lasted Winter two days and one night.

Winter didn't smoke. He was a sober man nowadays—drinking was too much trouble. Alcohol didn't suit him. Drunkenness had lost its charm. He'd given up sex with other people for the same reasons.

His new habit, eating, replaced both drinking and sex. He weighed well over 150 kilos.

When people talked about the famous author, their comments generally went something like, "What of it? Why not enjoy life, right? If you like good food, why not eat your fill?"

Martti Winter was no gourmand. He didn't have expensive tastes, didn't like Chinese food or care to hear about French cuisine. He hated shellfish, caviar, and complicated seafood dishes. He never drank wine with dinner. He liked to eat simple, uncomplicated foods: chocolate, pastries, ground beef, French fries, macaroni, chocolate mousse and sausage.

He found his way to the buffet table and started to eat a cream pastry topped with three green cherries and flakes of chocolate. The filling was marzipan.

He remembered that the woman with the freckles was an amateur actor in Rabbit Back. She was the fourth hanger-on he'd fended off that evening. There was a time when he'd positively collected actresses. There was something quite special about them—they seemed more complete and clear than other women and at the same time unreal. But it had been a long time since he'd had it in him to really react to a woman's sexual signals.

He had noticed the moisture on the actress's lips, sensed the shape of her flesh, smelled the perfume that only partly succeeded in concealing the aroma she naturally secreted. In theory, he would have liked to bed many of the women he met. In practice, sex with a stranger was rather laborious, messy and tiresome. He would have to look people in the eye whom he would prefer not to know if he saw them in line at the market or the corner kiosk.

Besides, Winter liked to keep his body private. It was like an untidy room—it was indecorous to invite strangers to see it. He didn't really think of his bloated form as his own anymore. It was thus natural that he didn't want to be seen with it.

He had adjusted to his fatness, of course. It was annoying that at this point he could no longer see his penis. If he tried to pee standing up he had to aim blind and usually wet the floor, and his shoes. A couple of days earlier he had thoughtlessly undressed in front of the mirror and recoiled at the sight of a large, leathery orangutan. In an expensive suit, however, he did look presentable. It gave his roundness a sort of dignity. He was convinced that it was best that he remain dressed in the company of others.

Winter turned once more towards his companions, excused himself, and withdrew to the bathroom. It was spacious but dark. A curved bathtub loomed at the other end of the room, white with copper legs.

Years ago, a young Martti Winter had walked into this same bathroom, and the memory returned to him now.

He's spent the entire Sunday at Laura White's house doing writing exercises. He comes into the bathroom deep in thought, pulls down his zipper—then suddenly realizes that he's not alone, because at the other end of the room, lying in a tub full of water with her eyes closed is the writer, Laura White, naked. Horrified at the sacrilege he's committed, he tries to quiet the pounding in his chest that's making the whole room tremble, until the water in the tub splashes on the floor.

Did she really open her eyes and look at the intruder? Did she smile at the boy mischievously and then close her eyes again?

Winter might have seen that happen but he didn't know anymore, not for sure. He had seen it in dreams hundreds of times and every dream was different.

He walked over to the bathtub, opened his fly, did a little work and let his seed run over the white porcelain. Then he ran water in the tub and watched the black hole at the bottom swallow the evidence.

He washed his hands and face, checked his hair in the mirror, and walked out.

Author Martti Winter isn't the only author at the gathering, of course. They're all here this evening, all nine of the old members of the Rabbit Back Literature Society, and one new one.

Do you see that housewifish woman over there? The blonde, chubby woman who looks a little grey and threadbare? Looks deceive: that is Arne C. Ahlqvist, one of Europe's most celebrated sci-fi and fantasy writers. Remember last summer's hit movie The Digger? *Hollywood based the screenplay on Arne C. Ahlqvist's novel* Excursion to the Sun.

Her real name is Aura Jokinen. She's something of an odd case among the writers in the Society. Her works are said to be too far from reality to be considered real literature. "Why doesn't she write about life?" the people of Rabbit Back ask. "Why come up with those strange tales of hers?"

Such questions come from those who haven't read the interviews she's given, in which she reveals that all her works are about her own complicated family relationships. In Anna magazine, the author said the following: "My last novel, Luna jacta est, seems to be about cyborgs, but if you scratch the surface you'll find my daughter's abortion, which was quite a shock to me and my ex-husband."

Also on hand are mystery writer Silja Saaristo and young adult author Ingrid Katz, who has kept a low profile for the past couple of years. Manning the punchbowl is a familiar face from television, satirist Elias Kangasniemi, whose TV commentaries once garnered a faithful viewership. Also familiar from television is the award-winning screenwriter Toivo Holm, making lively conversation with all comers.

If you observe the festivities, you will make a surprising discovery. The members of the Rabbit Back Literature Society don't seem to be talking with each other. They pass close by each other now and then, but never look each other in the eye, never indulge in conversation. One could very easily assume that they don't know each other at all.

EXCERPT FROM ESKO HARTAVALA'S ARTICLE
"THE LAURA WHITE INCIDENT",
FINLAND ILLUSTRATED WEEKLY, JUNE 2005

People were starting to wonder at the absence of the hostess.

Martti Winter assured those who asked him that Ms White would be joining them very soon. The night was still young. She had simply lost herself in writing the much-anticipated book that was to appear next fall—which according to the publisher's press release was to be titled *The Return of Emperor Rat.*

Ah! the people sighed, casting a look of enchantment up the stairs.

It was said that *The Return of Emperor Rat* would be Laura White's last book in the Creatureville series. Winter had asked the authoress about it a few days earlier at a party thrown by the mayor. White had smiled and said, *Martti, dear, we should never talk about what we're writing, or our writing might turn into nothing but talk.*

One of the caterers came up to Winter and tugged on his sleeve.

"Ms White has a terrible headache," she whispered. "Do you know where I might find something she can take for it?"

"I doubt that headache medicine will be much use for one of her migraines," Winter said. "She should lie down in a dark room. And she shouldn't be disturbed unless she specifically requests it."

"But she was sitting in her office and getting ready to come downstairs just moments ago, and she is the hostess of the party, so perhaps I should take her some painkillers…"

Winter broke away and moved clumsily among the crowd, accidentally elbowing and shoving some of the guests—he was attempting out of old habit to slip through gaps that were much too narrow for his present shape.

He drank some wine for the sake of form, then ate that much more intently. As he did he was dimly aware of meeting teachers, journalists, local politicians, theatre people, members of book clubs and amateur authors who were very excited about him and his literary career.

As always in these situations, he was also approached by those who thought of him as some sort of messiah, who tried desperately to make an impression upon meeting the One True Writer.

They quoted aphorisms to him, recited homespun poetry, and performed lines from plays they had in desk drawers at home.

Winter strove to be the humble, grateful, polite author and take his admirers seriously, but he couldn't stay focused on anyone for more than a moment. *Ah, you're writing a play? Wonderful. I hope you finish it. By the way, do you think that's sachertorte or just ordinary cake? Are the chocolate-covered almonds all gone?*

A couple of times he almost ran into another Society member, but an imperceptible course correction on both sides always saved the situation.

Then he noticed Ingrid Katz.

She kept flashing into view all over the room, and Winter became nervous when he realized that there was no point in trying to escape her. Her top knot kept coming closer, slicing across the room like a shark's fin.

Winter filled his plate and left the drawing room. He found a quiet place in a back room where he might continue enjoying the party.

Ingrid Katz appeared in the doorway.

"Have you seen the new demigod anywhere?" she asked.

Winter waved his cake spoon and grunted as some icing fell on his expensive necktie.

"Ella Milana? Isn't she somewhere in the crowd? I just met her a moment ago."

"What about Laura White? I haven't seen her once today."

He touched his temple. "Migraine."

"Ouch," Katz said.

Then she walked over to the fireplace and stooped to dig around in her bag. "Does my fellow author happen to have a match?" she asked at last.

"Your fellow author doesn't smoke anymore," Winter said.

"Ah. That's something new. We'll have to talk about that. But I should find a match so I can burn these books."

Winter glanced at her. She had a bundle of books in her hand and a meaningful look in her eye. He didn't feel like interpreting what it might mean, however. He took another bite of cake and smiled a little.

"Children's book author and librarian Ingrid Katz burning books, again," he said.

Katz clicked her tongue. "I've already burned four this week. You know, some people might take an interest in the whole thing."

"True," Winter said, "some people might."

"But not you."

"Well, I could, but I don't feel like it. Everyone has their own interests. Some collect butterflies, you burn library books. Look on the mantel."

"Why?"

"Matches. Listen, Ingrid, do you know anything about animal psychology?"

"What?"

"Dogs, to be precise."

She snorted and started piling the books in the fireplace. Soon the fire was blazing happily.

As she left, she said with a pinch of regret, "Martti, if you were any less interested in what was happening around you, you'd be indistinguishable from a leather sofa."

Winter enjoyed his solitude, quiet and cake, which contained a particularly well-made layer of marzipan. Then he noticed that Ella Milana had appeared in the chair beside him.

"Oh! Evening," he said.

"Evening yourself," Ella Milana answered.

Winter smiled encouragingly at the girl and made a note of the lovely curve of her lips. He thought that he might fit them onto the main female character of the novel he was working on, if he ever bothered to finish it.

"Exciting night. For you, anyway, I assume. Congratulations again, both for your story, and for the status it's brought you."

"Thanks," Ella Milana said.

Winter continued eating his cake, supposing that she would return to join the other guests. She was beginning to make him nervous.

"Have you played any interesting games lately, Mr Winter?"

"Uh, I think the young lady is overestimating my athletic condition," he answered. "Or are you thinking more of something like chess or checkers? Noble games both. Unfortunately I can never remember which piece goes where."

Ella Milana's expression told him immediately that she wasn't referring to any such commonly played game, but rather to The Game.

"Ah, you mean The Game," he said finally, reluctantly. "Who told you about it?"

He stood up slowly and with some difficulty and set his plate on an antique bureau. The girl looked at him excitedly. He turned with his side to her and wished she would go away. But instead she came closer, her dress rustling, an impudent smile on her face, veiled in strawberry-scented perfume, slightly drunk.

In his comic novel *Hidden Agendas* Winter had called such an attitude "the tenacity of a small animal". In the same book, it was said that the only way to fight "the tenacity of a small animal" was by cultivating a well-practised "old barge" approach.

74

"A woman named Arne Ahlqvist mentioned it," she said. "She welcomed me into the Society and asked if I was ready to play a couple of rounds of The Game with her, and some other nonsense. Then she saw someone she knew and left before I could ask her to explain. I asked Ingrid Katz about it, but she said that although she could answer me, I ought to ask you if I wanted a proper answer. She said you 'take a great interest in people and the things people do' and would be happy to initiate me into the procedures of the Society."

Winter made an indistinct noise and then started humming to himself. He closed his eyes. Then he smiled as if he'd just remembered an amusing anecdote. He turned, wagged a finger at Ella Milana, and stiffened where he stood. For a moment it looked like he was about to tell some hilarious story.

Then he let his face darken and his finger fall and turned away, as if he'd just remembered something extremely worrisome.

His next manoeuvre would have been to walk away shaking his head, sad-faced, but Ella Milana appeared in front of him.

"My dear Mr Winter, everything you've written, I've read. I read *Hidden Agendas* twice, so I recognize the 'old barge' trick very well when I see it. What was it Douglas Dogson said about how to fend off 'the tenacity of a small animal'?"

"I haven't the faintest," Winter said. "I don't read my own books or think about them after I've written them. I've never learned to quote books by heart, not even my own."

"Is that so?"

"Besides, I don't understand people who read a book for pleasure and then ruminate on the book's ideas. Paper was invented so we wouldn't have to keep all those thoughts in our heads."

"Be that as it may, the Douglas Dogson strategy isn't going to work on me. I know your books better than you do."

Winter shrugged. "I didn't think it would work. I've never tried it in real life. It worked in the book. Listen, could we talk about this some other time? There's so much going on, and it's almost time for you to go and meet Laura White. It seems to me that Ms White would want to tell you herself what The Game is. She's the one who thought it up. It's not exactly simple. In fact we have a rule book for it. You'll no doubt have your own copy soon."

Ella Milana's eyes widened. "A rule book? What kind of rule book?"

Winter took pleasure in her impatience and started to feel more warmly towards her.

He'd noticed before that people in their twenties, whenever they were with someone middle-aged, seemed to feel it necessary to find some way to point out the difference in age every five minutes or so. If they didn't mention it outright, they managed it by means of a polite distance. Unlike others her age, however, Ella Milana seemed to think that they were both originally from the same planet and century.

Winter decided to like her.

"This kind," he said.

He showed her his worn copy. He'd been carrying it with him for thirty years—out of mere habit these days.

"Can I look at it?" the girl breathed, groping for the book.

The palm-sized volume was covered in brown leather. The spine had small, gilded lettering that read RABBIT BACK LITERATURE SOCIETY: GAME RULES. NOT FOR NON-MEMBERS!

"Remember, you can't show it to anyone or talk about The Game to non-members," Winter said. "You'll understand why once you've read the rules. The Game is a way for the Society to exchange useful information which would otherwise be difficult to obtain. There's nothing wrong in it, but some of it might be a bit bewildering to ordinary people."

Ella Milana looked past him, squinted and walked over to the fireplace.

"Has someone been burning books?" she asked. "It looks like there were books in here."

This upset Winter. He didn't want to have that bothersome conversation.

"Ask Ingrid Katz. From what I can tell, she's keen to talk about it."

The woman from catering appeared in the doorway, cleared her throat, shifted her weight from one foot to the other, and announced that the hostess was finally about to make an appearance.

Winter walked through the doorway into the drawing-room without waiting for Ella Milana.

The orchestra had started to play again. Conversation stopped. Expectation quickened into silence. All eyes were directed towards the top of the stairs.

Laura White was standing there.

She looked down at the expectant faces, and they looked back.

Look, there she is—Laura White herself. Beloved author, fascinating woman. Her reputation ripples around the world, and there she stands, flesh and blood, looking at all of us with curiosity.

We can see her face, her eyebrows, her lips. Her delicate chin. Her hair. We see her hands and feet and slim figure in a white dress. We see the marks of age, the small flaws in her beauty. But above all we see her specialness, shining through her whole being.

Soon she will be among us. Perhaps she'll have coffee and cake and talk with us. We'll try to say something meaningful, something that will make her notice us and think we're interesting.

We'll probably not succeed in standing out from the crowd, but that's all right. The main thing is that we've experienced this night. As one of the teeming mass of people in the room, we've been allowed to touch the famous author. What does it matter if she doesn't remember our name a moment later? Perhaps some part of us will remain in her mind. Perhaps we'll find a piece of ourselves in her next book, and perhaps, through her, receive a piece of immortality in return!

EXCERPT FROM ESKO HARTAVALA'S ARTICLE
"THE LAURA WHITE INCIDENT",
FINLAND ILLUSTRATED WEEKLY, JUNE 2005

Martti Winter saw the new member of the Society slip through the crowd and stop at the foot of the stairs. Everyone else stood motionless. The room was thick with veneration. You could hardly breathe.

All children devoured the Creatureville books. Adults read them, too. There was a new Creatureville cartoon that was shown on television all over the world. Laura White's creation had long fed the spiritual soil of Rabbit Back and her books and merchandise had spread around the globe.

There she stood.

Everyone knew she had a serious migraine. It was said that there had been times when such attacks had nearly killed her. Everyone was relieved to see the hostess of the evening there at the top of the stairs.

Laura White was the only woman dressed in white. It was one of the unwritten rules, as was the ban on bringing any mythological figurines into her house. Any ladies who had mistakenly come in white had been informed of this rule and had their slip of etiquette corrected with a colourful shawl or other accessory.

Laura White's dress left her slender arms and legs bare. She smiled, but it was clear that she still had a headache. The pain dimmed her eyes and doubled her over slightly.

She wasn't going to let it spoil the evening. Her audience sighed with relief.

She touched her forehead with her fingertips, nodded and started her descent.

Like many others, Winter thought afterwards of those five steps that Laura White took before she fell.

The first two steps had meaning, naturalness. Her left hand slid along the dark, lacquered banister. Her head was slightly tilted, her face shone with intelligent irony.

She smiled at the people. She noticed the new literary talent she had discovered at the foot of the stairs. Ella Milana had at this point risen to the first step and Winter wondered if the girl would be able to wait at the bottom or if she would break into a run up the stairs like an eager child.

Laura White's right eye closed for a moment, as if she were winking. Then it opened and her head jerked in a way that showed a sudden pain.

She quickly touched her hair and lowered her hand back to the banister, achieving a sedate expression again.

The third step was unsteady, as if she couldn't see her way down. She tried to smile broader than before, but panic burst through her smile.

With her fourth step, Laura White collapsed.

She stretched both hands out in front of her.

She was like a sleep walker in a farcical pantomime. She blinked her eyes, opened them wide, and dropped into the emptiness above her audience's heads.

As Laura White's foot took that last step, the thing happened that everyone later tried so hard to understand, to explain, to analyse.

Suddenly the whole house is full of wind and snow.

Right before our eyes, a snowstorm bursts in from the upstairs room behind Laura White, howls down the stairs, and covers everything we can see in the blink of an eye.

One of the upstairs windows must have blown open and a sudden storm must have come up and made its way into the house.

Some claim that a sort of whirlwind of snow burst through the front door of the house.

In later police interviews some rather dubious claims are made, but people tend to say all kinds of things when they're tired, and they often repudiate their testimony later.

All agree, however, that at half past nine in the evening, just as Laura White is coming down the stairs, there is a sudden snow flurry in the house. It lasts at least thirty seconds, at most three or four minutes. When it finally subsides, there is no sign of Laura White.

The snowstorm that appears in the house rushes from room to room. It strikes people's faces and leaves a mark. It tears clothes and draperies and breaks household articles. The orchestra's instruments are destroyed as people stumble and crash into them.

The storm slams into people, flings them around, forces its way into their clothing. It blinds them, fills their consciousness with its

*furious howl. Some try to use others for protection, some hide behind
furniture or under carpets.*

*All the doors and windows of the house burst open. The window
panes shatter. The curtains float into the dark winter night as if the
house were saying goodbye to a lover.*

It all ends as quickly and unexpectedly as it began.

EXCERPT FROM ESKO HARTAVALA'S ARTICLE
"THE LAURA WHITE INCIDENT",
FINLAND ILLUSTRATED WEEKLY, JUNE 2005

The party guests looked around them.

The house was full of snow. Martti Winter didn't know what
to do so he just watched as those who'd fallen stumbled to their
feet and adjusted their clothing. They counted their buttons,
straightened their socks, skirts and neckties, shook the snow
from inside their clothes.

Someone picked up some snow from the sofa, made it into
a ball, and then was embarrassed, not knowing why they'd
done it.

One woman found a small mirror on the floor. She started
to straighten her dishevelled hair and smeared make-up. A
moment before she had looked like a blooming forty-year-old.
She shook her head at her image in the mirror. It would be so
hard to put it back together in all this mess.

Some people tried to close the windows but their glass panes
had fallen out. They drew the curtains over them. The musicians
slipped on the snow. The bassist found a woman unconscious
inside his broken instrument and made a feeble attempt to
help her up, then decided to leave the task to the professionals.

"Where's Laura White?" Ella Milana asked Winter. She was

holding up the bodice of her dress with one hand—the thin straps had broken. There was ice in her hair.

This question of the authoress's whereabouts was repeated many times. They searched for the evening's hostess in every room. Some doors were locked, and were only broken open when she couldn't be found in any of the others. Her name was shouted. They looked on the balcony and in the garden. They opened the wardrobes. They searched under the furniture.

Some stood looking at the staircase is if waiting for Laura White to somehow appear where she was last seen. Perhaps her disappearance was part of the plan and she would appear again at any moment, smiling, ready to accept their applause.

Martti Winter made his way across the slippery ground in front of the house. People wandered here and there around him, lost, stupid, bustling about. Winter didn't know what to think. The whole situation seemed ridiculous, like one of those group games Laura White used to like to organize.

He didn't want to play any more.

He stopped at the pond. The ice had been cleared of snow. Lamp-posts and lime trees along the shore formed a jumble of light and shadow. The pond wasn't a pond anymore so much as a little ice rink reflecting the golden warmth of the lamps.

Laura White's winter parties always included skating on Nixie Pond. Guests skated in twos and were offered hot cocoa, with whipped cream on top if they liked. There were a couple of benches set up on the shore now, as well, and a long table and a large wooden box full of skates.

Farther off a police car splashed blue light. Someone was trying to move it out of the way of the ambulance, rocking it back and forth, the motor screaming. People talked into radios and cell phones. Search parties were formed and the first of them left to sweep the surrounding area.

Winter was hungry.

The police had already talked to him. He hadn't known what to tell them, had no idea what had happened. He wanted to go home to eat and sleep.

He sat on a bench, kicked off his dress shoes, and searched the box for the skates he had always used. He stumbled onto the ice and lurched forward.

The ice of the pond crackled as he slashed sharply over its surface. Decades ago, in an interview in *Rabbit Tracks,* Rabbit Back historian P. Mäkelä had spoken of the history of Nixie Pond. It was said that numerous people who didn't know how to swim had drowned in the pond in the early 1800s, including five children, and that someone had once spotted a bizarre creature there, which dived into the water and never resurfaced. Mäkelä had said the story had numerous sources, and emphasized that stories of water nixies should be taken for what they were worth, but that the drownings were well documented fact.

The problem was that, impressive as the story was, this Nixie Pond hadn't been built until after the war. Laura White's father had dug the hole for a root cellar originally, but had left the work unfinished in 1951. After that, water started to collect in it.

Winter had once discussed the matter with a place name researcher. According to him, someplace in the vicinity was another Nixie Pond, the original one, where people had drowned in the 1800s. For some reason the original pond had been forgotten and its name had been transferred to Laura White's pond. This was apparently quite common with place names.

The ice was clear and the water beneath it black. Winter skated onward, clumsily kicking up speed. His legs were shaking. When he was ten years old, he had been a little afraid of the skating evenings on the pond ice, although at that age he didn't believe in water nixies anymore. When the other young members of the Literature Society were with him, as terrified as he was, the fear had only made the whole thing more exciting.

Winter remembered how Ingrid had once collided with him. They both fell, and their mouths knocked together.

He remembered how Laura White used to clap for them from the shore and urge them to ever more reckless tricks. *Skate! Skate, my future authors! Get moving, or the nixie will get you!*

Winter felt dizzy, staggered and fell. He shrieked like a little girl and landed on his side with a thud.

He yelled with pain, gasped for breath. His ribs tingled and sent a shock through his nerves. His ankles were starting to swell inside his skates.

The ice grew colder. The frosty air went through his clothes to his skin and seeped into his body. He felt sick to his stomach. He trembled. He tried to get up, but couldn't make his limbs obey him.

His cheek was flattened against the ice. The cold penetrated his flesh, reached into his gums and the nerves of his teeth.

From the corner of his eye, he saw a shadow. It was moving under the ice, rising towards him. The water was black, but the shadow was still blacker. He couldn't quite make it out, but it came up quite close to him and tried to press against him, wanted to come into his arms.

Then it whispered something in his ear in a blind black voice.

*

84

"What happened?" someone was asking.

Winter opened his eyes. He was lying on the front steps of the house. Two men held him by the arms. One was wearing a yellow scarf that hung in front of Winter's face and fluttered in the wind.

Behind the men appeared the old café owner, Eleanoora Kauppinen, looking pale and sickly. She looked at him, shook her head, and continued on her way. The chaotic circus of police lights and bustle continued around him.

Winter wiggled his legs and realized he was still wearing the skates.

"I hurt my leg," he said.

They started taking the skates off.

"Did I faint?"

"You fell on your side on the ice," one of the men said. "And you didn't get up. When we came to where you were, you were out cold. It might be a good idea to go to the hospital."

"It's nothing," Winter said.

The yellow-scarfed man looked serious. "A person can't live without their brain. You may have a concussion. A relative of mine once hit his head on a sailboat boom and forgot five years of his life, just like that. Turned a nice guy into a real prick, to put it bluntly."

Winter finally got his shoes on his feet. He took a few steps and then stopped to look around him.

More cars were arriving, others leaving. Three parties on snow-mobiles were headed into the woods. Their headlights stabbed through the night and retreated in distant, random twinkles.

Ella Milana strode past him, stiff and silent. Ingrid Katz hurried after her, hissing to Winter as she passed, "I'll take her home. She must be quite shattered."

8

THE SEARCH was still going on the next morning. The news about Laura White's disappearance spread rapidly and shocked the community.

New theories to explain the incident were reported constantly. The woods were searched by helicopter with a thermographic camera. The snowmobile teams searched as far as Rabbit Bog during the night and went back again in daylight for good measure, checking on new tip-offs they'd received.

The searchers found two elk carcasses, five stolen bicycles, and some old moonshine stills. Their most interesting find was the remains of an abandoned car. It was a white Renault, a model called a Quatrelle. The woods had made it their own. There was a tree growing out of the hood. Later it was learned that the car had been stolen in June of 1984.

The perplexing thing was that the car was sitting in the middle of dense spruce forest. There was no sign of any road that it could have driven to get to where it was.

"There's no rational way of explaining it," one of the searchers commented in *Rabbit Tracks*.

The article included a plea to the unknown person who had stolen the car, asking them to send a letter, anonymously if they wished, explaining exactly how the car had got there. There was also an assurance from the owner that they held no grudge against the thief, and that the statute of limitations had long ago expired in any case. A reward of a free, one-year subscription to *Rabbit Tracks* was offered to anyone with information on the matter.

The searchers also found dozens of stray dogs. For some reason the dogs of Rabbit Back wouldn't stay at home. Some of them eventually tired of roaming and returned home, but others enjoyed the freedom and forgot their masters entirely.

It was common knowledge that packs of wild dogs lived in the woods around town and sometimes came skulking around people's houses. Many were afraid of them, although they were hardly any sort of menace. Hunters had been given permission to shoot stray dogs, and sometimes the men in town talked about knocking off so-and-so's mutt.

One of the search party, a dentist and violinist in the Rabbit Back Chamber Orchestra, thought she had seen her own dog, a golden retriever named Stradivarius, in a pack with five other dogs. She went after them on her snowmobile and was very nearly led into a blind ravine.

She managed to jump off at the last moment, but the snowmobile fell over the cliff and was completely destroyed.

"What Rabbit Wood takes, Rabbit Wood keeps," said the unemployed logger who came to pick her up.

Many people had been lost in the woods over the years, and not all of them had been found. Berry pickers, mushroomers, and hunters were warned not to go too deep into Rabbit Wood by themselves because the area wasn't well mapped and there was no way of locating every ravine and boghole.

Children's author Laura White was not found in the dark halls of the forest.

*

The case became a regular feature in the press and was talked about on radio and television. The evening tabloids whipped up their readership with increasingly attention-grabbing headlines.

WHERE IS LAURA WHITE?

LAURA WHITE KIDNAPPED?

WHO KILLED LAURA WHITE?

The police expressed indignation at the press's hastiness. There was nothing to indicate that anyone had orchestrated a kidnapping of the famed children's author, and there had been no pronouncement of her death. She remained at large, of her own volition.

Months passed, and there was no trace of the missing author. It was assumed that her body was lying somewhere. It could be anywhere in Rabbit Wood.

Laura White's books were read with very mixed feelings. It was difficult to concentrate on enjoying the story when you knew the writer was lying dead somewhere in the vicinity, eaten by dogs, her body disintegrating.

Children suffered from nightmares. One first-grader told the rest of his class that he'd had a dream where Laura White's dead body climbed into his window and started reading the Creatureville books to him. The next night another child who'd heard the story had her own version of the dream. The school sent home a note asking parents to calm their children and warning them about what they talked about within their hearing. The teachers forbade pupils from talking about their nightmares at school.

The statement from a police spokesman two days after White's disappearance was replayed now and then on television. According to the spokesman, Laura White would no doubt be found soon, or at most in a short time—people don't just cease to exist, especially not world-famous children's authors, he argued.

9

As INGRID KATZ drove her home from the party, Ella Milana replayed her glorious future as an Laura White-trained author.

It was a future of ecstatic reviews, interviews, glittering publishing events, grants and prizes. Above all, it was a future filled with metres of shelves of books with her name on the cover. All of it had just been proven a mirage, which only deepened its bittersweet glow.

Two hours earlier she had been waiting at the foot of the stairs, looking into Laura White's eyes, preparing the greeting she'd written and practised for a week to make it sound as natural as possible.

Ms White, I want to thank you for giving me this opportunity. I don't know what it was that you saw in my story, but if you see the tenth member of the Rabbit Back Literature Society in me, I won't question it…

"Are you pissed off?" Ingrid Katz asked cheerily, putting on her turn signal and slowing down to make a sharp left turn.

Dark figures moved about in the road. Katz put on the brakes. The car skidded a little, then stopped.

The headlights shone on two large hounds and a spitz. The dogs looked at them, jumped over a snow bank, and disappeared into the darkness of the fields.

Ingrid Katz laughed, shifted into first gear, and stepped on the gas. Sharp gusts of wind shaved snow from the side of the road and tossed it up in white clouds of powder.

"It's OK to be pissed off," Katz said gently. "It means you're still alive."

The librarian's Ford smelled like liquorice. Ella glanced at her and thought it best to put aside self-pity. "Well, Laura White is missing, and I'm still sitting here. I have no cause to complain."

Katz laughed. "Well, yes. We'll all pray for her and light candles for the next few weeks and probably go to dozens of memorials. It's all part of the process. And so is being pissed off. I know you're angry. Don't try to be so mature and brave and keep things in proportion. It's a bore. You were about to achieve something great, and it was taken away from you. You've experienced quite a personal loss this evening and you have to be pissed off. Say it out loud. It'll make you feel better. Trust me."

Ella shook her head. "I prefer not to use that kind of language," she said, and hated herself for her affected tone. "Not that there's anything wrong with it. It's just not in a teacher's vocabulary. If I use crude language when I'm not at work, it's only a matter of time before I start swearing in class. I may not be working in the field I'm trained for, temporarily, but that doesn't mean…"

She trailed off, tired of listening to herself. She stopped talking and started thinking about where she was in her life. She could apply for numerous positions and leave Rabbit Back. That's what she had originally intended to do. But then her future had seemed to point to the Society and becoming an author, guided by Laura White. And she had made her decision, and Laura White had sent her a lovely letter promising her a stipend for as long as her training lasted.

"Shit," Ella said.

"There you go," Ingrid said happily. "When life gives you plums, spit out the stones."

There followed a moment of silence.

"If it's any consolation," Ingrid continued, "there's one thing you should remember. Even without Laura White teaching you, you're still a member of the Rabbit Back Literature Society. That's something, isn't it? Your name will be on all the official lists with the nine other members. I added it this morning. And whenever someone writes the next history of Finnish literature, it will say that the tenth and last member of the Rabbit Back Literature Society was Ella Milana."

Katz stopped the car and turned off the engine. They had arrived.

"I think your mother's expecting you. There are lights on in the kitchen. Try to explain what happened, somehow, although I don't think that'll be easy."

"Why not?" Ella said. "There was a party, then there was a snowstorm in the house and Laura White disappeared right in front of everyone's eyes, and the tenth member isn't going to be trained after all. That's it in a nutshell."

"You got farther than your dad did, in any case," Ingrid said.

Ella was already getting out of the car. She stopped, lowered her bum back onto the seat, and looked at Ingrid.

"What did you say about my dad?"

Katz froze. Her right eye darted nervously as the light hit it.

"I thought you knew," she said.

"Knew what?"

"That Paavo Emil, your father, knew Laura White many years ago. And us—the members of the Society. He used to go around with us. A very strong runner. The Flying Rabbitbacker.

He wrote some poems for Ms White and tried to get into the Society. But he didn't get in. She liked him tremendously and his poems, but she thought his true nature was to run, not to write."

Katz took out a bag of liquorice and offered some to Ella, who declined. She filled her mouth with the sweets, obscuring her speech.

"Your father had talent, but you've succeeded where he failed—you made an impression on Laura White. Tonight you lost a teacher who could have sped things up for you, but hey—you're just as talented as you were before. The great author and creator of authors wouldn't have chosen you out of all the people who've tried to get into the Society over the years for no reason."

Ella sat without moving.

"Do you have all your things?" Ingrid asked, peeping into the back seat. "Didn't you have a handbag with you? I brought one to the car anyway…"

Ella nodded her head, which was now full of such heavy thoughts that she couldn't speak. She showed Ingrid her handbag and suddenly remembered that inside it, along with her handkerchief and coin purse and keys, was a small leather-bound book.

The rules of The Game.

10

E LLA MILANA and Marjatta Milana would have missed Christmas altogether if it hadn't been marked on the calendar.

Some local organization had made it their business to worry about the Christmas joy of widows and orphans and brought them a package in a cardboard box. It had gingerbread, tarts, fruitcake, traditional Christmas casserole, a ham roll, a couple of women's magazines and a chocolate elf. They tried to eat the food, not wanting to be ungrateful, but being the recipients of charity lent it all an unpleasant aftertaste.

They gave each other wrapped presents, no longer remembering what they contained.

Later Marjatta Milana put a big pile of decorative pillows on the sofa because it had been looking so unused. Ella came into the dark room, lost in her own thoughts, and thought she saw her father lying on the sofa. "Don't start bawling," her mother barked from the kitchen table where she was going through the papers concerning her father's death.

A dream Ella had the night before Christmas Eve also gnawed at her holiday mood. In it, Santa Claus came to their house, and behind his beard she could see Paavo Emil Milana's rotting face. He brought them a sack of mythological figurines and a card for a free mythological mapping. "*Sorry Santa's a little dead,*" he said behind his beard, "*but the damned garden gnomes gave him a good knocking around. They're all communists, you know, every one of them. But now Santa would like to hear a poem or two. Can anyone think of a nice poem?"*

Then the dream changed, and Ella was lying in bed listening to Laura White's dead body as it climbed the ladder to her bedroom window. In the dream she knew that Laura White was going to each house where she sensed there were Creatureville books. She also knew that the author didn't mean her any harm; she just wanted to read the books she'd written when she was alive, over and over.

On the floor there was a copy of *Rabbit Tracks* with a lead story urging locals to be understanding towards Laura White's dead body if it should break into their homes. After all, it was "the body of the most beloved Finnish children's author in the world".

Ella woke up. It was still night. She imagined for a moment that someone really was scratching and tapping on her window.

It was just the crackling frost. She buried her head in her pillow and went back to her dreams, which no longer contained any restless undead.

Over the long Christmas holidays Marjatta Milana shovelled the paths in the garden. It was a little more pleasant than crying in the kitchen. Ella sat in the house, where she still felt like a guest, even though she did partly own it. She sat perched at her desk, holding her temples and thinking. She wasn't going to make a move until she had analysed the situation thoroughly.

The night after Christmas, she woke up in her bed and opened her eyes. In her sleep, she had realized that a person is made up not just of her physical parts and her memories, but also her future.

A person's future was part of her, just as much as her hands and feet and reproductive organs. But an individual future was such a large part of a person's time that you couldn't see it all in one moment, and without any information about it people ended up trying to guess the true nature of their future.

If this theory was correct, a person's future could be thought of as a kind of soul that defined one's ultimate being on the axis of time.

When she'd returned to Rabbit Back, Ella had consisted of lovely, curving lips, faulty ovaries, and a future as a language and literature teacher. Then her future had been operated on and she'd received a new diagnosis: she was going to be a member of the Rabbit Back Literature Society, an author trained by Laura White.

At first she shrank from her new future, because it was a considerable shock to her identity, but gradually it had started to appeal to her more and more. She had even looked through the *History of Finnish Literature* for the section about Laura White and the Society she had formed around her, and got excited imagining how in the next printing they would include her name, Ella Milana, as the Society's tenth member.

What was more, her being, spreading itself across the axis of time, was actually different now. She had experienced a similar shock as a child the first time she'd stood between two mirrors and seen her own profile. Before she saw it, she had imagined it very differently.

Our individual futures are never what we imagine them to be.

For instance, she had once imagined that her soul, her individual future, her most fundamental being, would include giving birth to several children in her thirties. She would have put it on her passport if she could. But then the gynaecologist had shown her, with the help of mirrors, that she was not the person she had imagined.

Once, at a lecture on aesthetics, she had admired a stranger, a man sitting to her right. She had watched him for half an hour, fantasized about him, and even decided to try to get to know him. Then he had turned, and from this new angle, he was unattractive to her.

It wasn't possible to see an image of the whole person at once, because your point of observation was at one point on the axis of time, and the thing observed was shot through with innumerable points of observation. Every day would present a new side to view, and a being that you thought beautiful might suddenly prove unbearably ugly to you.

Falling in love with a person's momentary being was as irrational as falling in love with the left side of his face, or the back of his head, or some other individual part of him. That was why Ella couldn't really blame her former boyfriend for not knowing how to love her once her childless future was made visible.

In the midst of developing this complicated theory, Ella heard a noise. This time she was awake enough to see that there really was someone peeking in at her window.

There was a dark figure standing on the fire ladder knocking on the glass.

Ella didn't move. She carefully tugged the covers up over her face until only her eyes showed. Then the moon flashed momentarily over the face of the knocker.

Unlike in her dream, it wasn't Laura White's body. It was the round, easily recognized hamster face of Arne C. Ahlqvist, alias Aura Jokinen, whom Ella had met at Laura White's party.

The woman pressed her face against the window and left a blind spot with her breath. Ella had read the rules of The Game. She knew what this was about.

The sci-fi writer had come to challenge her.

The rules of The Game stated how the challenge should be made:

> *Every member of the Society has an unlimited right to challenge any other member to a Game. The challenge must be performed between the hours of 10 PM and 6 AM, and The Game itself, with both players taking their turn, must be played immediately upon making the challenge. The challenger has a right to make every attempt to challenge, using any means available, provided that delivering the challenge doesn't cause unreasonable harm. The challenge shall be considered delivered when the one challenged perceives the presence of the challenger and the challenger perceives that he or she has been perceived. Once a challenge has been delivered, the one challenged cannot refuse The Game without forfeiting membership in the Society.*

Ella closed her eyes tightly and pretended to be in a deep sleep, trusting that a middle-aged woman with a family wouldn't stay hanging from a ladder in the freezing cold for very long. She hoped with all her might that her mother, asleep across the hall, wouldn't be awakened by the knocking and come rushing in to confuse the situation.

The figure finally disappeared, and Ella was calm again.

11

T HE CHANGE to her personal future was a deep disappointment to Ella, and she was also upset by many everyday worries. The bills had to be paid and the groceries bought. There wouldn't be any open substitute positions until next fall, and her stipend had disappeared with the snowstorm. She made a long and thorough examination of her personal future and realized that she had to earn some money somehow.

One thing she didn't want her future to include was unemployment, which for her had always meant a descent into dispirited listlessness.

Eventually it sank in that she couldn't change the cards she'd been dealt. She just had to play them.

When Professor Eljas Korpimäki heard a few days before Laura White's party that his favourite former student was going to be a member of the Rabbit Back Literature Society, he was thrilled.

"That's incredible news. You should show Ms White your dissertation. It's quite a competent bit of research. Maybe sometime in the future you might agree to let me interview you about your experience. I just happen to be about to embark on a new project on Laura White. Thank you for calling and telling me. It's always so heart-warming to hear news like this. By the way, would you tell Laura White hello from a humble professor who is still the world's leading Laura White expert? You might also mention that the same professor was just in

Tokyo delivering a lecture on her works. If she would just relent and grant me an interview…"

When the media announced that Laura White had disappeared without a trace, the professor called Ella in quiet bewilderment, lamenting the fate of everyone involved and wishing his favourite student the best in the future. "Perhaps we can discuss what happened later, when you're back on your feet. I don't want to trouble you any more for now."

Ella called him a couple of days later. She enquired whether he would be interested in paying her for a research project on Laura White and the Rabbit Back Literature Society.

He could hardly contain his joy. Two days later he called to tell her that everything had been arranged handily.

"I put some weight behind your grant application, and did what I could to get assurance from my contacts that your funding was basically guaranteed. We'll have to wait for the allotted time, of course, but there shouldn't be any problem. You'll get a stipend from the university for your first few months of work. It's a time-sensitive topic, after all, the fact-finding, in light of recent events. But are you quite sure that the members of the Society will agree to be interviewed? At this point the whole affair is still at the level of the women's magazines."

"Yes, they'll talk to me," Ella promised.

She would receive funding for a year of work. She was guessing that a year of The Game would get her all the information she needed from the writers in the Society. After that she would find a teaching position at some school far from Rabbit Back.

Ella was afraid of The Game. It certainly wasn't an easy way to gather information. But the idea of it was also exhilarating.

If The Game worked the way she imagined, based on the rule book, she would learn things that would otherwise have been left to speculation for all eternity.

She could dig up anything she wanted from the Society's past.

12

Ingrid Katz closed up the library at eight and sent the intern home.

She climbed the stairs to the third floor and walked around the upper level to see everything below from a bird's-eye view. This walking inspection was more a ritual than a necessary act. As always, she reminded herself that all this was her responsibility. Then she went back downstairs.

It had been a satisfying day: she'd had to remove only one book from the collections, and for merely ordinary reasons—a patron had dropped it into a bowl of berry porridge.

Ingrid Katz closed the main door, checked to make sure it was locked, and stopped for a moment between the marble columns to breathe the outside air. The columns had once made her feel like the keeper of a sacred temple. That feeling had faded now. They were just pillars of stone. When she was feeling glum she even thought that the books were just bundles of paper with text printed on them.

She walked around to the back of the library where her Ford had its own parking space, and opened the car door. It hadn't frozen shut this time.

She sat in the car but didn't yet start the engine. As was her habit, she paused to acknowledge her negative thoughts and go through them one by one.

Today one of them was the recurring thought of changing jobs, leaving the library for someone else to worry about. She let the idea take over, let it feed her desire to do something else, anything else. Well maybe not anything. What she wanted was to write, to write freely, to write something meaningful. She wanted to write. She did, after all, work among great books, in a virtual garden of creativity, when you thought about it, but she herself hadn't been able to write anything for a long time. She had been scraping together a modest children's book, but she had stalled even in that pathetic attempt.

She nevertheless *knew* that she could write something wonderful, something unprecedented, if she could just get started. A great novel that would win at least the Finlandia Prize, and maybe even be an international success, a hit with readers and critics, and sell so well that she could build her family a large house in Rabbit Back's best neighbourhood.

But all her energies were taken up with preventing the library from careening into chaos. Books were being ruined all the time. And they were stolen. Faulty works appeared on the shelves constantly. The budget was cut every year. Another part-time library assistant had been laid off and replaced by an unpaid intern who let loose flaccid farts between the stacks, thinking no one would notice.

Ingrid seized her unpleasant thoughts, shoved them in an imaginary garbage bag, and flung them from her mind.

Then she cast off her skin. She was no longer Ingrid Katz the librarian. She was now Ingrid Katz, wife and mother, who was just getting off work, about to be greeted with smiles.

As she started the car she looked around the library grounds. It was dark in the shadows of the trees; there could be anyone lurking there. For several days she'd had bouts of paranoia like she hadn't felt in years. She glanced in the rear-view mirror once more to make sure she didn't have any extra passengers in the back seat. She was conscious of the fact that this was disconcerting behaviour, but on the other hand she did have past precedents for it.

She drove straight home and greeted her family. She came home every evening in time to put her children to bed. She'd promised her husband she would.

Ingrid Katz had birthed four children in all. The first two had been made by a more or less mutual understanding. The last two were a gift to her husband, who had always wanted a super family.

She liked the children, too, of course.

"This is the life," her husband would say as they sat surrounded by their children.

One time Ingrid had answered, "You don't read books." She'd meant it as an accusation, as the worst sort of insult. She said it maliciously.

Her husband laughed. "Books," he said. "There are a lot more important things in life than books. The children, for instance."

This evening the children wanted their mother to read old fairy tales to them. She shook her head and read to them from her unfinished children's book. They fell asleep so quickly that she wondered if she ought to add some more exciting scenes. She tucked them in. After she'd gone to the bathroom, she put on her winter coat and looked for her gloves. She'd put them in her coat pocket, but now they were gone.

"Damn it," she whispered, standing in front of the entryway mirror. She stood looking at her reflection. When had she started looking like that?

"Are you looking for your gloves, honey?" her husband asked from the kitchen. "I put them on the bathroom radiator to warm for the morning. Are you going for a walk again? Did you remember to take your vitamins? You ought to take some or you'll come down with something among all those books."

"I remembered," Ingrid lied. "Yes, I'm going out. It's too bad one of us has to stay and watch the kids. I'm going to the kiosk to buy some liquorice and brush off the book dust."

As she went out the door she asked, "Do you need anything from the kiosk?"

Her husband thought about it. Finally, he said he didn't need anything. Ingrid Katz left. Her husband never needed anything from the kiosk, she knew that without asking, but ritual required her to ask. Their marriage was a careful construction of interlocking rituals, and was rather precious for that. Sort of like Midsummer or Christmas.

It was nine o'clock. The ritual of her evening walk required that she be back by ten. Then her husband could go to bed and she could sit up on the sofa reading for a couple of hours. She wanted to wish her husband goodnight. That was how they did it.

Ingrid walked here and there through the familiar streets of the town. A few dogs came to meet her. A small, mixed-breed mutt stopped in front of her and growled, but a sarcastic snort sufficed to send it on its way.

Ingrid liked her walks through Rabbit Back. They always skirted close to the centre but it was easy to imagine that she was walking in a great forest, far from civilization.

There were seven statues altogether along her favourite route. They were part of the Rabbit Back art campaign. The idea

was to make the whole district into one big gallery. You might
see a statue at the foot of a tree, in the shrubbery, on the shore
of the pond. Some of them were grotesque—frightening, in
fact—others comical, graceful, even provocative, like the bare-
breasted water nymph beside a certain small pond.

The model for the buxom water nymph had been the artist's
own daughter, who taught the younger grades at Rabbit Back
School. Ingrid saw a crowd of little boys gathered around the
statue to admire the artist's work.

Beyond the water nymph and the crowd of boys Ingrid
reached the lonely portion of her walk. The path narrowed,
there were fewer ponds and the trees grew thicker.

She glanced around. She didn't want to be surprised, not
when she was already feeling paranoid. She also didn't want to
see every statue too clearly. There were two malevolent-looking
goblins along this stretch, not to mention the grotesque figures
her imagination made from the snow and shadows. Ingrid's silly
children's author's head slipped easily into monster stories that
she used to frighten herself.

*A little girl named Ingrid was walking down the road, and little
did she know that there lurked a monster...*

She stopped twice under street lamps to listen and look to see
if anyone was following her.

Then she saw coloured lights in the dark. The little shop signs
gave her a happy feeling. The signs in Rabbit Back were nostalgic,
old-fashioned: HELI'S SALON, read one, and Ingrid remembered
that she ought to make an appointment for a cut and dye.

*

Exactly an hour after she'd left the house, Ingrid halted at her front door. She dug out her house key and started to fit it in the lock.

Suddenly there was a movement in the darkness.

She spun around and stared hard at a nearby bush. It seemed to have moved about half a metre. Nonsense, she thought. Then the bush started rolling towards her.

She dropped her keys, her heart lurched and started to pound in her chest. She looked at her watch. It was 10:01.

It was happening again.

Her hands and feet went bloodless and she felt dizzy, awful. She closed her eyes and turned her back on it, forcing herself to smile nonchalantly.

Then she felt a breath on her neck whispering the dreaded words: *I challenge you, Ingrid Katz*.

She turned around slowly, her eyes wet, a strained smile on her lips, and saw Ella Milana's amused face before her.

Ella watched as Ingrid gradually recovered.

Katz was slumped sideways on the porch steps, pale and breathless. At the library and the party she had seemed stern and brisk. Now the irony was crumbling and dropping away. Ella wondered if she'd gone too far. But Arne C. Ahlqvist had clambered up a ladder and scratched at her bedroom window in the middle of the night to get to her.

"Sorry to startle you," Ella said, "but I had the impression that this was how you did it in the Society."

Ingrid waved a hand at her. "I won't claim otherwise. It's just that I've been out of practice for a while. It's such a crazy thing to do. Dreadful, really. Utter foolishness. It's no wonder

you can't talk about The Game to outsiders. They'd laugh
at us, shut us up somewhere, the lot of us. But those are the
rules. Laura wrote them, and it's not our place to change
them around." She searched in the snow for her keys as she
muttered this, her face lighting up when she found them. "But
we can, in theory, be civilized about the whole thing," she
continued. "We could use the phone, for instance. 'Hello, this
is fellow Society member so-and-so. Could you possibly join
me for The Game tonight after dinner?' But we hardly play
The Game at all anymore. It's been more than three years
since I last played."

Katz thought for a moment and then said, "We can play at
the library, if you like."

Ingrid jangled her keys, opened the door and hung her coat
on a hook. "You're the challenger. You decide where we play.
The children's section? The reading lounge?"

They passed the elves, gnomes and nymphs standing in the
dark and Katz led them between the shelves to a reading corner
with a table and two bar stools. In the middle of the table stood
a small stone figure of a woman with plump breasts, wide hips,
and butterfly wings.

Ella liked this spot. She lost herself in looking at the floors
opening up above them and the skylight, the winter night falling
through it into the room in a grid of light.

"Do you have a handkerchief?" Ingrid enquired, taking off
her glasses and placing them carefully in their case.

Ella took out a red scarf and tied it around the librarian's
eyes, as the rules of The Game instructed.

"I hope it's not too tight," she said.

"No," Ingrid answered. "You managed to get a rule book from somewhere, then?"

Ella could smell liquorice on her breath. "Yes," she answered. "Martti Winter loaned it to me. I'll return it when I get my own copy, of course. That's promised in the rule book: *Every member of the Rabbit Back Literature Society shall receive one copy of the rules of The Game for their own study.*

"You can blame me for that," Ingrid said. "I'm the one who put you up to asking him. I suppose you've read the part about how to present the questions as well?"

"The rules say that I can ask you anything at all and you have to answer with absolute honesty," Ella said. She had the rule book in her bag, just in case. "If I'm not satisfied with your answer, I ask again until the answer sounds sufficiently believable. You're expected to try with all your might to be completely open and honest. If I get a sense that you're not making an effort to answer honestly, it's my right and responsibility as the challenger to help you by any possible means to find the truth within yourself."

Ingrid thought for a moment. "You haven't been trained in The Game," she said at last. "Are you quite sure you can follow through all the way to the end?"

"When I've got my answers from you, I am indeed ready to answer any questions you may have, if that's what you mean."

Ingrid shook her head. "That's my responsibility. What I'm worried about is whether you're ready to get the truth out of me if I don't answer truthfully enough. I have to know if you can honour the spirit of The Game to the last. You should understand that once a question has been asked, you have a duty, to both of us, to make sure that I give a complete and honest answer. You simply cannot content yourself with anything less than the whole truth."

Ella felt her palms sweating. "I've read the rules," she said, "and I understand them."

Ingrid's mouth grinned. Ella wished she could see her eyes.

"But I find it hard to believe that you have it in you," Ingrid said. "I'm sorry, but I don't believe you can play The Game properly. Laura White hasn't trained you."

Ella bit her lip. "Are you trying to make me say that I understand the meaning and the demands of Rule 21?" she said.

Ingrid Katz nodded.

Rule 21 wasn't an easy one. Ella had read it through many times until she was sure she understood it.

Once she'd read Rule 21 it was easy to understand the rituals associated with challenging someone to The Game. People could more easily free themselves from their inhibitions at night, and once you had the other person in your clutches, like a predator, it was easier to temporarily abandon common courtesy.

Ella took hold of Ingrid's lower lip. Then she twisted it until the woman let out a high-pitched cry of pain.

A drop of blood rolled down her chin. She pushed Ella's hand away and gave a squeak as she felt her lip with her fingers.

"All right," Ingrid said, mollified and a little frightened. "You understand Rule 21. So let's play."

Ella asked her question.

She had formed it carefully beforehand so that it wouldn't be too broad or vague, precisely according to the rules.

"I want information about those books you took off the shelves and destroyed. You weren't honest with me about them. Tell me the truth now."

Ingrid Katz turned pale under the scarf. She made a nervous movement, touched her swollen lip again, and said, "I've tried not to think too closely about it. This is the one thing that Martti Winter doesn't know about me, as far as I know what he knows and am not just thinking I know. But all right. The Game has started, so I'll spill."

13

Ingrid Katz Spills

E LLA STOPPED HER and asked her what she meant by "spill".
Ingrid's mouth smiled. "It's one of The Game's more
recent terms. You draw it out, and I spill it. I spill, I spilled, I
am spilling. At some point we wanted to distinguish between
playing The Game and telling stories, because storytelling is
an art, but The Game is something else entirely.

"You see, The Game doesn't produce stories, it produces
material for stories. That happens when you break open the
stories and let their unformed essence spill out. That's what The
Game is for. Everybody has valuable material inside them that
The Game can help to draw out."

Even with her eyes covered Ingrid Katz seemed to sense
Ella's confusion.

"I suppose it sounds a little tasteless," Ingrid said apologetically. "I may have been the one who suggested the term. You
won't find it in the rule book. I was thinking about collecting
sap from trees. It seemed like a beautiful idea in a way. To go
to the woods and make a little hole in a tree and come away
with something valuable without doing any damage. Arne C.
was very enthusiastic about the term, but she has her own ideas
about it now. She suggested we call The Game *Nosferatu*, but I
let it be known that I would quit the Society the second such a
name was adopted."

Katz began spilling by telling Ella that she wasn't the only book thief. "You wouldn't have got it into your head to sneak in after those books if I hadn't committed my own book theft a good thirty years ago."

She hesitated.

"At least that's one way to look at it," she added uncertainly, "now that I'm putting my feelings into words. It's weird. I've never let myself think it through to the end until now."

She said she'd been twelve years old. It was the first week of July. "We—Martti and I—were spending the morning on the hill by the school. We started acting childish, making rivers and dams, the way children do. We were going to Laura White's house but first we wanted to play in the mud. It was like that on the hill, a good place to dig rivers in the dirt. It was nice. It was exciting

to see how the water would go where we wanted it to, and we decided to go to the dead rat's grave before we went to Laura's house; we thought we still had time. Martti had on a new pair of leather shoes and they got all dirty, of course. He tried to make light of the whole thing, said, "It's just a pair of shoes," but I knew that his mother was going to tear into him. I promised to take his shoes to my house and ask my father to do something with them. My dad was a cobbler. He had a shop where the Brumerus kiosk is now...

Well, Martti was very grateful, just sighing with relief, even though he tried to hide it from me. And...

Ingrid is quiet for some time, then says, "I'm sorry. Maybe all this doesn't have anything to do with the books. I don't know. But I'm trying to go back in my mind to that day, and one detail leads to another, and so on.

"It's extremely difficult to remember things correctly. I

remember that day in one sense, but of course it's not clear, not a whole film in my head that I can just reel out for you. There are breaks in the film in several places, part of it's dim, some of the story is jumbled, a lot of it is faded almost completely away. There are alternate versions of some of it. The days get mixed up. I remember the feelings, but are they the original feelings or are they the feelings I have when I remember it?

"You must have noticed sometimes how when you tell a story you make up all kinds of additions to it, partly because it improves the story and partly because there are always gaps in your memory. You can't do that in The Game. The Game isn't for telling stories. In The Game you leak out whatever is deepest within you, nothing more and nothing less. But I'm sure you read about it in the rule book, so I'll stop explaining. Please be patient, though, and don't pinch my lip quite yet. I'm rummaging through my head as I talk and gradually I'll muddle into a deeper memory and some superfluous things might come out in the meantime. Anyway, I do remember the rat… I got it

for my birthday. A dead rat. Or that's what I thought at first, when I found a package on the kitchen table with a dead rat in it. I thought it was one of my father's deep lessons. He was always playing those kinds of tricks on me. I found out later that he had found the carcass in the cellar and swept it up into the first piece of paper he found to take it outside, and then forgotten it on the table when he went out to his workshop.

I didn't know what to do with it. I imagined my father would ask me in the evening what I'd done with my gift, and I ought to have a thoughtful answer. That's the way my father was. He was always inventing different challenges and tests for me. So anyway, I decided to give the rat a proper funeral. I went and asked Martti to come with me.

Martti was excited. He came over and put together a little coffin for it and it was the finest little coffin I had ever seen.

He made a fabric lining for it out of his handkerchief. I said wouldn't his mother be angry with him for putting an expensive handkerchief in a rat's coffin, but he didn't say anything. He was so serious.

That happened in the morning. When Martti and I were on our way to Laura White's house we decided to go by the rat's grave again. We had put a sort of little cross on it. We made it out of popsicle sticks, I think. When we were at the grave, Martti started crying. I was shocked, wondering what was the matter. He explained that he was imagining his mother lying dead under the ground.

I told him that his mother was alive, unlike my mama, but his tears just kept coming. I socked him in the arm as hard as I could. I said he ought to save his crying for when there was a reason to cry. That was one of my father's sayings. I made it my business to instruct Martti.

He got angry and ran away towards Laura White's house. I remember I stood there for a long time before I realized that he had left me standing alone at a rat's grave. So I walked after him.

The way to Laura's house seemed terribly long. When I got there, I walked around in the garden for a while trying to decide whether to go inside at all. I went to the edge of the pond and was about to rinse my face with the cool water, but then I was startled by a branch or a reflection and I ran to the porch. The pond in Laura's garden made all of us nervous—it was fun to skate on in the winter, but during the summer we didn't go near it. I don't know why.

When I think about it now, we could have swum in it. Don't children usually enjoy swimming? For some reason we just never did. Maybe it was because of Laura. She hated and feared the water. She never went swimming and probably never went boating either, and she preferred not to go near deep water, and we probably got that attitude from her.

Anyway, I went inside after all and I heard voices from farther inside, from the corner room. The others were there, already reading their stories out loud. I think I heard Martti's voice above the others, and oh how I hated him at that moment. And to top it off, it hit me just then that we were supposed to write something about our mothers for that meeting, and I hadn't written a single line. I wanted to cry.

I was all mixed up. I didn't know if I should go in where the others were or just go home. I may have had a fever, too. I was shivering. It felt like something had shut me off from everything. And then I went and looked around the house, although I was a little bit afraid to walk around by myself. I'd never really looked around Laura White's house before, and now I had decided to do it for the hell of it, just because I got the idea in my head.

Ingrid Katz stops speaking and points to her mouth. "Excuse me, but could I have something to drink? There's some water in the back room, I think. All this talking is drying out my mouth. I haven't talked so much at once in a long time. My job keeps me quiet most of the time. Since the signs specifically prohibit talking."

Ella fetches a paper cup of water from the back room. Ingrid sips it, apparently pondering what to say next.

"The next thing I have any complete memory of is running away from the house with my heart pounding and two books in my hand. The other children are still in the corner room with Laura and I have

those two books in my hand. Jesus.

What happened in the house is a little dim and confused. I was walking around, opening doors and peeking into places. I remember peeping into some drawers and seeing a wonderful music box which I would have liked to have for myself. It had a ballet dancer. And I remember a big chair that I sat in for a while. It had a strange smell, sour and damp and sort of mossy. I closed my eyes and imagined I was in the woods, and I think I may have fallen asleep in the chair. Then I can almost remember that I went into another room that I thought led into the entryway, but I ended up right back in the same room I'd left. I felt sort of lost. But I've always had a lousy sense of direction.

I have to say now that I can't be sure of the rest of this. It's in my head, but I don't know if it's a memory. I mean, it could just as well be some dream or fantasy. I put it in one of my children's books and worked on it so much that I don't really know how much of the original memory is left.

But I do remember something like this—there was a colourful place on the wall where the light was really interesting and I had a delightful thought that, hey, it looks like there's a door there, and then I touched the wall with my fingers and it gave way and suddenly there was a door opening in front of me.

All these books appeared in this room. And I stepped inside. At some point I started to feel bad, I got dizzy and shivery and wanted to throw up.

I don't remember anything about the room itself, I just remember the dream I've had many times. In the dream, the room is full of water and I'm swimming from shelf to shelf looking at the books. And in the dream I see one book on a shelf that I've been looking for everywhere for a long time, and another one that I really must have, and then I swim towards the door with the two books in my hand and I'm about to drown because the books weigh so much.

And then I always wake up.

Ingrid grows quiet again and seems to be gathering her thoughts. "A lot of overlapping, hellishly unclear memories," she laughs. "It's annoying! It's such a mess! Like at first there are a lot of films overlapping each other, and then I'm running out of the house with the books under my arm, feeling thrilled and guilty at the same time, horrified and confused, like you are when you have a fever. And then the memory breaks off."

Ella rubs her brow, trying to make something out of Ingrid's story. "So what does this have to do with the library books?" she asks.

"I'm not sure," Ingrid says, "but at my deepest, I feel like it's related. If you'll wait a moment, I have another memory. In this one, I'm coming out of the rain into the library. I remember the cold and the wet, remember how

water is dripping off me onto the library floor. I'm quite wet and shivering. The stolen books are under my dress, against my stomach, and I so want to get rid of them.

And I don't remember what books they actually were, although I know I looked at them. I had dreams about them, but it's hard to remember dreams precisely later on; they disappear completely as soon as you start to focus on them. But I did still remember that, at least in my dream, there was something weird about the books, something that made it so that I couldn't possibly keep them. One of them frightened me, something about a dead emperor—don't ask, I really don't know—and the other was a bit hazy, fluid and wavering, and when you read it you started to get dizzy and see double, or triple.

I waited for the old librarian, Birgit Ström, to go somewhere, then I went into the back room and closed the door behind me. I thought she was going to have a poo. Sometimes she would take a long time in the toilet and the smell of her poo would spread out over the library. I ran, all wet and chilled, to a book trolley and shoved the books in with the others and my hands were shaking terribly, and I guess after that I just left. I don't remember anything more.

Ingrid grimaces and her voice becomes thin and old as she continues. "Those trolleys were for the books that had already been returned and were waiting to be shelved in different parts of the library. So the books I put there infected all the other books on the trolley, and they spread the infection through the shelves. That's how it all started."

Ella leans forward and stares at the librarian's dry lips. "You called it an 'infection'," she says. "What kind of infection do you mean? Some kind of mould?"

Ingrid looks limp. "You've seen what an infected book looks like. I don't have a name for it. In my head I sometimes call it 'the book plague'—on those rare occasions when I dare to think about it. Or maybe you could call it a 'book mutation'. If you wanted to talk about it at all. Maybe the world is what it is. But there are things you can't talk about. You just keep quiet about them, and I would put this on that list."

Her face grows tense.

"I don't know what exactly it is. There are changes in some of the books. They somehow become… how shall I put it… fluid. And your Dostoevsky was a particularly bad case. It changed even more before I burned it."

She stretches her mouth into an ironic smile. Ella wonders if the air of the library is getting thinner or if she's just imagining it. She feels like the blindfolded Ingrid is leading both of them to the edge of some kind of cliff.

"I noticed when I was in school that there was something strange about the books in the Rabbit Back library. I didn't talk to anyone about it. I felt from the very beginning that it was my particular problem." Ingrid thought for a moment, then changed the subject. "When I was younger I once had a little trouble, the kind of thing that can happen to a girl who messes around with the wrong kind of boy. I knew it was there but I didn't want to think about it. I just shut off my mind until I'd gone to the doctor and bought the pills, and when I took them, I thought about something else altogether."

A stony silence fills the library. Ella looks up at the ceiling. The skylight looks blacker than before. The night huddles tighter around the building.

If she really listens closely, she imagines she can hear the books quietly rustling on the shelves.

"After high school I went to university and studied library science," Ingrid recites, through rigid lips. "I came here first as an assistant, and then, when Birgit Ström died, I became the librarian."

Ella opens her mouth to speak, but the words evaporate from her lips into the dry library air. She shifts in her seat. Her ass is numb.

"All right," she says wearily. "I don't really understand what you've told me, but I accept your story."

Ingrid Katz shakes her head. "I haven't told you a story. The Game isn't for stories. If only we could tell each other stories! Telling stories is nice. It's nice to embellish them with all kinds of things, and leave out the embarrassing parts. You can make stories logical and understandable. But if we play The Game right, all that comes out is what's inside you, nothing more and nothing less. I spill, you spill, we spill."

She takes a deep breath and stands up.

"You'll come to realize how The Game works," she says, her voice lively again. She takes the scarf off and hands it to Ella. "In your head, you have a clear, rational version of things. You know—your own story, the one you tell in public. We all dress ourselves in stories. Then you start to spill, and for a little while afterwards you don't understand what you're really saying anymore. And finally, always, the thing that is most shocking about spilling is you yourself. That's the true nature of The Game. Here. Put this over your eyes. It's your turn. I want your father's death."

14

AFTER THE GAME, Ella Milana slept for a week.
Her mother came to stand outside her door now and
then, to bring her a sandwich and let her know what was happening in the outside world.

There was going to be a fireworks show to celebrate the new
year. Marjatta Milana bought a raffle ticket when she went into
town. The principal called five times to ask about the essays,
which Ella still had not returned. Marjatta shovelled new paths
in the snow and kept the old ones clear as more snow fell. She
drove away two aggressive dogs that were hunting some small
animal among the currant bushes. There was a good programme
on television, which Marjatta ended up watching alone. There
was a proper meal waiting in the kitchen.

A postcard arrived from Ingrid Katz. Marjatta Milana read
it aloud, wondered that her daughter seemed to have taken up
sports, and pushed the card under the door. It read: *You may feel
achy after The Game. It's normal, and will pass.*

On the seventh day Ella got up, dressed, took her bag and went
out. The first flakes of a new snowfall were drifting to the ground.
The drifts were full of shovelled paths. Ella walked along one of
them to the shed, searched for a canister she knew was there for
the lawn mower, came out with it and doused her bag with petrol.

She struck a match under the apple trees. Her mother
appeared on the steps and rocked back and forth as she watched
her through the branches.

The match flew in a graceful arc and landed in the bag. The flames swirled higher than Ella had anticipated and she fell backwards onto her bum in the snow.

"What exactly do you think you're doing?" her mother shrieked. "Destroying a good bag! Aren't your students' essays in that bag, the ones the principal was asking about?"

"They're infested with mould," Ella coughed, waving the smoke away.

Her mother bustled over, grabbed her under the arm, pulled her to her feet, farther from the pyre, and tossed snow on the hem of her coat, which was smoking. Ella watched with satisfaction as the papers burned in the bag.

"I noticed it a couple of days ago. I don't know where it came from, but I certainly can't take them back to the school or give them to anyone. You know how these things can spread like wildfire."

A week earlier, when The Game had ended and Ella had left the library with Ingrid Katz, Ingrid hadn't offered her a ride, explaining, "I need oxygen. Need to clear my mind. Recovering from a spill takes time, and I have to come back and open the library in a few hours."

When she got home, Ella wandered into her room and tried once more to get to work grading the essays still in her bag. She couldn't understand anything she read. The pupils' texts were more confused and shapeless than usual, positively incomprehensible in places. She was beginning to suspect that she'd suffered some sort of attack of the brain, but then she noticed that she was able to read other texts without difficulty.

The problem wasn't her; it was the essays.

She watched the burning bag now, no longer baffled by the book plague Ingrid had told her about. At first it certainly had bothered her, but then she'd come up with a clever theory about the state of everyday reality:

Reality was a game board for all of humanity to play on, formed from all human interaction. You could in principle make it up out of anything you wished, provided you all agreed upon it. But it was easiest if everyone used square pieces, because they would all fit perfectly together and form a seamless whole.

So square pieces had become the standard. Ella guessed this had happened sometime in the Middle Ages, or perhaps it came with the knowledge gained during the Enlightenment.

Occasionally, however, an unusual piece might fall into someone's hands. The board had to be made according to strict standards, though, if you wanted to avoid problems with the rest of the world. So you had to disregard the non-standard pieces, had to maintain the right attitude about them.

And that's how Ella handled the troubling question of the book plague.

The highest flames swirled up from the confiscated comic book. Its pages showed vaguely duck-like figures behaving bizarrely. She hadn't looked closely at them since she'd come home from The Game, spent.

It was just a dream, the duck dressed like a sailor splitting an older duck's skull with an axe and doing it again to another duck that happened along.

The page crinkled in the fire for a moment and was devoured.

Ella Milana sat at her desk planning her research project.

Her first stipend payment had arrived in her account that

day, so she had to make a start. She stared at her own reflection in the window, forming her first question about Laura White.

She also had to decide whom she would challenge next. She couldn't challenge Ingrid Katz again until Ella herself or someone else was challenged. The rule book said: *You cannot challenge the same member of the Society a second time until you have challenged someone else or until you yourself are challenged by another member of the Society.*

Ella examined the printed list of Society members Ingrid had given her. It had a picture of each member, including Ella. Her picture had been taken at a local photo shop a couple of days before Laura White's party. She looked like a hopeless, overeager idiot.

The list included contact information for each member. Except for the screenwriter Toivo Holm and the author Anna-Maija Seläntö, who lived in Sweden, all of the members were living in Rabbit Back, including Ella.

This was the list of all the members of the Rabbit Back Literature Society:

MARTTI WINTER

INGRID KATZ

HELINÄ OKSALA

AURA JOKINEN

SILJA SAARISTO

ELIAS KANGASNIEMI

TOIVO HOLM

OONA KARINIEMI

ANNA-MAIJA SELÄNTÖ

ELLA MILANA

Ella looked at the photographs. She stopped at Martti Winter and thought at first that they had mixed up the pictures. Like the other members' photos, it had been taken years ago. Instead of a fat, worn-out man, the photo showed a fine-featured, almost beautiful youth.

It was the same photo that was on the inside covers of his books. Ella suddenly remembered how in high school she had read his entire oeuvre, occasionally falling into a reverie over the photo of the lovely young man who'd written them.

She had always known that Martti Winter and several more of her favourite writers lived in Rabbit Back. It hadn't meant anything to her. They might as well have been on the other side of the planet. Rabbit Back wasn't a particularly large town, but like all towns it was made up of numerous compartmented social strata. The writers in the Society and ordinary people sometimes encountered each other on the street or in a shop, but that was an optical illusion. Even if the two people saw each other, even if they said hello, no real encounter had occurred. The writers simply lived on a different plane of existence than other people.

Ella took Martti Winter's novel *Hidden Agendas* down from the shelf and opened it. There was the photo on the inside cover—a soft-focused studio portrait, sensitively lit and no doubt retouched. The picture let you know that the author wasn't an ordinary person, he was some kind of literary god made flesh, an enlightened, more evolved being. Ella remembered how Silja Saaristo had greeted her at the party: *Ella! Welcome to the demigod gang!*

Ella's finger ran down the list of names. All of them had spoken to her at the party. She must have made a clumsy, childish impression. She wasn't used to that kind of attention.

She thought about how Arne C. Ahlqvist had greeted her. Something about it had bothered her at the time. Because of her schooling, something had caught her attention, something that other people wouldn't have taken any notice of. She had almost started a discussion with her about comma placement, because Ahlqvist had said to her: *It's so nice to meet the new tenth member of the Society.*

As a language and literature expert, Ella, of course, would have put a comma between *new* and *tenth*. Without a pause there, or some kind of emphasis, indicated in writing by a comma, the sentence seemed to mean that it was nice to meet a new tenth member *who had replaced the old tenth member.*

And there had never been any more than nine members in the Society until Ella Milana joined.

Ella knew she was splitting hairs. Was she ever. It was like a sickness only lang and lit teachers contracted, and she knew exceedingly well that people just said things sometimes, that speech was imprecise, as well it should be. And she would have forgotten the whole thing if she hadn't suddenly remembered another peculiar conversation, one that included a strange adverb.

Oona Kariniemi was known for her profound love stories. At the party, Kariniemi had been talking with four older men when she noticed Ella, waved and darted between the men to come and talk to her. *Are you* the *Ella Milana?* she had screamed, a wine glass in her hand. *I knew it! That story of yours in* Rabbit Tracks *was excellent. You use the language beautifully. We've never had any real language professionals in the crowd, just us writers, but we've got along somehow. Of course our editors have had a lot of cleanup to do, ha ha. But hey, it's really great to get some new blood in the Society. Thanks to you we have a tenth member again.*

She had definitely used the word *again*.

Ella picked her phone up from the bed, searched for Ingrid Katz's number, hesitated a moment, then pushed the green button. She made a face at her reflection in the black window.

Ingrid answered on the fifth ring. "Evening, Ella," she said, a little breathless, apparently on her evening walk. "How can I help you?"

"Good evening. Sorry to bother you, but could you please tell me: have there ever been any other members of the Society besides the nine of you?"

The librarian's breathing rasped over the phone. "You're a lang and lit teacher. You must have a copy of *A History of Finnish Literature* on your shelf." Ingrid laughed. "Look in there, if you don't remember."

"I already looked at it, and it says that there have never been more than nine members. But is that information correct?"

There were several seconds of silence on the other end. Ella started to grow nervous.

She had felt a little silly when she'd dialled Ingrid's number, doubting the official history because a science fiction writer making a passing comment had left out a comma.

Five endless seconds later Ingrid said, "If it's in the book it must be true. You're the tenth member. There were always nine members before, nine writers in training, plus their trainer, Laura White."

Ella's mouth was dry. "I hope you won't be angry if I don't believe you," she said. "You're a terrible liar. I can tell from your voice that you—"

Ingrid coughed. There was another pause.

"Listen, if you really feel that something is being kept secret from you, go ahead and use The Game. But if I were you I would think twice before I decided to spill who knows what just to check some information that can be found in any literary history."

15

ELLA MILANA trained her binoculars on Silja Saaristo's house for three days. The house was on the east side of Rabbit Back, near a wooded knoll. The nearest neighbours were half a kilometre away. Ella parked the Triumph a little distance from the house and conducted her surveillance from inside the car. She ate sandwiches and drank coffee from a Thermos.

Then she thought of something that might prove useful. She took a day off from her stake-out to check her theory by reading a book she had started a few days earlier. She was delighted to discover that she didn't need to go undercover. The answer was in the book.

As she drove up to the house with the headlights off, Silja Saaristo was standing on the terrace in the glow of the porch light. She was smoking a cigarette, wearing a bathrobe, and holding a glass of wine, all according to schedule. Saaristo was on her way to her evening bath, and was exposing herself to the cold to better enjoy the hot water.

She never locked the door until she went to bed around 11:30. The lock was sticky and stubborn, and since she went out to smoke about once every hour, it was easiest to just leave the door unlocked.

It was now ten past ten.

Once she went back inside, Ella waited a moment and then made her move. She lit her way with a penlight. She walked calmly across the garden, slipped in the back door, purposely leaving it open, and went to a dark corner to wait.

A cold current of air blew into the house. Saaristo would soon notice it from her bath and think she'd left the door open herself.

Ella waited fifteen minutes. She stood in the shadow of a bookcase, shifting her weight from one foot to the other.

A cat appeared and wrapped itself around her feet.

Silja Saaristo toddled into the living room in her robe, her hair wet, calling the cat and hoping that it hadn't gone out the open door. She pulled the door closed and locked it for good measure, but then stood looking out the window at the snow on the terrace.

There were strange footprints in it.

Saaristo stood stock still and lifted her hands to her cheeks with a look of intense concentration.

As Saaristo started to turn with a wary look on her face, Ella smiled to herself in the dark. Her heart was thudding but she was sure that Saaristo's heart was pounding even harder. Ella sniffed the air and let herself imagine she could smell the other woman's fear.

The mission had been greatly aided by her hunch that Silja Saaristo had planned her own murder, in her novel *Lament of the Departed*—the very novel that Ella happened to have started to read the week before. It was all in there—the bath every evening, the hourly cigarette, the sticky lock on the terrace door, the door left open, tempting her out of her bath, the worry over the cat, the footprints in the snow, and the dawning suspicion.

Ella did not, however, crack open the skull of the lady of the house with the heavy table lamp that stood on the bookshelf just within reach and was described in great detail in the novel, tape-wrapped cord and all.

Instead she whispered a challenge in the darkness.

16

S ILJA SAARISTO offered Ella some tea and crackers with cheese, salami, and fresh peppers on top. When the crackers were eaten, Saaristo brushed the crumbs from her lap. Then Ella smiled, leaned towards her and tied a blue handkerchief over her eyes.

"I was just reading one of your books, although I don't usually like mysteries very much," Ella said companionably.

She had decided to behave as politely as possible to her fellow Game players. The Game gave Society members the right to invade the peace of the each others' homes, and even to use violence, within the parameters of Rule 21, but be that as it may, one could still do the whole thing civilly and politely.

"Oh? Which book?" Saaristo asked.

"*Lament of the Departed*," Ella said. "I might start reading more mysteries. It's no wonder you won a prize."

"I haven't finished another book since then," Silja Saaristo sighed. "And that came out two years ago. Or was it three?"

The cat jumped up onto the back of the sofa, walked the length of it with its tail erect, and dropped out of sight again.

"It's been a while since I played The Game," Saaristo said. "I was actually starting to miss it."

Ella asked her question.

Silja Saaristo tilted her head, her mouth in a tight line, sniffled and finally started to speak:

"Well, yes, there were actually ten of us at one point, although we never talk about it. I think we all still feel a bit bad

about what happened to the Society's most talented member, and then we all understand each other so well that we decided to forget the whole thing. And the death of a child is always such a hard thing, especially for other children.

I think I was the seventh member, if I remember correctly. Yeah. When I was invited to join, there were five of the present members—Ingrid Katz, Toivo Holm, Aura Jokinen, Elias Kangasniemi, and Anni Seläntö. Something like that. Ingrid, Toivo, and Aura all joined at the same time, when they were eight, and Ms White invited the others one by one after that, whenever she found someone good enough—she monitored school essays, from what I understand. But the member chosen sixth is completely forgotten nowadays.

After he died, nobody talked to us about it. It may be that no one outside the Society knew he was a member. I think some of the group went to the funeral, though. Maybe they did. I didn't. I can't stand funerals—a carcass in a wooden box, everybody sniffling and sobbing. I didn't even go to my grandma's funeral, although I think church is lovely, so beautiful and peaceful. I told everybody I was sick.

He came from someplace else—he didn't go to school with us. He may have lived in a different district. I don't think we ever knew where he lived. Anyway, he sort of came and went as he pleased—sort of an outsider, if you know what I mean. Some thought he was mysterious and interesting, but I thought he was just stuck up. He had a sort of a smirk.

Sometimes we tried to get him to tell us where exactly he lived. He wouldn't say. We might have left him to himself, but the thing was, he was clearly the most talented one of us, a real prodigy.

Martti was the second-best writer in the Society, but this other boy was something else entirely, in a whole different league. We were all ordinary kids, talented kids maybe, but still, just kids. This boy was like some fucking Mozart, writing incredible stuff when he was just little.

I don't remember anymore exactly what he wrote, but when I heard him read his stories out loud in Laura's reading room I remember thinking, "Fuck, thanks a lot, guess I'll give up writing now." And I wasn't the only one. That much talent piled up in one person can be fucking depressing for other people. You can start to think, Fuck, I wish he would just die.

He always had this diary with him where he wrote down all his thoughts and ideas. He would never show it to anyone, the fucking diva. Not to me, anyway. I did try to get him to show it to me a couple of times and I promised that if he did I would show him anything he wanted to see.

This all probably sounds pretty terrible. I wasn't a little harpy, honest. Ha ha, I just wanted really badly to see his diary. You understand, don't you? He was so secretive about it. We were just kids, and all kids play doctor at some point, do naughty sorts of things like that, but it was all quite innocent, really.

I was going to Sunday school at the time, although I was supposed to stop when the Society was meeting—we always met on Sundays at Laura White's house to read the stories we'd been assigned and practise writing. I always pretended to be a cool customer, an experienced girl, but I can tell you now that I didn't officially lose my virginity until I was eighteen.

Maybe kids are different today. Less innocent. That's one reason I've never wanted to have kids. I was pregnant once, though. It's wonderful. Being pregnant suited me. I used to take my clothes off and look at myself in the mirror, just so I'd remember. Think about it—your breasts grow and your body starts to change and you don't have to deal with your period for a while… I knew the whole time that I was going to have an abortion before it was too late, so I felt a bit crummy, but I wanted to get as much

THE RABBIT BACK LITERATURE SOCIETY

out of it as I could anyway. Experiences are important, especially for a writer, but of course you've probably…

…I'm going off on a tangent. So I was nine when I joined the Society. Once—it was in the winter, I remember, all of us marching to Laura White's house in our knitted caps and mittens… Anyway, Ms White gave us a sort of murder assignment.

We were supposed to choose one member of the Society and write a story where something bad happens to them. She said we could choose someone we envied or secretly hated a little, and get our revenge out through writing. She emphasized that it was all just a game and that none of us should get mad about it.

Martti Winter was already a member by that time—he joined a little while after me—and I think I remember that Ingrid and Martti agreed to think up something really awful for each other, although I don't know if there was really any bad feeling between them. I didn't want to make any agreement like that, I just wanted to do the writing the way it had been assigned.

And I envied that talented kid something awful. I'd been in the Society for a year or so. I decided to murder him in my story. I remember I actually giggled when I started to write it. The rest of my family was wondering what little Silja was up to, cackling to herself. They were terribly proud of me for getting into "Laura White's Writing Club". They could never remember the name of the thing. Or maybe they didn't want to remember it—the name was a touch pompous for such a little tyke.

I wrote at least five different versions of the story before I got it right. I don't remember what happened in the best story, but I do remember that in one of the rejected versions I invited the wunderkind for a walk along the railroad tracks, knocked him down, tied him to the tracks, and stayed to wait for the train. Kind of like in an old black-and-white film, the Keystone Cops or something. Ha ha. A typical kid's fantasy, isn't it? But

I wasn't satisfied with anything that didn't feel believable, even back then. So I thought up something better.

But those murder stories were never read at the meeting. Because he really did die. It kind of took the fun out of it. I burned my story in the woods. I felt mean for having written a story like that.

I don't remember now whether we ever knew how he died, but anyway, Ms White called Ingrid, and Ingrid and Martti came to tell us one Sunday morning that the meetings had been cancelled for a while and that our most talented member was dead. The Society was on hiatus for several weeks—at least we didn't meet at Ms White's house, and the cold winter got colder all the time—you couldn't even go outside—but then over the spring we gradually forgot about it and everything continued as it was before, like nothing had ever happened. And we never said a word about that boy again.

Do you want to ask me anything else? Nothing else comes to mind right now about him, but if you ask me something, I can try to remember.

Actually I do remember that I must have been somewhat traumatized by the whole thing. My mother once told a humorous anecdote at a dinner party about how when I was that age I used to wake up in the night in a panic and shout, "Murder, murder, he was murdered." She meant that I was already becoming a crime writer. I don't remember it at all. She says that no matter how many times she asked me, she never got any explanation for why I was screaming murder in the middle of the night.

Anyway, none of us felt like making much noise about the fact that the boy who died was a member of the Society, or even that somebody we knew was dead. We had an agreement not to. We met at this place in the middle of the forest, skied there a couple of days after it happened, and we vowed to each other that we would keep quiet about it, on threat of I don't know what. We thought that if our families knew that somebody in the Society had died they might get the idea that the Society wasn't good for children and forbid us from participating. Some of our families had, in fact, already complained that it took up too much of our time and our school work was suffering, and we didn't want to give them any more grist for the mill. We all wanted to be writers, more than anything, ever.

I don't think there was much talk about the death of the genius in Rabbit Back. He must not have been from Rabbit Back, or at least he wasn't well known here. And then Jaakko Lindberg, the teenage son of a doctor, an upstanding member of the community, broke into a store and stole some beer and got drunk and got run over by a train, which was lucky for us, in a way. He was pretty much smashed to bits, and that became the only subject of conversation for quite a while.

I actually went with a couple of friends to the railroad tracks to look for pieces of Jaakko, which they said had been left there, although we didn't find anything, thank goodness. We'd heard a story that his parents had promised a thousand marks' reward to anyone who could find his face. It was pretty grotesque because I'd had a bit of a crush on Jaakko, although he was a lot older than me. But the rumour of the reward and the missing face proved to be a wild goose chase. It was something the kids invented. Somebody's parents had been talking about "losing face" and it started this whole story, can you believe it?

By the way, I already have a question for you. Sorry for saying this—it's none of my business, since you can ask anything you want in The Game, but your questions have been quite easy. I remember whatever I remember and spill it for you. Flimsy memories. The Game is usually played rougher, with more present tense than past tense.

So I ought to tell you that what I'm going to ask about isn't nearly as easy as reminiscences like these.

Silja Saaristo is quiet. She seems contented, cheerful.

Ella slurps her tea, which has gone cold, and gathers her thoughts for a moment. Saaristo is right. Ella spills from deeper wells in The Game, and all she gets in return are vague bits of Society history, the confused memories of children, tenuous recollections.

But although spilling has proven more painful than she had imagined, The Game is nevertheless progressing just as she wanted it to progress.

The individual pieces may not be very useful from the point of view of literary-historical research, but the picture that's gradually emerging from them is a unique whole, the sort of history that no one could possibly collect, no one but Ella Milana, the tenth and final member of the Society—an outsider admitted to the inner circle.

After all, she can support herself for the next year just collecting information. That means a lot. Even if she never gets particularly deep with her research, she can at least pay the bills, and her inheritance taxes, and have some money to save.

If she does her work well, if she finds even just one precious nugget, she might be able to give up teaching forever and have a place in the academic world. How many times has Professor Korpimäki tried to persuade her to throw herself into literary research?

Ella, you have the research bug, and I don't say this to just any student. Your thesis doesn't need a lot of padding to make it a dissertation, and if you decided to continue what you've made a good start on, you can trust that I'll do everything I can to help. You're right that the world of research is sometimes a façade hiding something rotten, but here in our department you will always have a friend as long as I'm here.

Ella can well imagine returning to the university to make a career in research. She has always enjoyed putting together puzzles, both metaphorical and concrete.

Once when she was six years old, she refused to leave a house her family was visiting because she wanted to finish a puzzle she'd started. The evening had run late because the puzzle was too difficult. It had ten thousand pieces. She'd finally fallen asleep still working on it and been carried home.

The next day she ran away, walked three hours, and rang their doorbell. *Hi. I came back to finish the puzzle.*

Ella doesn't really know why she became a teacher instead of a researcher. Maybe she thought it would be easier for a teacher to have children and support them.

Most of Laura White's Creatureville books were quite ordinary children's stories. The characters were eccentric and had silly, exciting adventures. But there was something extraordinary about them. A woman from Rabbit Back wouldn't have become a world-famous children's author if there weren't. This extraordinary quality lay in their mythological layers, as Ella Milana's master's thesis had shown.

Of course, Laura White's success could also be explained by her ability to express "a childlike sense of wonder combined with sly observations about life", as the *History of Finnish Literature* put it. But "no other writer's books succeed in using old folk mythology in the multifaceted, enchanting, and surprising ways that Laura White's books do", as Ella declared in the introduction to her thesis.

Ella's own favourite Creatureville character had always been Crusty Bark, although most children shied away from him.

Crusty Bark wasn't exhaustively described in any of the books, but he was apparently some kind of small tree that had to keep moving constantly so he wouldn't take root in one place and forget the rest of the surrounding world.

Crusty Bark didn't speak or understand speech, although he did enjoy the company of the other inhabitants of Creatureville. The only way to communicate with him was to take a nap at his roots, be visited by a dream, and talk things out using his personal symbolic language.

The dream images that Crusty Bark offered gave White's books "a certain gothic gloominess that sometimes deepened almost to horror", according to Ella's thesis.

One entire chapter of Ella's thesis was dedicated to Crusty Bark. In it, she managed to link Crusty not only to many Finno-Ugric myths, but also to mythological stories of farther flung cultures, such as Japan. Some of Crusty Bark's adventures were also connected to Estonian legends of a wandering forest.

The creature known as Dampish, on the other hand, had to go about in a bucket. His advice often rescued the other inhabitants of Creatureville, but even he had a dark side. He tempted smaller creatures into his bucket, and the books were never explicit about whether he drowned his victims.

In one of the Creatureville books, Mother Snow says that Dampish is "just a confused little water sprite that we should all love very much". The comment precedes an adventure in which a half-dead field mouse searching for medicine for her sick litter makes the mistake of consulting Dampish and has to be rescued from his bucket.

In her thesis, Ella points out that "a water sprite is an unusual choice for a character in a children's book, since in the old beliefs water sprites are the ghosts of the drowned, who envy the living".

In the fifth book of the Creatureville series, Dampish himself comes to harm. Bobo Clickclack, the most human and at the same time the stupidest of all the creatures, tries to put out a fire and accidentally throws Dampish into the flames. Mother Snow baldly states that Dampish is no more, and Bobo Clickclack spends the rest of the book in the throes of terrible regret.

As a child, Ella was shocked by Dampish's fate. She expected him to return somehow at the end of the book, but it didn't happen. "The only happy ending offered the reader is the soothing of Bobo Clickclack's guilt." Even as she was writing her thesis, Ella found Dampish's fate unfair, altogether too dark for a children's book, but on the other hand "the episode provides fascinating interpretative viewpoints".

Ella had also thought a lot about the character of the Odd Critter and its hidden symbolism. The Odd Critter was always cloaked in some kind of disguise and tried to look like something other than what it was.

In her thesis Ella wrote: "In the Odd Critter's habit of constantly inventing new names for places and things one can see complex commonalities with phenomena of a postmodern era. Like the modern person, the Odd Critter is lost everywhere it goes, and tries constantly to spread to others the same confusion, the same feeling of estrangement from which it suffers."

As a child, Ella had been particularly amused by the story that began with the Odd Critter showing up in the middle of a peaceful day and announcing, "Help! Help! The dreaded and terrible Emperor Rat is after me and will be here any moment!"

The inhabitants of Creatureville panic and flee in a mad

rush to East Meadow. Gradually, however, they realize that the Odd Critter invented the whole thing just to remind them that "anything at all could happen at any moment".

Ella is caught up in her research ideas for a long while, smiling to herself, until Silja Saaristo interrupts her reverie.

"Hey, Ella, if you don't have anything else to ask me, what do you say we put this rag around your head?"

"Wait," Ella says, rubbing the bridge of her nose. "You join the Society when you're nine, and a year later, the boy dies. So that was what year?"

"I was born in the year of our Lord 1961, so it would have happened, let's see, in 1972."

"What was his name?"

"I honestly don't remember."

"And you don't remember how he died?"

"I don't even remember ever hearing how he died," Saaristo says. "I guess my interest in various causes of death didn't come until later."

Ella strokes the curve of her lip with a finger. "Did he drown? Car accident?"

Silja Saaristo shakes her head.

Ella wrinkles her brow. Then she draws breath in through her nose, filling her lungs.

"I'm invoking Rule 21," she says, leaning towards Saaristo, taking her cheek between her thumb and forefinger, and squeezing and twisting it until the surprised woman bends over sideways with a gasp.

When Ella lets go, Saaristo rubs her cheek grumpily. "God damn it, I always get Rule 21. Same thing with everybody. The last time I played this Aura Jokinen nearly tore my ear off. What did I do wrong, anyway? What story do you want to hear?"

"The way I understand this Game of yours," Ella says calmly, "you aren't supposed to tell me any 'story'. You have to spill. I draw, you spill. You know how The Game is played." She pauses for a moment, then continues. "I know that you're going to draw me out and make me spill like I've been stabbed and after that I'll be a wreck for a couple of days, and that's fine, because it's in the spirit of The Game. But before we do that, I want to see you spill. This isn't a friendly coffee klatch. That ended when you put the blindfold on."

"Yeah, but I've told you everything I know," Saaristo protests. "There's nothing more."

Ella leans back on the sofa and breathes in so hard that her nose whistles. "That dream you had," she says. "When you woke up in the night and screamed that the boy had been murdered. Tell me about that."

Silja Saaristo rocks herself and sniffles like a little girl. "I don't remember it at all. My mother told me about it."

"Do you have any yellow?" Ella asks, smiling coolly, keeping her voice controlled. She wants to hide the fact that her own words shock and surprise her. Didn't she want to treat her partners respectfully, play a sort of civilized version of The Game, which, judging by its rules, was a barbaric, frightening invention?

"Yellow? You want me to take yellow?" Saaristo says in bewilderment. "Isn't tearing my face off enough? I know I started the whole yellow thing, but I don't think it's such a good idea now."

Ella doesn't say anything. Saaristo knows the rules.

"Well, then," the woman sighs at last. "There's still some in the medicine cabinet, I think. Top shelf, in the back, behind the hairspray. Bring the wine bottle that's next to the tub while you're at it, so I can have a glass first. If it'll help me spill enough to satisfy you, so much the better."

Ella wouldn't know anything about yellow if Ingrid Katz hadn't told her about it at the end of their Game. The official rules didn't mention it.

"I'm telling you this so you won't be surprised if someone asks you to have a glass of yellow," Ingrid explained as they went down the library staircase, adding that she herself had never thought it was a good idea, but had given in to the will of the majority.

Silja Saaristo had launched the idea sometime in the 1980s, Ingrid said.

Saaristo had discovered yellow on a trip to the United States. After that it was provided to the Society by an animal doctor—confidentially, of course.

The official name was sodium pentothal. It weakened the central nervous system, slowed the heart rate, and lowered blood pressure. "If you take too much, you fall asleep. The right amount will give you diarrhoea of the mouth, which is, of course, useful for our Game."

"Diarrhoea of the mouth?" Ella exclaimed.

They were standing between the marble columns. Ella felt strange talking about such a thing in a place devoted to cultural enrichment. "Do you mean it's a…"

"A kind of truth serum, yes. I tried it once. I found myself thinking out loud. It won't prevent you from lying, but it does help you spill the truth, if talking about it is difficult."

*

The bottle contains small, yellow crystals. Ella Milana drops one into the wine and hands the glass to Silja Saaristo. Saaristo, still blindfolded, drinks the entire contents and sets the glass down on the table next to the teapot and the plate of crackers.

Ella watches as she relaxes, seems to sink into the sofa. She wonders how many laws they're breaking. Teachers probably aren't supposed to do these sorts of things.

Silja Saaristo smiles faintly. "Sooo. Not too bad. Feeling mellow. Very mellow. No tightness in my head. What else do you want to know? More about my dream? I honestly don't remember anything about it. Nothing at all, really. I remember it through my mother's eyes, and how do I know she didn't make the whole thing up to amuse people at parties? But hey, there is one thing I can tell you. I didn't feel like talking about it just now because I didn't want to talk bullshit, because I really don't know anything. We're just talking about my feelings, which I can't logically defend, or Freudian slips or something. I don't know. Ask the Freudians, maybe they would know."

Saaristo breathes for a moment, her mouth gaping open, and Ella thinks she's fallen asleep. Then she continues speaking, in a low, drawling voice.

"But you know, whenever I start talking about that boy that died, and I try to say 'he died,' my tongue ties itself in knots, and it's like it wants really badly to say 'he was murdered'."

17

WHEN ELLA MILANA left Silja Saaristo's house, she had a headache and a cinnamon jar. The mystery writer had wanted to give her the cinnamon jar and a pinch of the yellow crystals for the next round, saying, "Thanks for the inspiring Game."

Saaristo started up her computer while Ella put on her coat and shoes. "I feel like writing," she explained, although it was half past three in the morning.

Ella Milana opened the door. When she turned to look, Saaristo waved, smiling brightly.

The Triumph waited at the dead end around the corner. Ella thought about what she'd gleaned from this round of The Game, as far as her exhaustion allowed her to think. Was the history of Laura White and the Rabbit Back Literature Society hiding a child's murder? Such a revelation would make news all over the world.

She wasn't thrilled. Not at all.

She'd wanted to do literary-historical research that might bring to light a few smallish skeletons—secret relationships, homosexuality, that sort of thing. Pleasant little scandals. Murder victims weren't the sort of thing she'd been hoping to dig up.

Amateur detectives in fiction had always annoyed Ella. They were so unrealistic. She didn't intend to be the Rabbit Back version of Miss Marple or a cheap Baker Street knock-off, and she really didn't like the idea of making the tabloids. That was no way to advance an academic career. She didn't want to be an instrument of justice. She just wanted to do some literary research and earn a living.

She felt tired, pessimistic and hollow as she scraped her departed father's Triumph free of ice. Maybe she should stick to interpreting Laura White's metaphorical language or break down and take a teaching post someplace up north. Ingrid Katz had warned her not to play The Game too much. Ingrid had stressed that recovering from it always took its own time and you could get overly spent in playing it if you didn't remember to take long breaks between bouts.

Ingrid was right. First Ingrid had drawn the death of Paavo Emil Milana out of her. Then Silja Saaristo had scraped up some inspiration using Ella's anguish over her childlessness. "I read your story in *Rabbit Tracks*," Saaristo said. "It's a nice little story, but you only put the tip of the iceberg in there. I want the rest of it."

A person shouldn't talk too much, Ella realized. With writing, you could construct a whole world, but talking too much could demolish it.

Four days later, Ella Milana woke up around noon and called the Rabbit Back library.

The library assistant told her that newspaper microfilms were only kept at the provincial branch. "But if you're looking for back issues of *Rabbit Tracks*, you'll have to ask at their offices."

Ella picked up the most recent issue from the kitchen table, found the phone number, and called. She made an appointment with the office secretary to look at the archives that very day.

The archives were contained in cardboard boxes in a back room at the newspaper offices. The box containing 1972 came out of the middle of the stack without much trouble, in spite of its difficult position. Ella gathered up the first part of the year up to May and began thumbing through the issues.

She trusted that deaths in the greater Rabbit Back area would have been noted in the paper. The first issue in April did, in fact, have an obituary for Jaakko Juhani Lindberg. There was a picture of Laura White on the same page. It announced that the authoress was holding a seminar on folk mythology in the school auditorium.

There were no other deaths of young people in the year 1972, assuming one could trust *Rabbit Tracks*. Ella checked 1971 and 1973, to make sure. She didn't find anything.

She thanked the secretary and left. The offices of *Rabbit Tracks* were located in an old veterans' housing bungalow on the main street of town. There was a cash machine across the street. Ella withdrew a little cash and went to Rabbit Market to buy some food.

She ran into the school principal at the dairy counter. They exchanged wary greetings. He said he had received her message. "It seems very peculiar for students' papers to mould like that," he said.

"It was a new one for me, too," Ella answered. "There was an old newspaper in the same pile with them, and the mould spread amazingly quickly to the essays. A horrible fungus. Definitely not something you want in the school."

It was good news that the only youth to die in Rabbit Back in 1972 was Jaakko Lindberg. Maybe the murder was just Silja Saaristo's imagination, rather than a suppressed memory.

Ella put aside Society matters for a while and started making dinner. Her mother soon came back from drinking coffee with their neighbour, Mrs Salmela.

"You made real macaroni casserole," her mother said. "It just occurred to me that I've never actually seen you cook anything. I was starting to think I would never eat anything I hadn't cooked myself."

They ate together. Ella's mother looked intently at her. Ella smiled.

The smell of cheese wafted over the table. Ella noticed her mother closing her eyes now and then to breathe in the smell of the macaroni as if it were the finest perfume.

Her mother tried to ask her about things. Ella tried to answer without showing that she was thinking about The Game. Her mother thought she'd been working altogether too much on her research project. Of course, she couldn't know that Ella had a gigantic, shapeless research subject that presented an unbelievable number of interesting things to find out and that working on it could make a person lose her bearings.

The Game demanded more strategic planning than Ella had imagined. After the first Game she'd wondered if she really needed to ambush every member of the Society and take them by surprise in order to play. It had been the custom of the Society from the beginning, and it had its own rationale, but couldn't even old habits be changed?

Before The Game with Silja Saaristo, Ella had gone to ring the doorbells of five Society members in all, including Saaristo. Every one of them had obviously been at home. Ella could see their shadows in the windows. She could hear noises. No one had come to the door.

She had asked Silja Saaristo about this when they were starting The Game. Saaristo had grinned under her blindfold. "That's the nature of The Game. It's nothing personal. We simply don't open the door for each other after ten in the evening. Even though both players end up spilling, it's always better to be the challenger than the challenged."

After dinner Ella emptied the dishwasher of clean dishes and filled it with dirty ones. She told her mother not to get up, insisting that she relax and finish her cup of coffee.

Ella noticed that she was enjoying handling the dishes. She listened to the clitter-clatter and then she looked at her mother and was surprised at the peculiar feeling that drifted up from someplace deep inside, like a belch, and suddenly she laughed out loud.

"Well?" her mother snorted. "What is it?"

Ella blinked, realizing that she felt calm and happy.

The feeling lasted about ten seconds.

When it had passed, Ella formed a quick theory about it.

Happiness is contentment—the feeling that a person is content with the prevailing conditions. But people have an inherent need to achieve, to strive, to work at something—to always be developing. A happy creature stops developing, so happiness is a product of being content and development is a product of discontent.

Happiness, in other words, is a temporary glitch in evolution.

Ella knew very well that she wasn't in danger of being content with anything. Her individual future was creaking and swaying like a rotting bridge. The Rabbit Back Literature Society's secrets wouldn't wait forever. She might be gathering nothing more than memories, and they dissolve and change constantly. If she didn't act quickly and decisively, Laura White and the Society's past would disappear, cease to exist.

*

The activities of the Rabbit Back Literature Society had never been documented. For instance, Laura White's method of training nine children to be writers was entirely shrouded in mystery.

White's own personality could also use some illumination. Professor Eljas Korpimäki had long complained of the fact that the authoress had never given a single proper interview. He called her "the world's most unknown celebrity".

Laura White was born in Rabbit Back in October, 1945, on the same day that women were given the right to vote in France. Her father, Aulis White, was a businessman discharged from the service for health reasons; her mother, Linnea White (née Nieminen), was an enthusiastic amateur painter. The White family lived from 1954 to 1960 in Switzerland, afterwards returning to Rabbit Back. Laura White published the first book in the Creatureville series in 1963, at the age of 18. It received little notice at the time, but the second Creatureville book, published just one year later, was a critical and commercial success. In 1965, Aulis and Linnea White moved to the French countryside but Laura remained living in the family home in Rabbit Back and continued serving as leader of the Rabbit Back Literature Society, which she had founded. A total of nine contemporary Finnish authors were protégés of the Society, including Martti Winter, Silja Saaristo, and Toivo Holm.

Ella Milana knew that if she wanted to learn about Laura White and the Literature Society's past, she had to divide the problem into sections and restrict and construct her questions in such a way that she drew out the essential and interesting information.

The most critical thing at this point was the question of the tenth and clearly the most talented member of the Society, who died before his time.

If she could find out whether the boy really had been murdered, nothing else would matter. Her literary historical research would end there and the police and the scandal sheets would lay claim to her research. It might mean the end of the Society.

If Ella could show that the child had died a natural death, the whole thing would still be a tragedy, something to think about, a footnote to write into her literary history, and the real research could begin.

Ella's phone started to make a racket just as she was drifting off to sleep.

She'd added the numbers of all the members of the Society to her contacts list. The display showed that the caller was Martti Winter.

Ella yawned and pressed the answer button.

Before she had time to say anything, Winter's breathy voice was spilling into her ear. Suddenly she was wide awake.

"It's out there again. It's standing in the garden staring at the house. I'm sorry to bother you again, but I really don't know what to do with the thing. I thought before that I wouldn't tell anyone about it, that it would make it easier to bear, but I was wrong. I have to share it with somebody." Ella opened her mouth but didn't know what to say.

"Ingrid?" Winter's voice said hesitantly. "Hello? Ingrid? Oh, hell, who did I call? Sorry, wrong number... I can't work these tiny buttons with my fingers..."

He hung up.

PART THREE

18

WHEN MARTTI WINTER WAS TWENTY-ONE, his mother, Laila Barbara Winter, married a street lamp manufacturer named Eino Korkeala and moved from the hinterlands to Helsinki.

Martti remained in his mother's three-storey stone house in Rabbit Back. The house was in Hare Glen, five kilometres from the centre of town. Just north of Hare Glen was where Rabbit Wood began, but the glen itself was park-like then, bright with leafy trees and meadows, before it grew wild and tangled.

Eleven years later Martti Winter's mother was vacationing in the Swiss Alps with her street lamp magnate when she swished right into the path of a snowmobile that shot suddenly out from behind a hillock.

At the funeral, Eino Korkeala talked about his wife's last days and graciously praised Martti's newest novel, which had received a great deal of attention in the media. Martti, who had just been weeping in the men's room, thanked Korkeala for making his mother's life a pleasant one.

After the funeral they never contacted each other again.

Martti had never had a father. The only daughter of a wealthy family, Laila Winter had got pregnant while on a trip down the Nile. She'd gone to bed with a man from Berlin while her parents were dancing on the deck of a riverboat. All Martti knew about his biological father was that he was named Hans, was "as beautiful as a fallen angel", and was a violinist.

By the time he was thirty-two, Martti Winter had already earned a tidy sum from his books and their translations and film rights. The inheritance his mother left him cemented his economic independence. He renovated the run-down house and had a three-metre-high stone wall built around the property.

Then he wrote more books, in his office. It was on the third floor, where he could see the garden as well as a large strip of the valley from its large, many-paned window. When there were no leaves on the trees he could also see five neighbouring houses, the one farthest away belonging to Laura White.

Martti Winter was now a decade older and twice the size he had been when he renovated the house.

He was hunkered on the sofa in one of his living rooms, popping French pastilles into his mouth and fiddling with the telephone.

He wanted to call Ingrid Katz. He had picked up the phone many times. If he did call her, she might get the wrong idea and go back to her old habits. But if he couldn't talk to Ingrid, he couldn't talk to anyone.

They had once been lovers. They had played The Game together hundreds of times, plumbed each other's deepest corners. Ingrid knew Martti almost completely, and Martti knew Ingrid—or at least he knew her as she was three years ago, the last time they played. Ingrid Katz's personality back then was marked by an unquenchable desire to monitor Martti Winter's life.

She had been trying to spark his interest in her book-burnings for a long time. Martti suspected she was trying to tempt him to play; she probably wanted to find out what new things had materialized in his life and in his consciousness lately.

The study of Martti's well-being had been an important project for her for three decades. Up until the past few years she had ambushed him again and again and made him spill. She kept herself up to date on things like his sexual experiences, his moods, his disappointments, joys, lifestyle, diet, illnesses and plans. She hadn't suffered from jealousy for a long time now, and didn't try to revive their old love affair. She also wasn't planning a novel. She just wanted to check in at regular intervals to be sure he was all right.

Martti Winter, for his part, decided to make sure that he would never have to play The Game with Ingrid again. He started avoiding her in public places after ten o'clock, and never went out anymore. He installed the best locks available on the doors so that she couldn't break in, although the rules of The Game allowed it.

One night she got into the garden, squirmed through the ventilation system into the house, came up the stairs, walked up to his bed and challenged him to a Game in the middle of a most delicious dream.

Once he had recovered from The Game, Winter blocked every possible route into the house and bricked over a crack he found in the garden wall. It wasn't a large crack, but a small-boned author could squeeze her way through it, if she wanted it badly enough. To make absolutely sure, he also had barbed wire and broken glass installed on top of the wall.

He wanted to keep his new thoughts and experiences, even though they weren't terribly important ones. He couldn't stand the incessant probing of his mind anymore.

When he caught a serious respiratory infection, however, he had to give Ingrid a key, because she came to tend to him and take care of his ongoing business. Once he had recovered, he thanked her and asked her to return the key, but she refused. When she saw his panic, she promised she would never use it to challenge him.

Ingrid kept her word.

She had a habit of dropping by and letting herself in—purportedly to rest her legs—but she never came creeping around at night.

She'd been up to something secret for a long time. Winter didn't want to know what it was. If she wanted to burn library books, let her burn them. He had his own life to live, and preferred to live in blissful ignorance.

Winter had given up human curiosity not long after giving up sex and alcohol and taking up eating. When his stomach was full enough it was easy to concentrate on the basics. Lately he had managed to keep things simple, with the exception of the custom-made pastries, which he preferred baroquely complex, extravagant and abundant.

At the moment, however, his composure was shattered. He felt a need to talk with someone. He was even prepared to play The Game with Ingrid if it would help him to bare his problem to someone who might possibly understand.

Winter heard a noise outside. He sighed, got up from the sofa, and walked to the window.

The front garden was full of dogs. Two of them were having a row, until one submitted and calm returned. In the area in front of the porch alone he counted seven of them. When one dog got up and disappeared from view, two more appeared. There were more behind a snowdrift, near the rubbish can, in the shadow of the wall. In the daytime they dispersed, but at night they returned.

Winter had ordered *The Big Book of Dogs* on the internet and learned over the past few weeks to identify them, first by breed, then as individuals. He wanted to know which dog to blame if he were attacked, to know which kinds of dogs were particularly dangerous.

After studying the matter he knew that among the dogs were Jack Russell terriers, cocker and springer spaniels, golden retrievers, Labrador retrievers, Finnish spitzes, Russian wolf-hounds, German Shepherds, Norwegian elkhounds, schnauzers, dachshunds both long- and short-haired, Great Danes and an extensive selection of mixed breeds. He had made a list of the dogs and reported it to the police. The constable who answered the phone sounded weary.

"Rabbit Back has stray dogs everywhere," the policeman said. "We have real work to do here, like a certain famous author's disappearance. Listen, if one of them bites you, call us again. And don't worry, they'll leave eventually if you don't feed them. Besides, doesn't your house have a separate back garden with a high wall around it? Go in the back garden if the dogs frighten you."

Winter watched the furry backs moving about below him. The dogs hadn't noticed him standing in the window. Or maybe they didn't care. None of the dogs had behaved aggressively towards him so far, although he had encountered some of them during the daytime, when he took out the rubbish. But there was something threatening about them. They were planning something, waiting for something.

They could smell his fear and he sensed their desire to sink their teeth into his soft tissue. When he was younger, Winter had been a tough fighter and had always been able to hold his own, if his opponents were human. But the smallest dog could strip him of every shred of confidence.

He'd once had a revealing dream. A German Shepherd in a necktie had demanded to see all of his personal papers and started to accuse him of tax evasion, although he had taken care to keep his taxes in order. He had been humiliated and cried and even kissed the dog's paw to make him relent. When he woke up, he found a wool sock in his mouth.

Winter drew the blinds over the window and walked to the opposite side of the house. The back garden, blockaded against the army of dogs, didn't cheer him at all. Unfortunately, the dogs weren't his worst problem.

His office window looked out on the garden, which was separated from the rest of the world by the wall. He rested his hands on the window sill and peeped out warily.

He had spent a large sum of money to light the garden over the past couple of years. In September, for instance, he had installed six new garden lights, the brightest available, making a dozen lamps in all. He had also scattered small lights here and there among the statues and shrubbery. In theory, the area inside his walls should have been the most brightly lit garden in the neighbourhood, a veritable sea of light.

As he looked out the window now, only one weak light shone below. You could just barely make it out in the snow and dark undergrowth. For some reason, his lamps didn't work for very long. They dimmed and sputtered, they lost power. In spite of his best efforts, the snowy apple trees, oaks, and maples stood dark in the midst of blackness and the garden, surrounded by its wall, looked like a tub filled to the brim with the heart's blood of a winter night.

He had once been proud of his garden. He used to walk among the plants and statues and sit in the shade of the trees. Sometimes he had developed his novels there, at other times simply enjoyed the warmth, the flowers, the world of sound the insects created, with its multi-layered, architectural dimensions.

He had thought of the garden as a carefree playground. He'd brought women there, sometimes in the heat of the day, sometimes even at night, when the air was warm enough. He remembered many of them lying naked in the multicoloured light. He particularly remembered a certain worker from the pensioners' department. After the act, she had pushed him off her, spread her legs and rocked back and forth, letting his seed trickle down into the earth, whispering, with her eyes closed, "Let this be our shared sacrifice to the powers that live beneath our feet."

He also remembered how disturbing it was, how he'd been compelled to flee into the house, saying he wanted to get them something to drink, and when the woman finally came after him, she seemed embarrassed.

"I don't quite know what came over me," she said. "Just an inexplicable whim, I guess."

That same summer the gardener had come twice a week to care for the plantings. Winter had ordered all kinds of beautiful stones to place among the plants and decorated the garden with statues. They were large, imposing works made by local sculptors.

He had once served Ingrid Katz some cider in the garden. She had looked around and said, "You've got your own little paradise here, Martti. Is it all right if I build a little fort there behind the geraniums and move in?"

Now he didn't dare go in the garden anymore.

There were no dogs in it, of course. The wall kept them out. He'd wanted to create his own little paradise where no dog could come sniffing out his emotions or brooding over who knows what.

But there was something even worse in that garden.

A couple of years earlier, things had been different. He had invited a person he'd met by chance, a woman who said she was a mythological mapper. He thought it would be amusing.

He brought her into his garden, and she took a nap. This, apparently, was the key to mythological mapping. She would sleep in people's houses and gardens and have mythological dreams.

Afterwards she said something about his "personal problems" and phantoms that are apparently attracted to repressed guilt. "For that reason, I wouldn't recommend hanging your certificate in a place of honour or anything," she said.

She had been awakened among the tulips by her own shouts, and wrote out the mythological certificate with a trembling hand. "Most people think garden elves and such are nice, but a phantom, well, that's not a terribly pleasant thing."

They were drinking iced tea at the garden table. Winter thought the tulips looked a little dried out. The mapper chattered away. She kept emphasizing that mythological mapping was, when you came right down to it, just a silly little game.

"You see, I've had dreams about gnomes and elves and things ever since I was little, but only when I was sleeping in a strange place. And that's how I got the idea for this business, a couple of years ago. But even I don't take it all very seriously, Mr Winter, I can assure you. I just happen to have dreamed, while sleeping in your garden, of a phantom that has chased away all of the other creatures. So that's what I'm writing here."

Martti Winter picked up the telephone. He reached a finger towards the buttons, then thought for a moment about the nature of The Game, and what he was about to do.

Nothing in the Rabbit Back Literature Society was given away for free. You had to play for everything. Even the smallest experience had exchange value.

Had it really been ten years since Winter had met Aura Jokinen in front of the dentist's office? He'd said hello and was going to continue on his way, but she mentioned in passing that she'd had a root canal and Winter asked, purely out of politeness, how the root canal had gone.

Aura had smiled and said, "The experience was excruciatingly interesting, particularly when the dentist bungled it a bit. What do you have to swap for it?"

Winter laughed. They looked at each other, and he realized that she was waiting for his answer. He shook his head. Then it occurred to him that a root canal would be a fitting symbolic element in the novel he was writing, and that he himself had never had the experience of getting a root canal.

He offered a sexually transmitted infection that he'd suffered from six months earlier. Aura was delighted, and promised to keep her windows open. Later, Winter ran into his intimate problem in Arne C. Ahlqvist's *They Shoot Centaurs, Don't They?* The tragic hero in the novel, Martian warlord C. Horace Patton, a half-human, half-horse product of genetic engineering, suffered from the same disease.

*

Winter just wanted to talk to Ingrid. If he had to agree to play The Game, to agree to spill, he would. Let her write his experiences into a gothic novel, or a tragicomedy. He didn't care, as long as he could talk to her. He searched for her number in his phone memory and pressed the call button.

Someone answered. He started to talk, his explanation confused. Then he realized he had called the wrong number, and he stopped talking and hung up after a short search for the button.

He was about to try calling again, but then he felt hungry.

Four years ago, in a period of severe distress, Winter had had a moment of enlightenment.

He had been thinking about suicide. First he considered hanging himself, then gassing himself with the car in the garage, but then, as he was sitting in his office near the open window, listlessly pounding out a novel, a liberating thought flashed through his mind.

An individual's life was based on, and geared towards, eating. Everything else was of secondary value. Even sex was only important from the standpoint of continuation of the species, and continuing the species was one thing that the individual known as Martti Winter had no intention of taking on.

He didn't long for death. His problem was thinking too much. He was always over-thinking things, and it was sapping his strength, day by day.

As he gazed into the distance, he could see that the world was full of people who longed for death because they couldn't bear the weight of their own thoughts. Thinking might be fun at first, but then you got hooked on it. People were even encouraged to do it in school, and in many popular pastimes. In the end, though, it made you miserable.

Winter didn't know many writers who weren't unhappy—and he knew a lot of writers, both in the Society and all around the world. The great majority of them suffered from alcoholism, mental health problems and stress. Excessive thinking was eating writers away from the inside out. Four writers he knew had recently committed suicide. Just two days earlier he'd learned that a Chilean colleague had shot himself in the head.

Alcohol only made a person's thoughts deeper and darker, even if it did offer a brief period of respite. The answer was to eat.

Winter had hit on something important: the happiest people were the ones who existed as little more than dimly conscious food-ingestion devices that enjoyed the occasional orgasm. Intelligence and thinking were really only needed for acquiring food. Once a person's belly was full and he had some food stored close by, thinking was reduced to a minimum and worries and needs could gradually be forgotten entirely.

So Winter escaped from the world and excessive thinking into his kitchen, his monastery. He had only to devote himself to eating, he needn't worry about anything else—not his unfinished novel, or dogs, or women, or the origins of the universe or the meaning of life. And he knew that in the end he wouldn't regret his sausagey fingers, or even his penis, left behind on the other side of his expanding corporeal self.

19

ELLA MILANA went to the grocery store, and there were three writers from the Rabbit Back Literature Society there. They weren't there together. Each was on his or her own mission.

Oona Kariniemi was standing in the middle of the fruit section with a large, red hat on her head. She was squeezing the plums and also watching an old woman who was taking some time to examine the pears. The woman's wrinkled face trembled with extreme concentration and deliberation. She went through nine pears in all before she found the perfect one and put it in her bag.

Kariniemi smiled and turned to look for another subject. Ella went around her at a suitable distance.

It was annoyingly difficult to get anywhere. People were milling around in the aisles, alone or with their families, clogging up the place, pushing past each other, peering around, babies crying, their mouths gaping, whining and bawling, the squeaky shopping trolley wheels clattering through the crowd, the air dense with odours, the ventilation inadequate for such a large number of people, splashes of coffee and something else, something sticky, on the floor, children shoving and Creatureville characters appearing from someplace to pass out sweets—Look kids! It's Bobo Clickclack and the Odd Critter—and when the Odd Critter took off its head to go and have a cigarette, Mother Snow came out from a back room to take over. Ella tried to move farther away but Bobo Clickclack was behind her and he elbowed her lightly between her shoulder blades. She turned around, angry and overheated, but he thrust a basket of sweets in front of her, so she took one, thanked him and kept moving. Then she saw another member of the Society. Elias Kangasniemi was standing in the baby supply section, expensively dressed, apparently absorbed in his cell phone, and just behind him a couple was arguing, holding a greyish baby and pushing a shopping trolley full to the brim with infant formula and beer, the man growling and the woman whimpering, and when she looked more closely at Kangasniemi, Ella was almost certain that he was recording their conversation with his phone because it was good material and he didn't want to miss a single word of it. When the couple moved on Kangasniemi followed them with his phone in his hand pretending to look at the shelves and Ella thought of what Douglas Dogson said in Martti Winter's novel *Hidden Agendas: Are writers the torchbearers of humanity? It's a romantic idea, but it's complete rubbish. We writers are the crocodiles in the river.*

There was a series of soft thuds from the fruit department. A member of staff came running because someone had caused an avalanche of oranges. The floor was covered in orange balls, which people were kicking around the store.

Ella closed her eyes for a moment and cursed the crowd. It was usually quiet in the market, the lines short, but the sign on the door explained the situation: RABBIT MARKET'S 20TH ANNIVERSARY! COME IN FOR COFFEE AND CAKE! She had seen the sign and yet she had come in anyway. Good Lord. She couldn't stand crowds.

She opened her eyes and started powering her way to the cashier, her temples throbbing. She didn't want any coffee or cake. She didn't want to do her shopping anymore. She was weak and sweaty, trying to find some open space, and when she passed too close to the shelf and something fell on the floor, she didn't want to know what it was. She hadn't had a proper meal and her blood sugar was low. She dug in her pocket, trying to find the caramel Bobo Clickclack had given her.

Then an orange rolled out from under a shelf, slowly, with fateful dignity.

She watched it come towards her, transfixed.

But her feet kept walking, and she stepped on it.

The next thing she knew, both feet were in the air. It was all so ridiculous! She expected to land on the floor with a flop and was surprised when she realized she was falling upward.

She woke up and found herself lying on something high in the air.

Gusts of wind tore at her clothes. There was snow in the air. She sat up, looked around, and realized she was still in Rabbit Market. She had flown up to the top shelf in the middle aisle. She thought for a moment and figured out what had happened: the store's super-charged ventilation system must have had a thrombosis that carried even the customers along with it.

The shelves were surprisingly high, at least ten metres up. The air there was thin, but it was fresher than down near the floor. The loaded shelves swayed in the wind. She felt like she was standing on the deck of a ship. She looked down at the people pushing their shopping trolleys. No one looked up.

Ella felt contented there. She could walk quickly on the top of the shelves to the cashier and get out of the place.

Someone whistled to her.

Three shelves away, near the coffee, was Oona Kariniemi, swinging her legs in front of the packages of Costa Rican. Her mouth was spread in an amused grin, her pearly white teeth peeping out between red-painted lips. Kariniemi winked at Ella, and Ella winked back.

There was a flutter somewhere above them. Elias Kangasniemi was gliding among the ceiling lights with his arms spread. His expensive wool coat flapped like outspread wings.

He noticed Ella, flew closer, smiled warmly, and tipped his hat to her. Gazing upward at him, Ella curtseyed. It seemed appropriate. She felt a respect for his flying skills.

"I was thinking I would write a novel up here," Kangasniemi shouted. "No rest for the weary."

Ella nodded, grinning. She was enjoying watching him fly. He banked, riding a current of air, manoeuvring adeptly through the falling snow.

Then he looked troubled.

Oona Kariniemi whispered that it wasn't polite to watch a colleague at work. She turned her back on Kangasniemi and motioned for Ella to do the same. Before Ella could obey, Kangasniemi opened his mouth and screeched like a hawk. The cry made one of the light fixtures rattle. The store dimmed and cooled a little. Then, stretching his arms in front of him, he shot away between the shelves.

Ella looked after him. Had he fallen? He soon came back into view, making his way upward again, panting and sweating into the air, dragging a fat woman with him. He wobbled, collided with a shelf, made a small turn, and finally landed next to Ella with his prey. The shelf shook. A package of cookies fell down into the depths and onto a customer's head. Ella heard a cry of surprise.

Elias Kangasniemi straightened his tie and said with careful articulation, "I don't know if you noticed, but this woman has a very interesting way of talking to people. I just had to have it. I'll probably throw the rest away."

He took a large hunting knife from under his coat, bent over the woman he'd just nabbed, then stopped and smiled at Ella in polite supplication. Ella remembered her manners and turned away, then became frightened when something large, cold and hard was pressed against her cheek.

The world reeled. She gulped for air as if she were just being born.

She was lying on her back on the floor. Around her were oranges, puddles and standing feet. Someone wondered aloud whether the former substitute teacher was drunk in the middle of the day.

Ella saw Silja Saaristo's face in front of her. She blinked.

"Honey," Saaristo whispered. "I have bad news for you."

Ella made a questioning sound.

"You're dead," Saaristo said. "You were shot four times, stabbed three times, and struck on the head twice, once with Mika Waltari's *The Egyptian* and once with *A History of Finnish Literature*. There seem to have been nine murderers."

There followed a moment of silence.

Ella looked at Saaristo. Her head buzzed hollowly. She felt a chill. "Dead?" she said.

Saaristo giggled. "Come on, you. You must have fainted."

Saaristo helped her up. The crowd went about their business.

"It was a lovely collapse," Saaristo said. "Like something out of an old melodrama. All that was missing were the smelling salts. It's no wonder you fainted in this crowd. Free coffee and

THE RABBIT BACK LITERATURE SOCIETY

cake will get the masses out better than resurrection day." She looked around, smiled broadly, and said, "But if you want to find characters for a book, this is a good place to do it, as I'm sure you've noticed. I found bits of a serial killer's mother, half of a hero's lover, and three whole peripheral characters today. A nice haul."

20

I N THE BACK ROOM OF the library was Ingrid Katz's desk
and its drawer, which hadn't been unlocked in two months.
There was only one key to the drawer in existence. It was hanging around Ingrid Katz's neck.

Two months earlier she'd had her interest piqued by a damaged book, a first edition of the first book in the Creatureville
series. It had been published in 1963 and its title was simply
Creatureville.

Laura White's works had always managed to avoid the book
plague, but a small boy had brought this copy of *Creatureville*
back and reported that the words were in the wrong order.
There was nothing in the book to read, and if you did read it,
it didn't make any sense.

Ingrid Katz checked and saw that the book had become
badly tainted. The words had changed places, the letters were
jumbled. If you stared at the text long enough you might even
see small alterations occurring before your eyes.

She had wondered for some time what would happen to
the books that had the plague if you left them alone. For years
she had been burning all the tainted books immediately, but
burning a first edition Laura White wasn't something to be
done lightly.

So, on a momentary impulse, she had wrapped *Creatureville*
in Christmas paper, shoved it in the drawer, and locked it.

She wouldn't open the drawer again today, or tomorrow,

and probably not for another month. She wouldn't do it until the time was right—when she was sure that enough time had passed, and sure that she herself was ready to see the result.

21

FEBRUARY IN RABBIT BACK HAD been dark, cold and snowy, and Laura White's body hadn't been found.

People had started to have dreams about it and talked about their dreams everywhere—in line at the store, at cafés, kiosks and bank machines. On her Thursday visit to Mother White's Café, Ella heard detailed accounts of how the authoress's body had been sitting in people's kitchens, living rooms, attics and nursery rooms, reading her own books aloud "through dry lips that rustled like paper", as one old man put it. Ella could see that the man's talk was alarming old Eleanoora, who was standing behind the counter trying to arrange the baked goods.

When she'd finished her coffee, Ella walked through the woods back to the village and popped into the bookstore to buy some notebooks and pens. The bookstore owner was recounting his dream of the night before to the sales clerk loudly enough that Ella could hear the whole thing as she walked among the shelves:

I heard a child screaming and I ran to the kids' room. Saku and Irina were in their beds, and at first I didn't see anything unusual. The kids didn't say a word, but I could see that they were quite white and stiff and their eyes were spinning in their heads like tops. Then I saw that Laura White's body was sitting on the wall, just as if it were a floor, you know what I mean? She was holding the Creatureville book that Saku got from his grandma last Christmas and reading it out loud to the children. And her voice was the most awful thing, like rustling dry leaves, and I knew that no one could make her stop until she'd read the book all the way to the end.

I woke up all sweaty. And it's obvious that my kids have had similar dreams. I wouldn't dare to ask them about it, but they've been sleeping with the lights on. I'm sure it won't be long before they clear up what happened to her...

March approached without any change in the weather. The sky was still lightless and the snow fell constantly. Rabbit Back wrapped itself in a blanket of unending dusk fringed with bad dreams.

It had been two weeks since Martti Winter had called Ella's number. Since then Ella had been laying out a strategy. She had to find a way to challenge Winter. He was, after all, the most important, best-known member of the Society and thus her most important informant. Unfortunately, he had no desire to see anyone or to play The Game.

Ella had been reading through the works of Laura White and the writers of the Literature Society, especially Martti Winter's books. She wanted to be up to speed when she did her research, and writers are known by their works.

She had driven past Winter's house three times, stopping to assess the situation. Martti Winter was no less careful than the other Society members after ten in the evening, perhaps more so. His house was a fortress. You couldn't just walk in. The front door was locked even in the daytime, and if the house had a back door it must open on to the back garden, which was protected by a ludicrously high wall.

Ella made a note of the fact that the house seemed to attract dogs. She couldn't imagine what that meant, but she wrote it down anyway. The smallest detail might prove significant, as any researcher knows.

She had also spent a lot of time trying to interpret what Winter had said on the phone. *It's out there again. It's standing in the garden staring at the house.* Those were his words.

Could he have been talking about a dog? It was possible, but why just "it" when there were dozens of dogs around? And how could a dog have got into the garden anyway, when it had a wall around it? Or maybe some member of the Society had been lurking outside, perhaps sci-fi housewife Arne C. Ahlqvist—she had been willing to climb ladders to try to get into Ella's window.

But even members of the Rabbit Back Literature Society couldn't fly over those walls.

As Ella left the bookstore, the snow began to fall more heavily. Large flakes landed on her face and melted. It occurred to her that it would be terribly sweet and uninhibited to stick out her tongue and catch snowflakes. After all, she'd done it as a child. At least she hoped she had—it seemed a beautiful thought.

For a moment Ella Milana wanted to be the kind of person who catches snowflakes on her tongue. For a couple of minutes she even tried in earnest to catch at least one snowflake, just to see what that kind of spontaneity felt like.

Then it occurred to her that thinking about catching snow-flakes in this way ruined any possibility of spontaneity. She let the snowflakes fall to the ground undisturbed.

Ella went into Rabbit Market. There was no free coffee and no overabundance of customers, which suited her very well. In the deli section, she filled her cart with items from her list. Then an idea occurred to her, and she wadded up the list and started gathering boxes of chocolates, marmalade, chocolate bars, day-old marzipan pastries and cheap packets of biscuits.

22

MARTTI WINTER'S PHONE RANG.
It was good news, from Rabbit Market. For its anniversary, the market wished to acknowledge its most faithful customers with special baskets of treats. Would Mr Winter be at home to receive a gift delivery?

23

WHEN THE BELL RANG for the fifth time, Martti Winter opened the door a crack and peeped out.

A delivery girl stood halfway up the porch steps with a basket in her arms and a billed cap that hid her eyes. Winter opened the door all the way. He was wearing an English smoking jacket and well-tailored trousers with suede slippers peeping out under the hem. He felt he looked respectable.

The girl greeted him and expressed her apologies, explaining that there were a lot of baskets to deliver and the other delivery girl had suddenly taken ill and unfortunately Winter's gift basket was the last one on the list.

She glanced at her watch. "It's already after ten. So late! I'm very sorry, Mr Winter. You must already be getting ready for bed at this hour…"

Martti Winter gave a vague smile, waved a hand and assured her that no harm had been done.

The delivery girl smiled with relief and handed the basket to him. He took it with pleasure, thanked her, wished her a pleasant evening and warned her not to get too close to the dogs, who weren't to be trusted.

As he turned to go back inside, the girl strode quickly up the last two stairs, grabbed hold of his sleeve and flashed a sheepish grin.

"Well, what is it?" Winter asked her. "Oh, of course. Forgive me, my friend. A little drinking money! Of course. Let's see what I have in my pocket. Well, well. A ten-euro note, it seems. Here you go."

But the girl didn't take the money. Instead she explained shyly that she had always admired his works, and that she hoped that instead of drinking money he would grant her another service. "I have a book with me, and I wanted to ask you to do one little thing that you really can't say no to."

Winter raised his eyebrows, flattered, but at the same time annoyed. "Can't I? Well, perhaps I can't. You'd like an autograph, I assume. Give me the book. I even have a pen in my pocket…"

The girl took a book out from under her coat and handed it to him. He stood staring at the book, still vaguely smiling, not knowing what to do with the pen in his hand.

The cover read RABBIT BACK LITERATURE SOCIETY: GAME RULES. NOT FOR NON-MEMBERS!

Martti Winter gave a snort as he realized what was happening.

The delivery girl took off her cap, lifted her face into the light and offered him a challenge.

Ella followed Winter up the stairs. He was puffing like a steam engine.

"I assume I can keep the gift basket? Because if I can, I'll be less upset. This style of challenge at least has the benefit of not requiring the challenger to crawl in a window or surprise you in bed or on the toilet."

"Of course you can keep it," Ella said.

There were a lot of stairs. On the second floor, Winter slumped onto a sofa, sweating hard.

"I haven't played in a while," he said between panting breaths. "I don't think any of us older members have. In fact,

I had started to think that The Game might have been played out for me."

He wiped the sweat from his brow and pointed a finger at Ella. "By the way, did you know that Arne C. Ahlqvist was hunting for you? She called me a couple of days ago and asked whether I'd had a chance to play with you. Aura is eager to play again since you arrived. She needs some new material for her novel. I don't know what the other members' plans are, but I'm sure the fresh blood is tempting."

"What's to stop you from playing with each other?" Ella asked.

"Nothing really, except that our jam jars are fairly emptied out, for each other. They say you can never know another person completely. With The Game you can, if you play it by the letter and spirit of the rules." He smiled sadly. "That's what makes it such a useful, but at the same time dangerous tool. You see, people dress themselves in stories, but The Game strips us naked at the first handshake. That's why we older members don't really enjoy each other's company. Elias Kangasniemi once described The Game as psychic strip poker around a glass table."

When he was able to breathe again, they went up to the third floor. The walls were of dark hardwood. The hallway was dim, although there were small lights lit everywhere.

"Of course, we might still be of interest to each other if someone happens to have an experience that would be useful," he said, glancing at Ella over his shoulder. "Four years ago, for instance, Helinä had some health problems. Breast cancer, in fact. She went through all the treatments—radiation, poison, surgery. Good material. Even I was on my way to challenge her a couple of days after she got out of the hospital. But it so happened that there were already two of my colleagues skulking around her house when I arrived—one of them sitting on the edge of the roof knocking on her window with a stick, and the other applying a screwdriver to the basement window. I left them to it and went home."

The stairs creaked under his feet. He huffed, staggered, leaned on the wall for support. He was doubtless significantly overweight, but he nevertheless was a surprisingly stylish figure in his tailored trousers and expensive-looking morning jacket—at least when he wasn't struggling, at the limits of his physical capacity.

Ella thought about the book-jacket photo. The man preceding her up the stairs was nothing like his youthful photo. But Ella didn't believe that the person in the photo could have disappeared completely.

Maybe you just had to look at him the right way.

They arrived at a door painted blue. He opened it and gestured for her to go inside.

"My office," he said.

Everything in the room was blue. The curtains were made of thick, blue fabric. The rugs were blue. The walls were covered in tapestries reflecting various shades of blue. In the corner was a cluster of three blue armchairs. On the blue bookshelf, all the books had blue covers. Even the computer on the blue desk was blue.

"Blue calms me," Winter said. "It's difficult to write a novel when you're very nervous."

They sat down on the blue chairs. Winter pointed to a blue drinks dispenser in the corner.

"I had that shipped from Japan last summer. It was a custom order. They didn't have any blue ones ready-made. Get us a spot of something if you would. The mugs are on top of the machine. I'll have cocoa. You can have whatever you like. There are twenty-eight drinks to choose from."

Ella dispensed some cocoa for Winter and a cappuccino for herself. The mugs were blue.

"If it's up to me," Winter said, "we may as well start at once. Have a stab at it. Make me spill."

Ella cleared her throat and felt her cheeks reddening.

"All right," she began. "My question concerns…"

Winter raised a hand. "Aren't we forgetting something?"

Ella felt even more embarrassed. She smiled feebly, opened her bag and took out a handkerchief. Then she held it out towards the man's boulder-like head, her arms straight, as if the blindfold could jump into place of its own accord.

"A pleasant coincidence," she chattered nervously, "that my handkerchief is blue."

A smile spread over Winter's face. "Excellent. I hope it's not too small. Please be so kind as to tie it on for me."

Ella's fingers were trembling as she wrapped the handkerchief around his head and tied it in a knot. The skin of his temples radiated heat against the inside of her arms.

24

Martti Winter Spills

M ARTTI WINTER sat across from her like a large animal
sent to slaughter—laid bare, helpless, awaiting the fateful
blow to the head. Ella cowered in his shadow, going over her
well-polished question in her mind.

She gathered her thoughts, focused on breathing evenly and
was able to make her voice surprisingly steady.

"There are nine known older members of the Society. But
at a certain point, there were ten of you. I want to know everything you know about the tenth member, the boy who died."

At first, Winter made no move.

Finally, he tilted his head and said, "Ah. *Him.* The most talented of the original members. You've dug him up. Good girl.
No fooling around with trivialities. Straight to the secret nucleus."

He smiled as he gave her this acknowledgement. But his
breath had the heavy, aching murmur of a wounded bull's. He
looked for a moment like he might collapse.

Then he started to spill.

"When I was invited into the Society, all of the other members
except for Oona were already in it. The Society had existed

*for two years. Laura White had, as you know, created it in 1968. Oona
came a few months after I did. Then we were all together. There weren't
any more members after that, not before you.*

I was nine years old, going into the third grade at Rabbit Back School. The invitation came in the spring, when I was still a second-grader. The invitation knocked my life out of whack quite a bit. You see, I was the star player of the school football team. I had a true natural talent in handling the ball, although I can imagine you would find that a bit hard to believe now. I could beat boys many years older and much larger than myself, coming and going. Even our teacher, Mr Vaara, said that Martti Winter was a boy who was going to be the star of the Rabbit Back league.

It was a pleasant time. School went fairly well and I was idolized, the way masterful football players always are at school. I've always remembered how Mr Vaara once said in religion class that God might have created the heavens and the earth, but when it came to football, even God couldn't beat Martti Winter. One of the girls in class had a father who was a pastor, and of course word of what Mr Vaara said got to his ears. Mr Vaara received some sort of reprimand from the principal, who was a regular churchgoer, but it didn't matter, because everybody knew it was true—I did play football better than God.

Sometimes I still dream about it. Running across the grass, the ball obeying my every thought, kicking, dribbling, heading the ball, in control of every possible move, and as I approach the goal I'm unstoppable, and I kick the ball right between the goalposts, and it flies up into the sky and never comes down...

Oh, well. Now I'm just blabbering. All this culminated on the day in May when Mr Vaara asked me to stay after class. When all the other students had left, he informed me that the authoress Laura White had approved me for membership in the Literature Society.

I was at a complete loss, of course. I thought, what the dickens is that? I don't remember applying to be a member of any society. The teacher looked very serious and asked whether I even knew who Laura White was. And I did know. She was that author woman who had written the Creatureville books. *The teacher said that she was a great figure and a magnificent person, a writer with incomparable insight into the human mind. And he said that everybody knew that the children who were chosen to be in the Rabbit Back Literature Society would one day become something important, and that I should be eternally grateful that I had been asked to join.*

I didn't understand any of this. The teacher babbled all sorts of things about the brilliant road of literature and how I had received a call to travel it. He even got a little teary-eyed about it, I think, and I'd never seen a grown man cry. Then he got out our composition books, those yellow-covered ones, and waved a bundle of them in the air and said that in any case they would have to get me a new notebook because Laura White had taken the old one with her.

The old fellow had a crush on Laura White. Everybody knew it. People laughed about it behind his back. Supposedly he had once tried to cuddle up to her at a party when he was tipsy, but a bee appeared from somewhere and flew between them and stung him on the lip. He had to mumble his way through the school day, his lip was so swollen. We practically died laughing, and he flew into a rage.

So Mr Vaara was excited, but I wasn't—at least not in the beginning. I went home and told my mother what my teacher had said. But she already knew about it. He had called her at home, and she was radiating happiness, buzzing with joy. She hugged me and said that she had always known that her boy would be a great man one day.

My mother had never been proud of me before. I mean, of course she thought it was nice that I was good at football, but football was just a game, when it came right down to it—that's what she thought. But this. She was completely excited that I had been anointed as a talented, promising writer.

So naturally I joined the Society.

I knew all the members by sight, and they all knew me. The six girls and boys in the Society were allowed to sit indoors and write during recess while everyone else was driven out into the rain. Everyone thought they were a bit strange and snobbish, but since they were, in a way, in a higher class, no one dared to tease them. We were aware that they were on their way to being something great and important. And of course everyone knew the beautiful woman who led the writing club.

We boys were infatuated with Laura White. When we saw her in town, we would each put on an act, hoping she would look at us running around and showing off, and when I met her for the first time face to face, of course I froze completely.

To tell you the truth, I don't remember anything about our first meeting. Maybe that says something about how nervous I was. I remember that my mother drove me to Laura White's house in the car, that I got out and walked past the pond to the house with the sun scorching my back and knocked, and Laura White shouted from inside that the door was open.

I went inside, walked through the rooms and saw her sitting in a white dress surrounded by wicker furniture. "Come and have some tea, Martti," she said, and I stumbled straight into her smile.

My next memory is of running towards home, thrilled. I was going to be a writer. The kind of person who writes all those books in the library and at the bookstore that everybody reads!

I had actually never read a single book in its entirety. Reading had never much interested me. But when I got home I went to the bookshelf, took out a book at random, and started to read. And when I got to the end of that book, I started another and then a third.

I didn't get to know the other members well at all in the beginning. I learned to remember Ingrid Katz's name first, and I even teased her about it. "Here, kitty, kitty," I would say.

But Ingrid was actually a bit taller than me then, and she pushed me behind a door and put her mouth up to my ear and whispered hotly that I'd better not try that again or I wouldn't like what would happen to me.

She always knew how to get to me, and the teasing stopped right then. Actually, we started to become friends, because I learned to respect Ingrid.

At first, belonging to the Society felt quite normal. It was like any other club. Laura White gave us writing homework, and we wrote stories over the week and then on Sunday we read them out loud and listened to what she had to say about them. Sometimes she commented on them, sometimes she didn't. Sometimes she asked one of us to stay afterwards for some guidance, and then she explained in detail what was good about the story and what could use improvement. And often she would ask us all kinds of things about the theme of a story, using questions to make us understand the texts better.

There wasn't anything remarkable about it, I suppose. Laura White knew how to write well and how to teach us to write well. The most important thing was that it made us really want to be writers. We wanted it more than anything else—so much that it was, in fact, unnatural for children, now that I think about it.

If any of us had doubts about the Society at any point, our environment made sure that none of us broke ranks. Adults treated us quite differently than they treated other children—almost deferentially. Laura had that effect on people. She told everyone that we were future writers, and everyone acted accordingly.

The Rabbit Back Savings Bank donated a typewriter to each of us and we thought they were the most wonderful things we'd ever seen. I still have mine in the garage somewhere. It's the one I wrote my entire first novel on. I did it for sentimental reasons—by that time I had a more modern machine I could use.

But amid all this there was one drawback. I lost my football stardom.

The ball wouldn't obey my thoughts anymore. It slipped, went in the wrong direction, and when I drove it towards the goal during break, it would just jump to someone else, and I would be left stupidly standing there with no ball.

It was a hard spot for me. I can still remember the expressions on the others' faces when I fumbled it out of bounds. They were disappointed, sad, sometimes even scornful.

My days of glory were over. I was left alone. My former friends asked me to go swimming or biking less and less often, until finally, when I tried to tag along with them uninvited, they had to spell it out for me. My best friend, Pekka Jansson, said, "Go play with your writing friends, Martti, since you're going to be such a great writer and all."

I gave him a bloody nose, and burst into tears to top it off. The boys shook their heads at each other and left without saying much. And then I left, just like Pekka told me to, and went to find my writing friends. What else could I do?

"This is certainly interesting," Ella interrupts, "but my question was about the tenth member."

"Yes, I'm coming to that," Winter says in a distant, distracted tone, no longer poised.

Ella understands that this is all a part of spilling. Spilling is not the same as telling stories. The spiller has to stop using words to build stories, to forget everything that makes a good story, above all to forget trying to entertain the listener.

"Things come out in the order they come out," Winter says. "So. I was

a better football player than God, but the Society was a different situation. I was a better writer than many of the others to start with, and some of the members envied me, most of all Silja Saaristo. Compared to the tenth member when he came, though, I was nothing. Absolutely nothing.

When I read my own stories aloud the others would sigh with envy and admiration, but it felt empty to me because I knew that as soon as that boy started to read his story, mine would be dust, nothing but horse shit, stuff no one would even remember.

I'm sure you've heard of child prodigies, kids who seem to have a natural command of something that it takes other people a lifetime to learn? That boy was like that.

The rest of us were all pupils at the Rabbit Back School, but the little genius was from someplace else. Sometimes he was gone for a long time and then he would appear again and read us his literary output. He didn't spend much time with the rest of us and I don't think he really talked with most of us either, although the rest of us became fast friends and did everything together for many years.

It was understandable in a way. The other nine of us felt like we were better than other people, somehow entitled, young gods, the miraculous future of literature. Damn. I'm sorry for laughing in the middle of The Game, but for kids we really were self-important little shits. And since he was many kilometres above us he had to maintain his dignity, maintain some distance from more mediocre writers.

That's how we understood it.

We also envied that boy so much that we were hardly likely to let him come along with us anyway. I'm sure he sensed that we were freezing him out. We would hardly even look him in the eye.

But I don't have any facts about him. I can dimly remember his face, or at least the impression it made on me. Once, for instance, I was looking at Ingrid when she was sitting on the steps at Laura White's house—I had a bit of a crush on her. Later I found out that she was utterly in love with me, but she couldn't show it because I was a year older than her, and at that age a year is a wide chasm. I was looking at her and thinking to myself that she certainly had a pretty face, when all of a sudden that boy was standing beside her and looking at me in a peculiar way.

And suddenly I thought that, compared to him, Ingrid was positively ugly. If Ingrid was pretty, then that boy had the face of an angel, that's how divine his features were.

Except that I didn't like his eyes. There was something disturbing about them.

I don't remember his name. I've tried to remember it over the years. I assume that all of us children knew his name, but when he died we agreed that we would never talk about him again, and things you don't talk about have a way of escaping your mind.

I've sometimes had dreams where he comes to my house and grabs me by the shoulder and kisses my cheek and whispers something in my ear, but I can never quite hear what he's saying. And I wake up from the dream covered in sweat every time, as if I'd had the worst kind of nightmare.

He died in the early spring of 1972. I was eleven years old at the time. Ingrid came over to my house in the morning and told me. Laura White had come to her house and told her that the boy was no more and that the meetings of the Society would be cancelled for a while.

I don't know whether Ingrid said how he had died. Maybe I didn't even ask. I have an idea that he drowned in the pond in Laura's garden. I don't know where I got that idea. I just remember that when I went by the pond a little while later there was a hole in the ice and I thought, That's the hole he fell through and drowned, him and his ever-present notebook.

Winter's speech grows ever more indistinct, as if he were speaking in his sleep. Now he rouses himself a little, slurps some cocoa, which has grown cold, thinks for a moment, and continues.

"Did I already tell you that Laura White taught all of us to carry a notebook? Right from the start. We were told to write down our observations about people and life and the world. She always stressed that a writer should know how to make observations about two things—meaningless details and the universe. She also said this: 'If you really want to say something, you have to give up words and forget yourselves.'"

Winter's mouth hung open. His tongue flicked against his dry lower lip.

"At the end of one meeting Laura said, 'Dear budding writers, beloved friends, in the end, you must learn to look at everything as if you weren't even part of the human race.' And she gave us an assignment, a different one for each of us. I was told to pretend for a week that I was a Martian observing a creature called a 'mother'. I actually ended up abandoning the assignment on the third day, when my mother grew worried and started to make an appointment at the doctor's for me.

"We wrote all kinds of things in those notebooks, as well as we were able. Most of what we wrote was quite trivial. Things like 'sometimes my mother cries secretly' or 'my mother left a strange-coloured stick in the toilet' or 'today in class a terrible-smelling fart came out of the teacher's bum and everybody pretended that they didn't hear or smell anything'.

"We spent those first years pretty lazily. Learning to observe took some time—but not for the tenth member, naturally. No, he was constantly writing in his notebook, everywhere he went, furiously writing, writing with abandon, the little Mozart, the gifted little shit."

Winter smiled self-mockingly under the blindfold, and Ella smiled, too.

There was a cry from outside.

From the garden. From inside the wall.

Ella turned to look. What an inhuman sound. The winter night flowed thick into her veins.

25

MARTTI WINTER heard the mug fall out of Ella Milana's hand onto the floor and roll under a chair.

The contents of his own mug spilled into his lap. "The neighbour's cat," he said, ignoring for the moment the cold cocoa seeping into his underwear.

She didn't answer.

"Did it frighten you? Such a horrible sound for a small creature to make." Winter laughed. "Let's continue the game, shall we?"

Silence.

He waited another moment and then tore the blindfold off.

She was gone. He heard her clumping down the staircase. There was no creak of the front door. Her steps continued deeper into the house.

She was going through the downstairs rooms towards the terrace, towards the garden.

There were far too many stairs in the house for a heavy-set, middle-aged man to catch up with a light-footed young woman.

When Winter finally made it to the first floor, his lungs were straining like sails in a storm, his chest convulsing. He resisted the urge to stop and rest and headed towards the piano room. He held on to the walls and tables for support, knocked a vase, a lamp and several boxes of chocolates onto the floor, panted, gasped, shouted, wheezed, falling more than running as he went.

He came to a stop in the piano room.

The double doors at the back of the room were open and freezing air rushed into the house. The furniture crackled around him—the piano, chairs, sofas and small tables flinching in the sudden cold like frightened animals.

Winter, too, recoiled from the open doors and the darkness beyond. He would have liked to bolt like a horse and run until everything went dark. He cleared his throat, willing himself to calm down, and stepped through the doors onto the terrace.

At first there was nothing to see but a blank square of frozen black. The world ended at the edge of the terrace. The darkness was too thick even for the creator. The work of creation had been abandoned right here.

But the girl was out there somewhere, where during the daytime there was a garden, statues and a high wall around all of it. As he stood staring into the dark, he could finally make out different shades of black—the night sky, the trees under snow, the carved figures between them.

The terrace pavement was covered in ice. It was a roofed terrace, so there was only a thin layer of snow on it. He could see footprints where she had run back and forth over the pavement. Winter walked to the right and then to the left, taking short, careful steps in his slippers.

He noticed a gap in the snow between two statues. The stone nymphs were smiling:

She's not coming back. She's stepped into the darkness and you're never going to see her again.

The tracks led to a wall of darkness beyond the lime trees. The terrace was surrounded by silence.

Winter felt very heavy and tired. He peered in the direction of the tracks and waited for his eyes to adjust to the darkness.

"Hey," he shouted.

An echo bounced back from the stone walls. His skin rose up in goosebumps. He was sure it had sensed him.

"Hey! Miss?"

A twig snapped somewhere. A sighing, sniffling sound rippled over the snow. Someone, or some thing, was wading through the drifts towards the terrace.

Winter went to the edge of the frozen pavement. His movements were like those of a child who can't swim and fears falling into the water. He leaned one hand on the iron railing, reached the other out into the darkness and closed his eyes. He stood waiting for the warm, human creature named Ella Milana to take hold of it. He closed his mind to all other possibilities.

"It's some kind of small animal," the girl said.

Her voice came from a few metres away, low to the ground. Winter sighed with relief and opened his eyes, but he still couldn't see her in the blackness.

"A squirrel or a bird, I'm not sure. I can't see anything. Poor little thing. It's injured. A cat must have caught it."

He was able to make out Ella Milana's pale face, then her dark clothes. She stood out against the dim garden like she'd risen from black water, carrying a bundle in her outstretched arms. For a second she looked like an icon of the Holy Virgin holding the baby Jesus.

Winter leaned out, took her under the arm and tugged her and her burden onto the terrace. As if by agreement, they quickly moved several steps away from the edge of the terrace and stood facing each other, the light from the house comfortingly close by. Their breath melted into one large cloud of steam. It prevented him from seeing at first what she was holding.

It had feathers. It was a magpie, or had once been one. You could hardly call it alive, although it was still breathing. It had no eyes. Its empty eye sockets were steaming. White bones jutted out where the wings should have been, and the bird flapped them up and down, as if it imagined it could somehow reach the outer perimeter of the darkness it had fallen into.

"Oh. Little friend," Winter whispered, laying a hand on Ella Milana's shoulder.

She couldn't take her eyes off the remains of the bird, still managing to cling to shreds of life. A wave of indignation rose up in Winter. Pathetic thing. Still alive, all torn up like this! Horrifying—absolutely obscene!

The bird stopped flapping its wings. It tilted its blind head, opened its beak and let out a little sound, like a child's babbled question. Ella Milana's arms swung apart in a broad arch and let the bundle fall with a thud onto the terrace. Winter lifted a slipper, placed it on the bird, and shifted his whole weight onto it. He heard a crack, then took two steps backwards.

They stood facing each other for a moment longer, looking first at the crushed bird lying wet on the ice of the terrace, then at each other. Ella Milana turned to look into the darkness from which she'd carried the bird. "What could do something like that?" she asked. Her voice was matter-of-fact, but her ashen face revealed her mental state.

Martti Winter rubbed his arms. The frosty air seemed to wrap itself tighter around them.

"A cat," he said. "They get over the wall somehow. Or maybe it was an owl. There are a lot of owls around here. They sometimes attack the cats. And vice versa."

Ella Milana turned to give him a doubtful look, but then nodded. "A cat or an owl," she said. "What else could it be?"

Martti Winter picked up the carcass and flung it back into the darkness, as far from the house and the terrace as he could.

They turned to leave. A black form flew between them from out of the garden. They recoiled. The dead magpie stared at them from empty eye sockets.

"Oh!" Ella Milana said.

Martti Winter felt like screaming. Ella Milana lifted her left foot as if to dance, pivoted and took a few curious, bewildered steps towards the garden.

The garden sighed and rasped in a sudden gust of wind. Somewhere outside the wall the dogs began to bark in unison.

Martti Winter filled his lungs with the cold, caught the girl under the arm and quickly slipped into the house. He dropped her on the floor, flung the doors closed, locked them and pulled the thick drapes over them. Then he turned his back to the doors and straightened his trousers.

"Ouch," she said, lying on the floor massaging her hip.

"Would you like some more coffee?" Winter asked solicitously. "Or cocoa? We seem to have interrupted The Game, so…"

Ella Milana scrambled to her feet, wiped her lovely, arching lips with her fingers and turned her head to look at the closed terrace doors. "Don't you think we should discuss what just happened?"

Martti Winter snorted and padded over to the piano. He sat on the too-small stool, rose a couple of times to adjust it, looked up at the ceiling and started to play the first bars of the *Moonlight Sonata.*

Then he switched to ragtime.

"What did just happen?" he asked as he played, grinning like a lounge pianist. "An evil owl murdered an innocent magpie. Or maybe a cat did it. That's that. Nature can be cruel."

"An owl or a cat! That was something else," she said. "Owls don't hurl dead birds around."

Winter continued playing.

"Another variation on the 'slow barge'," Ella Milana said sourly, laying a hand on the piano.

Winter grew distracted for a moment looking at her, particularly at her delicate fingers tapping the top of the piano. He lost track of the notes, so charmed was he, suddenly, by the young woman's presence. A peculiar passage came into his mind, something he had read somewhere, or was it something he'd written himself? *She isn't beautiful, not like the girls on magazine covers who stir heat in the viewer, jealousy, a desire to possess. Her charm is akin to that of a meadow of flowers veiled with morning mist, with all its sounds and scents. Impossible to grasp, yet it awakens a great and unrequitable longing.*

"Fine," she said, with a click of her tongue. "We won't talk about it. We won't discuss it. But maybe we really ought to stop The Game for now."

Winter batted his eyes, lifted his sausage-like fingers from the keys and rested them in his lap. "My spill ended when you ran into the garden," he said, staring at his fingers. "Now it's your turn."

"I suppose so," she said.

They went back up to the third floor and into the blue room. The handkerchief was tied over Ella Milana's eyes, and the second round of The Game began.

"I would guess," Winter began. Then he was silent for several seconds. He made a decision to continue the manoeuvre he'd already begun, something they had developed when The Game was in its early stages. They called it "the x-ray manoeuvre", for obvious reasons.

"I assume that you sometimes take all of your clothes off and stand in front of the mirror naked, looking at yourself. I want to know everything you see, and what you think about what you see."

26

E LLA MILANA was at the front door, ready to leave. Martti Winter looked worriedly at her and began to hold forth on the nature of the x-ray manoeuvre.

"On the one hand, it's a somewhat crude game, but on the other, a sort of extreme verbal strip game, exciting and humiliating and every possible thing in between. Silja Saaristo used it for the first time in 1978, with Ingrid Katz as her subject. Ingrid used it on Elias Kangasniemi, and Elias used it on me. That's how it started. The wisest thing is to think of it as a rite of initiation. It's something we made up, so we use it. Would you like me to offer an apology? I can do that. I'm sorry I used the x-ray manoeuvre on you."

Ella didn't answer. She was looking for her gloves on the wooden hat shelf, but found them in her coat pocket.

"At this point you ought to be aware that there are a lot of other tricks you can use in The Game. If all this is too much for you, then stop playing."

He looked her in the eye with a twinkle that suddenly melted into genuine regret.

"Oh, little Ella. All this must be devilishly difficult for you. You've thrown yourself into The Game cold. The rest of us at least had a chance to grow into it gradually. When it began it was quite innocent. Laura didn't create it so it would become like this. When it began, we were children. But we changed, and The Game changed with us. Have you been offered the yellow yet, by the way?"

Ella nodded. She had, in fact, just taken sodium pentothal, and she could still feel its effects. She pressed her lips together and held her tongue captive between her teeth to keep from continuing to babble. Escaped thoughts flocked into her mouth like seagulls.

As she opened the door, Winter seemed to remember something. He asked her to wait, disappeared deeper in the house for a moment, and when he came back, breathless, pressed a photo album into her hands.

"Take this. I dug it out a couple of weeks ago just for you, to give you some idea of what the Rabbit Back Literature Society is. Take it with you. You can borrow it as long as you don't lose any photos. And under no circumstances are you to give any of them to the newspapers. None of us want to see these in the evening tabloids. I've put labels on some of them to give you a sort of tour of Society history."

Ella took the album under her arm, nodded and walked out. The dogs stirred in the darkness.

"If you have any questions about any of the pictures," Winter added, "just call. Or come to visit, during the day. We can drink coffee and chat. You don't need The Game to have a conversation."

Ella went down the steps and stomped her feet to disperse the dogs.

"A Dalmatian, a corgi, a Labrador retriever, and a mixed-breed spitz," Winter said from behind her, proud of his expertise. "Perhaps a cross between a Finnish spitz and a Norwegian elkhound."

The dogs remained at the edge of darkness.

Ella wasn't afraid of dogs, but she did feel uncomfortable under their reproachful gaze, as if she were the intruder.

Martti Winter shouted, "I'll certainly understand if you don't want to come! The Game has that effect. Once you've played The Game with someone enough, you can hardly speak to them anymore. I was just thinking that if we're not yet that far gone, it would be nice to chat."

Ella stopped and considered the emotional state that shone through his voice. "Yes, I'll come," she said, without turning around.

Ella Milana lay in her room for five days. Her mother tried three times to take her temperature. She said she was tired, needed to recharge her batteries for a while.

Mostly she didn't think about anything. She just lay there looking at the ceiling and lamented the hollowness of her being. She was a clay pot, and she'd been broken in pieces. There used to be something inside her, and now that it had spilled for the use of someone else, all that was left was a cracked, dried-out shell.

Sometimes her mind would slip into going over The Game again—first the round she'd played with Ingrid Katz, then the one with Martti Winter, in some moments the time she spilled to Silja Saaristo about her barrenness, and she thought about how ugly and defective she had felt listening to her own words.

The things she'd spilled about her father's death now belonged to Ingrid Katz—all of her rottenest, most repulsive, most horrible thoughts. She would have liked to leave them to rot in the back of her mind, but they had come out right after her beautiful thoughts, and the moment they had crystallized into words she had started to upbraid herself for them.

She had managed to conceal her callousness from herself, but when she played The Game she vomited it all out. She'd heard herself say that her father's death and funeral had meant no more to her than when an appliance that has been malfunctioning for a long time finally breaks down completely—mostly a relief rather than a loss. She'd listened like a bystander as she said that she had tried to grieve like she was supposed to, had even cried, but not for her father. For something else. She simply didn't know how to grieve that difficult, irritating stranger they'd called Paavo Emil Milana.

Even at the funeral, she had been thinking about everything else. As she laid a wreath on the coffin she'd been thinking about shaving her legs and buying her own mug to keep in the teacher's lounge. All of these thoughts had spilled not just into Ingrid Katz's but also Ella Milana's ears, and once exhumed, they were difficult to bury again.

She had even spilled the fact that it was sometimes a struggle to remember exactly how her father had actually died—of a heart attack in the middle of the garden. She remembered much better a dream she'd had a couple of days after her father's death.

In the dream there was a man who looked like dry leaves and rustled in the wind with an annoyingly loud noise. People were walking by with their hands over their ears, glaring at him angrily. Then the wind grew stronger and finally it was so furious that it carried the rustling man away with it. The people walking by stopped and applauded and Ella woke up clapping her own hands together enthusiastically.

Winter had drawn out her nakedness the way it was in her own head. Ella had never experienced such nakedness, even at the gynaecologist. When she realized what was expected of her, she pretended to have a coughing fit and surreptitiously popped a yellow crystal. Only then was she able to get through the x-ray manoeuvre.

And she had spilled it all for him—her skinny shoulders, her slightly too big but pleasingly round ass, the red, irritated skin of her hips, the half-moon birthmark on the inside of her left thigh, her perky, pink nipples, which would never feed a baby, and the veins that shone under the skin around them, her comically undisciplined pubic hair, the soft asymmetry of her labia and the bumps left where she'd once shaved them with an old razor.

She had even spilled that perfect, arching line that she formed by twisting her upper body forty-five degrees—sometimes when she was alone she would look at it too long in the mirror, startled at the clarity of her own gaze.

She'd talked about how she used to let her gaze sink through her skin, peel away the flesh and tear away the muscles until she could see the reproductive organs that would never produce life, whose presence she could never forget, even for a moment.

Ordinary people could never surrender so much of themselves as the writers in the Society did—not even the most impassioned lovers, in spite of their claims of melting into each other and becoming one. The writers in the Society wrote stories, but they didn't dress themselves in stories with each other, and that nakedness was hard to comprehend.

Ella lay in her room and gradually rewove slender new stories inside her to replace the ones that had been torn to bits, and her condition started to improve.

Her mother put something down at the foot of her bed, on top of the blanket, and said, "You left this in your father's Triumph."

She didn't open her eyes, but once her mother had left she moved her foot and something heavy thudded to the floor.

Once she opened the album, she couldn't contain herself. She flipped back and forth through it, peering at the yellow labels, too impatient to stop at a single photo.

The first few pictures were black and white, the rest in colour. They had been taken by multiple people. Some of them were carefully composed and well photographed, others were clumsy, crooked, over- or underexposed.

Finally Ella made herself take a breath and started to go through them one by one. She got out pen and paper and concentrated on each one carefully, making notes and observations, as a researcher should when analysing her subject.

She hadn't yet sent anything to Professor Korpimäki because her material was still too amorphous to provide a basis for even a preliminary report, but she might find something more substantial in these photographs.

On the first page was a picture of Laura White and three children. They were standing on the steps of Laura White's house. White had a slightly reticent smile on her face; the children were glowing with pride. The authoress was wearing a white dress that left her arms bare, and one hand rested on the shoulder of a boy in a billed cap. Two little girls in dark dresses stood holding hands.

The yellow label read: *Ingrid, Toivo and Aura with L.W. shortly after the founding of the Society, May 1968. Picture taken by Mr Vaara, who had a habit of popping in at Laura's house "in a collegial capacity" until L.W. apparently made it clear to him that he was disturbing the children's lessons.*

At the bottom of the page was a picture of Laura White captured in the act of twirling around in a summer meadow with her hands stretched towards the sky. Her figure was blurred to mere motion and her features were unclear—you could see the limbs of the trees through her furiously spinning face.

I believe this picture was taken by a professional Rabbit Back photographer named Kaarle Kellokumpu, Martti Winter's yellow label read. *Apparently L.W.'s presence addled the man's head and he succeeded in adjusting his camera in such a way that she became partially transparent.*

The album contained many photos of the Society children in nature, exploring rivers and streams and large boulders. Ella recognized Martti Winter at about the age of ten, sitting on a branch of a birch tree grinning, and the little girl holding on to his ankles was clearly Ingrid Katz. The yellow label confirmed this. *The Rabbit Back Literature Society on a picnic. We had thousands of picnics where we ate a snack and wrote short exercises and sometimes wandered deeper into Rabbit Wood. Wonderful outings, where we saw all kinds of strange and beautiful things. Afterwards I tried a few times to find the places where L.W. had taken us, but unfortunately I never did.*

In one dim, black and white photo, Laura White was walking in the deep forest with a dreamy expression, followed by the nine young members of the Society, of which only the features of the first three could be easily made out—they were Ingrid Katz, Aura Jokinen, and Silja Saaristo, sticking out her tongue. On the yellow label, Martti Winter had written that he'd taken the picture himself, in July of 1971.

Ella covered her mouth to keep from shouting out loud. There were nine children visible in the photo and one, Martti Winter, behind the camera.

Ten children in all.

So obviously one of them was the gifted child, the one who died less than a year after the photo was taken.

Ella looked at each child in turn and was able to identify four more of them with near certainty: Anna-Maija Seläntö, Toivo Holm, Helinä Oksala, and Oona Kariniemi. The two that remained were fuzzy, dim figures in shadow, one of which could be tentatively identified as Elias Kangasniemi.

The other was the tenth member of the Society, the dead boy.

Ella started to look for him in the other photos. There had to be a better picture of him somewhere! A photo might give her a chance to learn his identity and the cause of his death.

She knew that he died in 1972. The members of the Society had been between the ages of 11 and 13 at the time. Halfway through the album they started to look like teenagers. The last photos showed what were clearly adult writers posing surrounded by their published books, with champagne glasses and cigarettes in their hands. There was a photo of Ingrid Katz and Silja Saaristo in the water, their breasts bare, and farther off stood Elias Kangasniemi, also in the water, scratching his pubic hair.

The later photos offered useful information, but for now she had to put them aside and concentrate on the early pictures, where she might find what she was looking for.

Of course, Ella didn't really think she would find a photo that would present the tenth member of the Society. The members who were still living had decided to forget their dead comrade and wipe him from the Society's history. She was almost sure that the album would have purposely left out the boy who had been made a non-person. She was counting on finding something that Winter and the other members hadn't noticed. She had a researcher's training, after all. The Society's writers weren't real researchers, trained to analyse their subjects systematically. They were like a bunch of Pizarros, making expeditions into each other's minds, unconcerned about the damage they inflicted.

The kind of people who make mistakes.

Martti Winter had made a mistake when he forgot that the shot he'd taken showed the tenth member, dimly visible.

She started to look through the pictures with a magnifying glass. She stopped only to resist her mother's occasional attempts to drag her downstairs to drink some coffee or eat some soup. She developed a pounding headache and nearly cut off the circulation in her back and legs completely, but she couldn't stop.

Finally, she let out a grunt. The magnifying glass fell to the floor. She clambered up with stiff, numb legs and hobbled across the room.

It was daylight outside. Where had the evening gone?

She went back to the album, picked up the magnifying glass and looked at the photo again. Laura White sitting on the lawn with Martti Winter and Aura Jokinen. The yellow label read: *A lesson in L. W.'s garden. L. W. finds a promising passage in young Winter's notebook, and a budding sci-fi writer grows bored.*

In the background was Laura White's house. Ivy climbed the wall and the house was surrounded by colourful flower beds. The sun was high in the sky, the shadows short. Laura White and Martti Winter were sitting on the shore of the pond, absorbed in the notebook he was holding as Laura White explained something to him. Aura Jokinen was looking away.

Ella followed Aura Jokinen's gaze with her finger. She did it again. The girl was looking into the house. The front door was half open. In the entryway, masked by light and shadow, stood a child leaning his arm against the wall and staring at Aura Jokinen. That detail had almost escaped her.

The magnifying glass revealed his delicate face.

He wasn't any of the recognizable members of the Society.

"Nice to meet you," Ella whispered to the boy in the picture, the first tenth member.

27

THERE WAS A SOFT PILLOW, hot drops of moisture on her thighs—the lewd remains of a dream. Her eyes opened slowly. Light reflecting from the walls and ceiling flooded over her. Too much light.

Images floated halfway between the dark and the light. She tried to take hold of them, but they were woven into the dimness, too delicate for her touch.

Her mouth opened in a yawn so wide that her jaw cracked; air rushed into her lungs and out again. Her breath probed the flesh it inhabited, measuring its outlines and outer reaches, focusing until the most important details were in place. Ella Amanda Milana. Lovely, curving lips, painterly nipples, defective ovaries.

When she had assembled herself, Ella Milana pinpointed her location in time and space and imagined she could feel her personal future snapping into place in her spinal cord.

She swung her feet to the floor and recommenced her literary historical research.

She went downstairs and found a letter that made her an heir of the missing authoress.

The letter had been waiting for her on the kitchen table on a pile of fresh advertising flyers, not far from the butter dish and the bread basket. It had been sent by one Otto Bergman, Master of Law, and was addressed to "Ella Milana, Member, Rabbit Back Literature Society".

"Something to do with the Literature Society," her mother had said from behind her newspaper. The kitchen smelled of toast. "Open it and tell me whether it's good news or bad news."

Ella ripped open the envelope. At the very beginning of the letter it mentioned that the same letter had been sent to the other members of the Society. It had the stamp of a law firm. The paper was thicker than ordinary letter paper, its texture unusual against her fingers.

Ella poured herself some coffee and sat down to read it.

"It says that Laura White has willed all of her possessions to the Rabbit Back Literature Society except for a sum to be spent on establishing an annual writer's grant. Her house will be separately transferred to the foundation and awarded to the members of the Society for their use in perpetuity."

"Well, well," her mother said. "But what does it mean?"

Ella kept reading. The letter said that every member of the Society would be paid a substantial sum of money once the will had gone through. The letter also emphasized that Laura White's death would not be declared any time soon:

Laws governing declaration of death set out the conditions under which a missing person may be declared dead. The general conditions are that a person has been missing for an extended period of time and has not provided information about themselves, or said person has clearly perished in a devastating fire or other accident likely to be an immediate danger to life. Because Laura White cannot be seen as having been the victim of such an accident, but rather disappeared at a party, and because it cannot be proved beyond a doubt that she did not leave the party of her own free will and that she is not, for her own reasons, remaining out of contact in an unknown location, her

death cannot be declared until her body is found or after the passing
of five years' time without any communication received from her.

Ella thought she could hear the most distant part of her personal future creak, give way with a bang as it once again changed its shape, and then quiver somewhere inside her spine. She felt a little dizzy.

When Martti Winter opened the door, the first thing he looked at was the pack of dogs in front of the house. When Ella Milana waved a hand and said she had come for coffee, he was visibly cheered.

"Marvellous!" he said, showing her in with a hand on her back and checking the dogs' positions as he closed the door again. "I'll make us some coffee and we can have a piece of cake and a chat!"

The low winter light filtered through the windows. Ella noticed that in daylight Martti Winter's home looked like a chocolate box—most of the furniture was confectionery in colour and shape, like dark and light chocolates.

He led her into one of the small downstairs rooms. Inside was a small, round table and chairs, a carpet the colour of vanilla ice cream and some small paintings. Ella sat at the table and set her bag down next to her chair.

On the table was a china teapot, a large chocolate cake, and a wide selection of sweet rolls, pastries and other treats.

"You were quite sure that I would come," she said with a smile.

Winter raised his eyebrows questioningly.

"The table's already set, I see," she said, pointing at the dishes of treats.

Winter nodded awkwardly and went to fetch her a cup and plate.

The two of them chatted about the weather, the passing of time, the stray dogs running around, the flavour of the chocolate cake and the mythological figurines scattered around the house. There was a knee-high, stone gnome in a corner of the room, grinning wickedly, and a wooden carving of a woman lolling near the door, a dazzlingly well-endowed figure, her lower body veiled by her hair.

"I didn't buy them myself," Winter said. "It's impossible to live in Rabbit Back without receiving them from everyone as gifts."

Ella wolfed down a meringue, talked a bit about Laura White's house, and then enquired, as if the thought had just occurred to her, whether it would be at all possible to get into White's house and look around.

"I was supposed to meet her, and then everything happened the way it happened..." she said, "and it would be so interesting to see the place where it all began."

Martti Winter pondered the question over two strawberry waffles and one caramel napoleon. "I understand, of course. You got the letter from the lawyer. And naturally I can see why you would feel a desire to see the house. The rest of us spent a lot of time at Laura's house in our day."

"I'm sure you must know the place through and through," Ella sighed.

Winter shook his head. "Not through and through. There are a lot of places in that house where we never went. We didn't run around the place. That was unheard of. We knew from the start where it was all right to go and where it wasn't. We always went where Laura told us to."

He sat sunk in thought for a moment. "So I can assure you that all ten members of the Society will better acquaint themselves with the place as soon as the estate is distributed—including you, naturally. That may take five or ten years, according to the attorney's letter."

"Yes. Ten years," Ella said. "I was thinking, though, that perhaps we could take a peek at the house earlier than that. After all, someone ought to check in on the place."

Winter smiled at her eagerness and explained with elaborate patience that the house was taken care of by a trusted employee, "Old Man Bohm", who lived nearby and went now and then to make sure the pipes hadn't broken and turned the place into a swimming pool. "I don't think any of us has a key to the house," he concluded.

Ella gave up the fight and led the conversation back to the delightful flavour of the cake, a subject on which they were in perfect accord, but she couldn't stop thinking about all the things that must be in that house—letters, notes, photographs, unfinished manuscripts, maybe even Laura White's personal diary.

"I had a question about one of the photographs," Ella said. She put the photo in front of him. It was the one of Aura Jokinen and Laura White together. "See the boy standing in the doorway?"

Martti Winter raised his eyebrows. "Why, yes."

"Do you think it might be the tenth member of the Society?" Ella asked. "The first tenth member?"

Winter looked at the photo up close, squinting, his mouth partly open. "It could be. It must be. As far as I know, no other children but the members ever visited Laura's house. She didn't especially like children, actually. She liked the ten of us, of course, but she thought of us as specimens. We weren't ordinary children to her. She said something once about how children—all children except us, of course—were in her opinion tiresome, noisy, stupid, soulless creatures who gave her a headache." Winter smiled. "That wasn't the sort of thing one put on the cover of a Creatureville book, of course. She just didn't want to have anything to do with children except at one remove, through her books. Once she actually said that she was surprised that it was children who read her books, since she had by no means written them with children in mind."

Ella asked whether the photo helped him remember anything more about the dead boy. Winter cut himself a fourth piece of cake and poured them both some more coffee. Then he looked at his guest with a sly smile and wiped his lips. A few crumbs fell onto the breast of his dark shirt.

"Do you mean that we should take a break from coffee and continue The Game where you feel we left off?"

Ella was taken aback by his gentle teasing. She was immediately conscious of the fact that her nakedness was his to control. His gaze at the moment was tracing her birthmarks and other distinguishing features with a sureness that was impossible to mistake. She felt herself at a disadvantage. She had a moment of panic, but then looked with cold, analytic eyes at the man who had won her nakedness from her.

What a big lump of a creature he was, with his pudgy hands, pumpkin head and gingerbread smile! Let him have the map to her flesh if it made him happy. It was nothing but a stripped doll in the clumsy, sweaty hands of an oaf who didn't even know what to do with it.

Gradually she felt a return of the strength he had momentarily stolen. He sensed the change; Ella could see it in his eyes, the same eyes that were in the photo of the handsome young author on the jacket flaps.

"Actually," she said softly, "I was thinking we could just talk about it like two normal people."

"I see," he said, surprised. "I can certainly tell you, at least, that I still don't remember the boy's name."

"Really?"

"Really. We never actually wanted to get to know him. He may have been a member of the Society, but he was never *one of us*. We didn't want to know his name. We didn't want to know anything about him."

Ella looked surprised.

"Think about it," Winter said. "A child on his way to becoming a writer, like us, and yet so far above us that we couldn't even imitate him. How could we possibly have liked him?"

"I assume you weren't overwhelmed with grief when he died, then?"

"Grief is the wrong word," Winter said with a vague look in his eyes. "We were shocked, of course. But we didn't grieve. On my own behalf I can say that although I wasn't glad he had died, I did feel liberated, in a way. Like I had escaped from his shadow."

Ella looked at the layers of chocolate cake. A disturbing thought came to her.

"Shall I put on some music?" Winter asked.

"No. Or go ahead, if you like."

"Don't you like music?"

Ella smiled. "Music is just sound at varying pitch to me. It crumbles in my ears like a rye crisp. And I didn't come here to listen to music."

"Why did you come, then?"

"To drink coffee and chat," Ella said. "You invited me. Have you forgotten?"

She looked at Winter. He had a surprised smile on his moon face that made her nervous.

"Well, what is it?"

"You're blushing."

"Blushing? Don't be silly. Why in the world would I be blushing over a cup of coffee?"

Then she realized that her cheeks were, in fact, hot.

"Like a little girl," he said teasingly. "What were you just thinking about? Tell me. I'll give you a cookie if you do."

"I wasn't thinking about anything," Ella said coolly, fearing that she was blushing even more. She was remembering with excruciating detail the dream she'd had the night before.

They looked at each other for a long time—a young woman with lovely, curving lips and a defective part at her very centre, and a massive man with old photograph eyes in a moon face and a half-eaten Danish in his hand.

"At this part of the movie the girl always gets up and leaves," Winter said at last. "In case you're not sure what to do."

Ella shoved the photo back into her bag and stood up. "Goodbye, Mr Winter. Thanks for the coffee and cake."

He walked her to the door.

Ella went down the icy steps slowly, a slight smile on her lips, until she saw a German Shepherd and a spaniel skulking on the other side of the snowy meadow.

"What draws them here?" she asked, pulling on her gloves.

"That I don't know," Winter said. "But you should come again, for coffee and a chat. Before we play each other out completely and stop saying hello when we meet. That will happen eventually, but we're not there yet."

Ella Milana returned to Martti Winter's house for five days in a row.

They drank coffee, ate baked treats and chatted. Ella enjoyed herself but didn't forget her research—at every visit she managed to gather useful information.

Winter talked more about how Laura White had taught him to look at everything with an outsider's eyes.

"We were supposed to look at ourselves that way, too," he said. "She would take us in front of a mirror and make us stare at our own reflection until it started to feel alien and peculiar. Then we were supposed to write a description of ourselves and imagine that it was written by someone else, someone who had never seen a human face before. She tore up my first five attempts. It wasn't until the sixth one that I accomplished what she was looking for.

"When I read it aloud to the others, Silja Saaristo ran out of the room and threw up. Laura looked ecstatic, her eyes were glowing, and she clapped. 'Look at Martti!' she shouted to the others. 'He has a writer's eyes.'

"I didn't show that piece to my mother. It used to make her cry when I made faces and twisted my eyes up. 'You're such a good-looking boy,' she would say. 'Don't deliberately make yourself ugly.' If she had read the description I wrote it would have broken her heart."

The story of the butterfly made a particular impression on Ella.

"Once Laura asked me to stay behind when the others were leaving. She gave me a caterpillar and said that my first task was to grow it into a butterfly. I put it in a pickle jar and gave it fresh leaves every day. I went to Laura's house every day specially to take care of it. Then the caterpillar made a cocoon, of course, and one day a butterfly squirmed out of it. It was a tortoiseshell butterfly. I was incredibly proud of it, almost as if I had created it myself.

"Then Laura picked up the jar from the table, held it between us, and asked me what my feelings were about the butterfly. I thought about it for a moment, and I answered that I liked it and cared a great deal about it, because I had raised it. She nodded. Then she gave me a little brown bottle and told me it was ether. She told me to pour some into the jar.

"I obeyed, naturally. The butterfly began to behave strangely, rolled over and felt the glass wall of the jar with its proboscis. Laura said, 'Look, it's dying.' And I looked.

"I was crying, and I was ashamed, and eventually my butterfly was lying dead at the bottom of the jar, and I still didn't know exactly what I was expected to do.

"Then Laura gave me a homework assignment. She told me to write about something. I asked what I should write about. She said, 'Anything.' The main thing was that I should write at least five hundred words, about anything at all.

"I went home and sat with the blank paper in front of me for what seemed like ages. Then I started to write. I spent several days writing that piece. I hardly took time to eat or sleep. I got up secretly during the night and wrote. When the piece was finished, I went to my mother, who was reading a book in the garden, and handed it to her."

Winter closed his eyes and smiled.

"It was about a cowboy named Billy James who had a horse that injured its leg. In the end he had to shoot the horse with his revolver. My mother read it with tears in her eyes, hugged me tightly, and said, 'Good gracious, Martti, that is what I call a real story.'"

Ella leaned forward, the half-eaten cookie in her hand forgotten.

"What did Laura White say about your story?" She was more spellbound than was perhaps desirable in a researcher.

"She said I should write it again. She told me to write the whole thing three more times. When I'd written the fourth version, she let me read it to the others."

They sat for some time without speaking. It felt natural that they should both think their own thoughts for a moment. Ella looked around. The room was high, the ceiling covered in chocolate-coloured panels decorated with skilfully carved reliefs of gambolling wood nymphs. Martti Winter said that he'd ordered them from a local woodworker with the proceeds from his first successful novel. The carvings were based on a dream he'd had numerous times.

"They would always lure me into their dance and then get me lost in a deep forest. It's in their nature. They want to seduce you, to cause your destruction, but most of all they want to be seen. I sensed beforehand that if I commissioned the work, I would stop having the dream, and that's what happened. But when I saw the woodworker later he said that he had started dreaming about the carving. I'll bet his dreams were just as damp and horrible."

Ella glanced at the clock and got up from the table.

Martti Winter said, "Ella Milana, my dear, will you come again tomorrow? I enjoy having someone to talk to for the first time in a long while. I had forgotten how pleasant a chat and a cup of coffee can be. For some reason you don't get on my nerves nearly as much as most people do."

"I may not be able to come," Ella said. "I promised my mother I would go with her to Tampere to see my aunt."

Ella broke that promise.

"I have a lot of work to do," she told her mother the next morning. "I'll drop you off at the station, of course. And if you plan to be in Tampere for the whole week I could drive there in the Triumph in a couple of days, once I've got my work where it ought to be."

"Well, let's do that, then," her mother sighed. "Though I don't see how your project's going to fall apart if you leave it for a few days. What you need is to meet some nice young man and do a little courting before you forget how. I didn't raise you to be an old maid. Even a wallflower has to bloom sometime."

Ella looked over her notes. She was delighted at how much information she had gathered just from chatting with Martti Winter over coffee and cake. If Professor Korpimäki started asking her for her Laura White material, she would at least have something. A lousy researcher she would have been, if she let such information go uncollected.

As she drove up to Winter's house for the seventh day in a row and walked to the door humming to herself, she noticed that there was a key left in the front lock.

A bicycle leaned against the porch, glittering with frost. Ella thought she recognized it.

She let herself in and listened to the silence for a moment. A plastic bag from Rabbit Market lay on the floor by the door, full of chocolates and other sweets. There was a pair of woman's boots in the middle of the entryway with snow still on them.

She heard muffled talk from upstairs.

Ella went up to the second floor. She could hear a woman's voice from a room she knew Martti Winter used for his daily nap—he had shown it to her a couple of days before.

She pushed the door open.

The venetian blinds cut the daylight into thin slices that painted stripes across everything in the room. The air was heavy and there was an odd smell that Ella didn't recognize right away. In the middle of the room was a heavy-framed bed. Martti Winter lay on it. His breathing was laboured. Ingrid Katz was bent over him like a hungry phantom groping for blood to drink.

"Is he sick?" Ella asked, stepping over the threshold.

"Ah, the baby writer," Ingrid Katz gasped. "Hello there. It's getting crowded around here."

Ingrid Katz and Martti Winter were nearly invisible, shadows cast over them like a pile of quilts. Ella squinted, trying to make out the scene. It occurred to her that Ingrid might be torturing or perhaps even murdering Martti Winter.

"Hello, Madame Librarian," Ella said.

Ingrid snorted. "There aren't any librarians here. Just I. Katz, author and member of the Rabbit Back Literature Society. I came to check on the condition of my comrade, to make sure he was all right."

Martti Winter let out a groan like someone suffering an agonizing death.

Ingrid Katz smiled and shot a quick glance at Ella.

"Our dear fellow author has eaten till he's a bit bloated and isn't up to his usual duties. I know him like the back of my hand, so I have a certain responsibility for him. I know him almost better than I know myself. And the same is true for him. He knows me. Don't you, Martti?" She smiled at him with tears in her eyes and whispered, "I know what makes him tick as if I'd built him myself. When you've learned a person's thoughts and needs through and through, you can never leave him for good."

Martti Winter whispered, "Ingrid, my call last night was a moment of weakness. I was terrified and alone. If you had answered, I'm sure I would have said right away that it was a mistake. You can't come here with your own key anymore. That's what we agreed on. You think you know me, but you don't, not anymore."

"Don't I?"

"No," he whispered triumphantly. "There are new things inside me."

He groaned again. Ella noticed now that Ingrid's hand was under the blanket, and she realized what it was she was doing to him.

She ought to have left. Everyone present, including herself, knew that it was the only sensible thing to do. Her feet wanted to leave; the door was waiting to be slammed. She didn't leave.

She stood in the dark room to watch the strange scene that her presence didn't seem to alter.

"Oh, you have new things inside you, do you?" Ingrid said, half teasingly and half sadly. "So you don't need Ingrid anymore?"

"No," Winter gasped. "I don't. Don't come here anymore."

"That's what he says now," Ingrid said to Ella. "Now that poor Ingrid has done her job."

"Naturally it was necessary to conclude what you started, without my permission and in the middle of my nap, but don't provide this service for me again, Ingrid."

Katz pulled her hand out from under the covers and wiped it with utmost calm on a tissue.

"If you can get the job done without me then naturally I'll leave you in peace. I apologize. I simply thought…"

"Thank you and goodbye," Winter said.

Ingrid nodded. "I do have a life of my own, after all, a family, children—and I'm a rather good mother. I try to live that life as much as I can. Except when I'm sometimes pulled into The Game, as I was the other day by our baby writer. And I worry about you sometimes. You know, I've been having bad dreams about you. We haven't seen each other in ages, you and I, and when you called, I started to think…"

"There's no need to worry about me," Winter said gently. "Go back to your family and your library. But first give me a few tissues."

Ingrid looked at Ella thoughtfully. Suspiciously, in fact. "But Martti, does this girl really like you?"

"You would have to ask her that," Winter said wearily. "But please don't."

Ingrid Katz walked twice around the bed and stopped at the foot, her hands on her hips. "Well, Martti, I'll leave you in peace. But you must promise that you'll be all right. And that if you're not all right, you'll let me know immediately. I don't need you, but I do need to know at all times that things are all right with you.

"Well, goodbye then," Ingrid said to Ella with everyday good cheer, as if she'd been there watering the flowers.

Then she calmly left, with a smile on her face.

Ella was left alone with Winter.

He was still lying motionless on the bed. The conversation he and Ingrid had just had seemed inauthentic to Ella, made of paper. As if she'd walked into the middle of a play. Maybe that's what happened when people became writers and knew each other so well that there was no need to speak anymore. Authentic communication was quickly replaced by written drama.

Ella adjusted the blinds to let more light into the room. She would have opened the window as well but she couldn't make the latch work.

There was a black and white photo on the wall of Martti Winter and Ingrid Katz at about ten years old. They were holding hands. In the background was Laura White's house and the swing in her garden. White herself sat on the swing holding a pen and a notepad.

Ella paced back and forth around the bed and looked at Winter from different angles, trying to teach her eyes to see his essence in new ways.

While she did this, she came up with the beginnings of a theory of the varying sources of human attractiveness. Attractive people come in two forms. Some people are attractive like beautiful objects that awaken aesthetic pleasure—they make you want to own them, and to be seen in their company. People like Martti Winter, on the other hand, are attractive like museums, or palaces, or other architectural structures that a person seems to return to again and again to walk around and enjoy the atmosphere.

"So you came today, after all," Winter said, turning his large head on the pillow to look at her.

"I should pour that glass of water over you," Ella said.

She tried to make her voice cold, but the words rang like a gust of July wind. She sighed and stretched her hand out into the darkness. She wanted to touch his face and turn it towards the light, wanted to see the eyes that looked out from the Martti Winter jacket flaps. But he took hold of her wrist, held it for a moment, and shook his head.

"You should go now. Come back tonight after ten."

Ella nodded and left.

That evening they played a round of The Game that brought the history of the Society into a whole new light, or rather threw it into an even deeper shadow, Ella thought later, sitting at her desk in a state of intellectual vertigo and aftershock.

Ella rang the doorbell. Martti Winter opened the door. He was wearing nothing but a wristwatch. The watch looked expensive and stylish. Ella guessed that it cost about as much as a mid-sized car.

She seemed to have lost her words somewhere.

Winter glanced at his watch, which Ella also tried to concentrate on. He said it was a couple of minutes past ten, and then he challenged her.

Ella nodded and glanced nervously at the dogs, who were staring at them from every direction. Winter's nakedness seemed to make them nervous, too. There were more dogs than there had been before. Ella and Winter went inside and the pack of dogs stayed safely outside. Ella breathed easier.

Her discomfort returned, however, as Martti Winter went up the stairs. His flesh filled her whole field of vision. She followed him, her gaze fixed on his heels like a vice. They went into the blue room and sat in their usual places. "*Ecce homo*," Winter said, and spread his arms.

Ella obeyed and looked at him, although she would have liked to look away. There was too much light in the room. He'd brought in too many lamps. There was something pornographic in the situation. She felt like crying. Winter picked up a handkerchief from the table and surprised her by tying it over his own eyes.

"I'm going to teach you a new manoeuvre. It's called the mirror. It's different from the other moves because the blindfold is tied on the challenger instead of the spiller."

"Why?" Ella asked, her voice squeezed into a tight bunch.

A grim smile oozed over Winter's face.

"That will become clear to you as we play. I'm going to make you my mirror. I apologize in advance for this, but…"

"The Game is The Game," she said.

He nodded. He was frightened now, too.

"I want you," he said, "to look at me as if you were my mirror, and convert my image into words and spill out everything that you think when you look at me."

28

Ella Milana Spills

E LLA SITS before his great nakedness, small and terrified.
Martti Winter says, "If you have some yellow, now would
be a good time to use it. If you don't have any of your own, I
have a bottle in the downstairs medicine cabinet. It clears the
mirror very effectively. There's a mini-fridge under the table.
You'll find some soft drinks there."

Ella's gaze wanders over his flesh. She doesn't feel well. She
opens the little blue refrigerator, takes out a bottle of Jaffa, finds
three crystals of yellow in her bag, and drops them into the
bottle. Then she drinks half of it.

"Spill," Winter whispers. "Be my mirror. Service your fellow
author, as the rules of The Game demand."

"I see a naked man," Ella begins, then clears her throat.

She concentrates. She closes everything out of her mind but
the rules of The Game. Nothing else matters but honouring
the rules of The Game. She has to build a precise picture of his
nakedness in her mind and clothe it entirely in words, without
concealing a single thought.

She relaxes as the sodium pentothal starts to take effect.
Words form in her mouth, syllables line up on her tongue like
the carriages of a mountain railway. She drinks the rest of the
soda and notices that she's already begun to speak.

"You're big. So big. It's bewildering how much skin you have, like the frame tent I slept in as a child with my parents, and yet you manage to fill it completely. Your flesh shakes like jelly when you breathe. Looking at you makes me think of a large, soft creature that's been brought onto land from the depths of the ocean. You're not meant for humans to see. You have

less body hair than I expected. I thought you would be covered in hair, but my goodness, you're as smooth as a child. I wonder if you shave your chest hair... but why in the world would you do that? You don't seem to care what you look like. The skin on you is like a baby's skin, pudgy, brimming over like a baby's skin does, and I wonder if you're even aware that you have a streak of chocolate under your double chin—there's no telling how long it's been there.

Your breasts are larger than mine, but you have nipples like a little boy; it's hard to even find them. There's something touching about that.

Your head is like a large boulder, heavy and lumpy, and you have a face like a gingerbread man. You have lovely hair, just like in your old photos— you probably take good care of it. But on such a fat head, there's something grotesque about it. Like your hair and your fat don't match.

Your nose is boyish, in a good way. A little turned up, small and delicate.

You have a certain sensitivity to your mouth, but mixed with weakness and decadence. When I look at your mouth for any length of time, it makes me want to hit you, hard, make you bleed.

Your mouth is like a greedy child's, like that of a child who's been spoiled with chocolate and ice cream, a child everyone secretly hates, even his mother. The worst part is that in those old photos your mouth is beautiful and sensitive, but now, with so much fat on your face, your original features have sunk into the fat and almost disappeared.

But at the same time, there's something about your delicate, degenerate mouth that's exciting. Do you remember how I blushed when we were drinking coffee? I was remembering a dream I'd had about you, or about your mouth, actually. God, what a dream!

I was at a party, lying naked on the buffet table among the cakes and pastries and goose liver, and you came up and started tasting me all over with your mouth, and then I think you took a bite out of me.

Ella continues looking and talking.

She goes over his arms and legs, gives a precise description of his ears and the small details of his skin, notices a pale scar on his leg, occasionally returns to fatty forms whose shapeless excess is simultaneously troubling and fascinating. Somewhere deep inside she realizes that her words are cruel, but her surrender to the yellow and the rules of The Game has done its work.

Martti Winter sits the whole time in his chair motionless, listening.

But the outlines get mixed up with the other outlines. You only get glimpses of your flesh; it's changing all the time as the point of view changes. Right now you've got the part turned towards me that's like a big tent full of bucketfuls of fat. But your entirety is spread out broader on the axis of time. Chronologically you're forty-three years old, and if I knew how to shift a little, if I stepped just a hair to the side of this present observation point, I could see you as a beautiful man, the same man who looks out at me from the jackets on your novels and the old pictures in the photo album.

A solid, muscular chest, a hard stomach, all that is just as much a part of you as the part of you in these few years where I've ended up, looking at you from this chronological angle.

As she spills, Ella gets up from her chair and comes over to Winter. Doing something can be spilling, too, she thinks hazily. She puts her hand on his chest, leans over, and kisses him.

He seems to answer her kiss from very far away.

Then Ella asks whether he's satisfied with her answer. He nods, brushes her cheek and asks her to present her question.

She backs up, her legs rubbery from the yellow.

She stumbles and falls towards Martti Winter. Her hands sink into the folds of his stomach up to the wrists. She's horrified, tries to get back on her feet, loses her balance again and falls face-first into his arms.

"Oops," she mumbles. "I don't seem to be all that graceful today."

A moment later, back in her own chair, having collected herself, Ella asks, "Do we have to play The Game to the end today? The yellow makes me tired. Maybe I could ask my question the next time."

"No," Winter says. He takes off the blindfold and looks at her. "If we don't play both turns today, as the rules require, we won't be members of the Society anymore."

To Ella's relief, he goes to get dressed. She's beginning to get used to his beanbag-chair shape, but she likes him better with his clothes on.

He comes back in gold slippers and black socks. The straight legs of his trousers fall over them. Ella remembers him talking earlier about his tailor. Under his luxurious smoking jacket she can see a white collar and an expensive silk tie.

"So," he says. "Make me spill. Shall I wear the blindfold again, or would you like to try 'the mirror'?"

Ella shakes her head and starts to tie the blindfold over his eyes. "I just want to ask you about one small thing so we can go to sleep. That's my right, isn't it? I have to make sure that you spill the entire truth, but the question can be easy and simple, can't it?"

Winter concedes that she is correct.

Ella continues.

"You actually answered this same question a year ago in a magazine interview. So, Mr Winter—where do you get the ideas for your books?"

Ella smiles.

She assumes he will be amused by the carefree superficiality of her question.

Wrapped in his blindfold, Winter turns pale.

29

Martti Winter Spills

"I GET THE IDEAS for my books when I ponder life and listen to Mozart."

It's a pretty little answer, simple, and pure rubbish, but those are the kinds of answers the women's magazines like to hear. As a professional gesture, Winter elaborates. He describes how the themes of classical music trigger a process in his mind that crystallizes literary, universal themes into thoughts, which in turn generate reflective stories. He doesn't fail to add piquant little details, of course, because details are extremely important, in stories and in lies—he says that he tried Bach once, but it sent him into meditations on theology, and he started musing on the state of his soul instead of writing.

Ella Milana doesn't believe him. The silence stretches out, agonizing at first, then terrifying. Martti Winter senses a change in mood. Ella is no longer in a hurry to get home.

Winter starts to sweat.

Ella finally says something.

"I'm sorry, what?" Winter asks.

"Rule number twenty-one," Ella repeats. She's standing right next to him now; he can feel her breath on his cheek and it causes him to shudder. She's no slouch, he thinks fondly, and prepares himself for pain.

"I'm going to start with your cheek," Ella whispers, "where I can get a good grip."

No secrets between players. That's the motto Winter used to recite when The Game was new, back when it used to unite them, and hadn't yet made them dread each other.

When Ella Milana has applied Rule 21 to Winter five times and got rubbish in response four times, Winter decides to end the farce he's begun.

He asks for a glass of soda and adds, "Be so kind as to pour a good dose of yellow in." His speech is indistinct because his lip and cheek are swollen.

Words start to fly out of Winter's mouth into Ella's listening ears.

No secrets between players. He's experiencing the joy of truly spilling. His words are like birds, or perhaps like bees on a hot summer day. He smiles as he talks himself into deeper memories, memories he thought he'd lost. With the blindfold over his eyes, past events start to flash in images around him. It's like he's leaning back against the axis of time she was talking about, bumping his head against the moment when an eleven-year-old Martti Winter read the last words of his piece, titled "My Mother", out loud.

> *And when my mother tucks me in at night and strokes my head, I remember that one day she's going to die and be buried in Rabbit Back cemetery, and I'll have to give her to the worms.*

The other six Society members clap.

Elias Kangasniemi shakes a fist at him and laughs, "Damn it, Martti, you're going to drive me to hang myself with those stories of yours!"

The others laugh to break the horror. Elias's father did hang himself when Elias was four, and he constantly cultivates a kind of gallows humour, although the rest of them aren't allowed so much as to mention a rope. Elias wipes his nose and looks out the window.

They're sitting in a spacious bay window-seat in the reading room at the south end of the house. The room is painted white. They're bathed in flooding, gushing, almost overwhelming brightness because they're surrounded by windows on all sides, even the ceiling. Behind them glows the summer of 1972. The skylight delineates the sky in a blue circle with birds darting through it. The other windows look out on the garden.

Her garden is a stormy sea of colour. Ingrid wrote that last week in a poem that Laura praised strongly. She said Ingrid had "learned the basics of metaphor beautifully". Martti thinks now that if the garden is a sea of colour, then perhaps the house is a ship where he and the other children are sailing under the leadership of their captain, towards some distant destination.

Through the window glass Martti can see the insects sway in the garden's eddies of hot air, their wings scorched, slightly mad. Laura White's house is cooler. The authoress pours raspberry juice into glasses and drops in some ice. A fan turns on the ceiling. Toivo told him that the fan is a propeller from a Russian airplane that was shot down and given to Ms White by some soldier.

Laura White nods at Martti's story. She's sitting in a wicker chair with one leg thrown over the other, dressed in white, and drops of sweat are running down her neck. She sips her coffee, places the cup in its saucer, rocks her head back and forth and says to Martti, "Your descriptions have improved tremendously. You've observed your mother very commendably. I especially like the way you described your own feelings, although there may have been a few redundant adjectives. Helinä, you can read yours next."

Martti doesn't listen to Helinä's story. He wants to savour the praise he's received.

But where could Ingrid have got to? She hasn't come yet. He's not angry at her anymore, although his arm hurts and he's sure he'll have a bruise.

He regrets now that he went and left her at the rat's grave. Now they'll have another several days of being angry with each other. It's stupid, since they both know that in the end they'll make it up again.

She was sick, too. In the morning Martti had felt her forehead. It was hot, and she was pale and sweaty. He told her to go home because she was coming down with something, but she wouldn't do what he said, wouldn't admit being sick at all. Five years ago, Ingrid's mother got sick, and died two weeks later.

Martti whispers in Laura White's ear that he has to go to the toilet. Helinä is still reading as he tiptoes out of the reading room and closes the glass door carefully behind him. He has to pass through several dark rooms. It feels tiresome because it's so easy to get lost in Laura's house.

Someone walking ahead of him opens a door and goes into one of the rooms they're not allowed in.

They were not specifically forbidden from walking around the house. In some houses you might be allowed to run around, but in Laura White's dark house one walked sedately, and behaved in a civilized manner.

After Martti met Laura White for the first time, he asked his mother to teach him good manners. "Ms White is a fine lady and if I'm going to start visiting her house every week I want to know how to behave, so I don't screw up."

His mother bought him *The Golden Book of Etiquette*. Laura White had the same book herself. Sometimes, when the children were at her house writing, she would sit nearby and study *The Golden Book of Etiquette*. Martti thought she must be an expert on etiquette. Sometimes she read other kinds of non-fiction, the kind that describe how the human brain works.

Humans are very complex and difficult-to-understand creatures, Laura once said. *The job of writers like us is to study a person until we learn to understand him and understand his life. We simply have to remember to maintain enough distance when we do it; otherwise we won't see him very clearly.*

Martti can see the person walking ahead of him clearly now. It's a girl, tall and thin, wearing a pretty red dress she got as a birthday present, and dirtied when she was playing this morning.

Oh Ingrid…

Martti runs after her, but stays out of sight. He wants to see what she's up to.

Ingrid is walking uncertainly. She staggers. Her thin legs peep out from under the hem of her dress. Martti thinks that her fever must have risen. Soon she'll probably faint and crack her head open.

But Ingrid doesn't faint. She just wanders, returns to a room she was just in, turns around, changes direction and runs back so that Martti has to dash behind a bent-legged sofa to hide.

Then she disappears without a trace.

Martti goes into the room after her, but the room is empty. He runs into the next room, and the next, and the next.

He's already on his way back to the reading room when a door on his right bursts open and Ingrid comes rushing out. Her hair is tousled and sweat is running down her pale face. In the dim light of the hallway he can see that her red dress is wet through with sweat. It drips on the floor.

She's holding something tight against her chest.

Martti calls to her. Something wriggles in his stomach. She stumbles in the other direction—first into the hallway, then into the foyer and out of the house, with Martti right behind her.

He bolts out of the dark house into the brightness of the veranda, and as he stops to regain his vision Ingrid runs down the road that leads across Hare Glen. She falls, scrambles onto her feet again, and continues her unsteady escape.

The sound of birds and insects surrounds Martti as he stands in front of Laura White's house wondering what to do. Shadows slip through the brightness of the garden; the weather is changing. Clouds are piling up in dark heaps that meld at the edges to form a stormy alliance.

Ingrid just stole something from Ms White's house—he saw it with his own eyes.

Of all the people in the world, his Ingrid has gone and stolen something from Laura White.

Laura White is particularly strict about her books. They're allowed to read her books, but they have to ask permission first, and under no circumstances can they take the books home with them.

She has books in her collection that are so rare that no one else anywhere has them, not even the largest libraries in America. Once she got so excited talking about her books and talked so quickly that none of the children could understand her. It frightened them to see an adult dash about and babble like that.

It's a play that Aleksis Kivi apparently wrote in 1873, if not earlier, and I found it on a shelf where I used to keep a catechism. The process is very exciting, although I don't really know what causes it.

She eventually got a severe headache and withdrew upstairs to rest.

When Ingrid wanted to borrow one of her books that wasn't even in the Rabbit Back library, Laura said no. The reasons she gave for this were left to occupy their minds for a long time. They were almost certain she wasn't joking.

I'm sorry, Ingrid dear, but it's an unconditional rule of mine. Books attract bacteria when you handle them. Every book has its own quite unique strain of bacteria, which changes slightly whenever a new person reads it. I'm sure you understand.

She looked at her hands and grew more serious.

I'm sure you all know the sign in the library encouraging you to inform the librarian if there are any infectious diseases at home. They understand what bacteria can do to a book. Books owned by different people should under no circumstances be kept on the same shelf, otherwise entire bacteria strains could be mixed. And books can't stand up to just anything.

Libraries are rather dangerous places, by the way, although they do serve a noble purpose. Always wash your hands when you read a library book, and keep library books separate from your own books.

The bacteria question has troubled them for a long time. They want to ask her if she's serious, but they're afraid to. Once when they asked her about her childhood, she answered a few questions gladly, then suddenly raised her hands to her temples and slumped half-unconscious onto the sofa.

Oh, children, she whispered, covered in a cold sweat, *my head is splitting. You'll have to be quite silent for a little while. But don't leave. Come closer. Take hold of my hand. I'm sure this will pass in a moment. Martti, my love, can you put your cool hand on my forehead? It helps. Don't be afraid. I'm in a little pain right now, but everything will be all right again soon.*

They've witnessed these attacks of hers four or five times. They've never spoken about them, not even among themselves.

There's a bicycle leaning against a tree. It's Toivo's bike, the kind with a long seat. Martti gets on the bike and follows Ingrid down the road, which meanders across Hare Glen like a gravel snake. Ingrid isn't at home or in her father's workshop.

Martti rides to the shore and pushes his way through the thick willows to their secret fishing spot. He can see their footprints in the sand, their shared fishing rod leaning against a birch tree. On the bark of the tree are initials, inside a heart. Martti carved his own into the tree and then Ingrid added hers, and the heart.

This is where Martti touched her bare breast after she had read an adult book called *Lady Chatterley's Lover* and wanted to write something like it. *I have to know what it feels like, otherwise I won't be able to write about it,* she said—it was five days ago now. She took off her shirt right in front of him, the midday sun casting steep shadows on her skin.

Ingrid's breast was small and the skin felt like warm rubber as he first prodded it and then squeezed it warily.

She's not here now.

Martti climbs up the hill to the water tower, too—Ingrid's magic place. The hill is a grass-covered cone with a fenced, level place on top. On the platform is a booth with a steel door that's always locked.

Ingrid likes to make up crazy stories about the booth: inside are trolls in chains, mad witches, ghosts and demons, imprisoned children, Russian prisoners of war. They come here to eat lunch when the weather is fine, share some liquorice from the kiosk on the shore. In windy weather they come up to the platform to send model planes flying in every direction.

They also tried kissing here last winter when they were supposed to write something about love for Laura White. After the kiss, Martti pressed his lips against the iron railing, and bled profusely when he tore them away again.

He doesn't see her here now.

He finally finds her in the east playground. A drizzle of rain is falling. Ingrid is sitting on a swing, half turned away from him, thrashing her legs. As Martti comes down the grassy hillside he sees what she's stolen from the house.

She's looking through a book and another one is lying on the grass, a cloth-covered notebook, the kind Laura White has given to all of them, telling them to take better care of them than they would their own soul. Martti has one, too, in a blue cover with gold letters that say: RABBIT BACK LITERATURE SOCIETY.

One of the notebooks was more green than blue. That one was for the proud, quiet boy, the best one, the one who died last winter, whom they decided never to talk about again.

All nine of them were at the secret meeting: Martti, Ingrid, Silja, Helinä, Oona, Elias, Toivo, Anna-Maija and Aura.

Laura White said that writers shouldn't talk to outsiders about their own affairs except through their writing. She didn't even tell the parents of the living members of the Society about the boy's death. The children knew that when people don't talk about something, it gradually ceases to be true. Within a few months they had succeeded in wiping the boy almost out of existence. It had been easy, because none of them knew how he died. They didn't want to know.

The dead boy's notebook was on the grass at Ingrid's feet. Martti didn't understand how she'd got it.

The dead boy had made notes in his book all the time and wouldn't show it to anyone except Laura White. He must have collected at least a thousand ideas for books in it, a thousand wonderful ideas. Every one of them would have given anything for just one glimpse into that green notebook.

Elias had once tried to take it by force. The boy flew into a terrible fit of rage and Elias was so afraid that he peed his pants.

Did you see his eyes when I tried to take his notebook away from him? I'm sure he would have killed me if I hadn't given up.

Suddenly Martti understands that his duty is to protect the Society. Ingrid is delirious with fever, and angry—she might do anything at all. Martti imagines the parents breaking into Laura White's house just as one of them is reading a story and tearing their children away.

Our child will not remain in a club where children are suddenly dying without warning. There are other hobbies besides writing. We'll buy a violin or an accordion and pay for some music lessons!

He raises his arm and is about to shout to Ingrid, then he slips, falls with a thud onto his back, and slides into a patch of thistles. The sky rushes open and rain starts to drum against the ground. As Martti struggles back to his feet he sees the red dress with the books running far off down the tree-lined road that leads to the library.

When Ingrid comes out of the library, Martti is hiding behind a tree. He watches as she stands in front of the building, damp and shivering.

Martti remembers what Laura White said about the library: *The building is quite pretty, almost worthy of all the books inside it.*

The authoress's words also reached the ears of Tuomo Lindgren, the owner of the stone works. A couple of nights earlier, Martti had gone to the kiosk to buy his mother some cigarettes. Lindgren was there, bragging drunkenly to his friends that he would "knock Ms White's socks off, make her eyes bulge right out of her head".

Hell, I've got my own stone works, after all. I've got the cash to do whatever I want, and I'm the kind of guy who, if I think something up, even God isn't going to stop me! I never read a book in my life, and I never plan to, but hey, if Miss Fancypants Author wants something to look at, I'm the man to do it, and you can bet it'll get done. Do you know how much it costs to ship those damn marble blocks all the way from Italy? Do you? I do, because I just went to the bank to pay a pretty big bill for marble, and it didn't even phase me. Ha!

Ingrid is standing in front of the building and her hands are empty.

She's left Laura White's books in the library.

Martti runs to her, his shoes splashing in the rain. Her shoulders burn under his fingers. "Ingrid! Ingrid! The books! The notebook! Why did you do it?"

Ingrid's eyes glisten strangely. She sighs, goes limp and slumps to her knees.

"I guess I don't feel very well," she mumbles. "But I'm not sick. I just need to rest for a while."

Martti leaves her and runs into the library.

He can see a book cart near the check-out desk. When he squints he can just make out the green-covered notebook among the others. It's the most important one. He has to act fast.

He glances behind him and sees that Ingrid is no longer on her knees—she's lying prone on the ground, her face in a puddle.

It's impossible to run in two directions at the same time. He knows that. But grabbing the book will only take a couple of seconds—he can do it and still help Ingrid up before she drowns.

He dashes towards the cart, then stops like he's hit a wall.

A long, grey face adorned with thick glasses appears in front of him.

Birgit Ström, the old librarian, is a friendly person, and she of all people knows to hold the young members of the Rabbit Back Literature Society in high esteem. On the other hand, she is merciless to anyone she sees as a threat to the welfare of the books.

Martti remembers a story he heard in town: The mayor himself once tried to walk into the library with an Eskimo pie in his hand. Birgit Ström craned forward from behind her desk, grabbed the ice cream, dropped it into the wastebin and welcomed the mayor to her "house of civilizing literature".

"I see our budding author is quite wet," Birgit Ström says, reaching her long arm out in front of him as if she were about to give him a hug. "Perhaps the bard should take a look at himself. Look how he's dripping on the floor! Drip, drip, drip. As we all know, books definitely do not like water. Perhaps our young writer should come back when he's a bit drier. Someone has already run through here all wet and left puddles on the floor. What a shame."

Martti stares at the librarian's breasts, which hang down like long beanbags. He spins around and runs out to help the sputtering Ingrid out of the puddle. Then he takes her home.

Martti searches the library for the notebook for four days. He goes through the stacks systematically, one book at a time. Sometimes he has to start over when he realizes he hasn't been thorough enough. Hopelessness and exhaustion creep up on him and he even considers asking the librarian for assistance.

But he rejects the idea, because if he did, the entire future of the Society might be in danger.

He spends all day Thursday and Friday searching, going home only to eat. Birgit Ström observes him and assumes he's performing some task given to him by Laura White, since he doesn't say anything.

Then the weekend comes and the library is closed. He returns on Monday and Tuesday, and late on Tuesday afternoon, when he's up to the letter J, he sees the notebook, with RABBIT BACK LITERATURE SOCIETY printed on its spine, peeking out from between two thick books. Martti can barely repress a squeal.

He checks to make sure Birgit Ström isn't in visual range and pulls the notebook off the shelf. Its cover is stuck to the book next to it. When he peels the books apart it makes a nasty sound and some of the green fabric from the notebook's cover remains stuck to its neighbour.

He looks to right and left, and up to the higher levels as well, where a golden light makes the dust motes dance, then stuffs the notebook under his shirt and walks out of the library.

The memory breaks off at this point. The boy with the book stops, leans forward on the axis of time, grows three decades older, and is sitting in a blue room wearing a blindfold.

Martti Winter finishes speaking. He lets the moment rest. There are no more words. "May I have some more soda?" he asks from within the darkness, which he has come to strangely enjoy. "And put a crystal of yellow in it."

A bottle materializes in his hand and he drinks from it.

"What happened then?" the girl's voice says.

"I didn't open the notebook," Winter hears himself say. "I didn't dare. I knew that if it was going to be opened, the whole Society ought to do it together. The book should either never be opened, or we should open it together and destroy it. That's what I thought. I went

to tell Toivo and Elias that we needed to have a meeting. I sent Toivo to tell Oona, Helinä and Silja. Elias told Aura and Anna-Maija. I told everyone that they shouldn't disturb Ingrid because she was home with a fever.

We met on top of the hill where the water tower is. It was getting dark, and the members had to make up all kinds of excuses for being out so late.

The sun was setting and the light shone only on our hilltop. All the rest of Rabbit Back was already covered in darkness. I told the others that I had the dead boy's notebook, but I didn't tell them where I'd got it. They didn't need to know that Ingrid had stolen something from Laura White's house.

They were all amazed, excited and afraid. I'm sure I was more afraid than they were, although I acted like a cool-headed leader. I insisted that not a word should be breathed about the notebook or our secret meeting to anyone who wasn't there. Not to Laura White, not to our parents, not to Ingrid. I'd brought Ingrid a big box of liquorice as a sort of secret recompense for what I was planning to do.

Ingrid said later that the last thing she remembered about that day was our argument at the dead rat's grave, and I saw no reason to tell her what went on while she was in her fever.

I made my comrades swear. Everyone spit on the same spot on the ground. Then we mixed the spit together and each one put their finger in it and put some of the common spit in their mouths. It sounds stupid and revolting now, but we all took the ritual very seriously. Even Elias didn't joke about it.

I said that I thought the notebook should be destroyed to protect the Society and that there would be no discussion about it, but that we ought to discuss whether we should read it before we destroyed it.

We knew that the most gifted writer in the Society had diligently filled up his notebook. We knew the kinds of stories he had read to us. He wasn't any older than us, but his stories were so great that all we understood about them was that they were extremely good and very deep. When we listened to him read them, we were all overcome with sacred reverence, even though we hated the boy himself.

We all understood that the notebook contained ideas for at least a thousand books.

I asked who wanted to read it, but no one dared to look at me.

Then I asked who wanted to go home and forget the whole thing, and no one said anything.

I got an idea and I said, Fine, this is what we'll do. Does anybody have a watch? Someone did. Good. I told them I would leave the notebook here on the hilltop overnight and go home. Each one of us would have an hour to come and read the dead boy's notebook, or not to come if they didn't want to. I would come last, at sunrise, and destroy the notebook. I could burn it in the sauna oven at home, since my mother would be heating it up the next day.

And that's what we did. The notebook was left on the top of the hill.

When day was breaking, I woke up on Church Hill, where I had been sleeping in some bushes, and went to get the notebook from the water tower, as we had agreed.

So I didn't know for sure whether the others had read the notebook or not, and we agreed that it was something we could never ask about in The Game. But I could see in their eyes later that they had read it, every one of them. I don't remember anything else about the book itself, but I do remember that it had amazing things in it, things that I couldn't even really understand at the time.

And every night, to this day, I still dream about that notebook. I tried for a long time to forget about it. I regretted reading it. In the end I did succeed in forgetting its contents. I don't remember what was in it, at least not when I'm awake, although I've tried a few times. But every night I dream that I'm reading the notebook that the dead genius wrote, the book Ingrid stole, that I and the others read by the water tower that night. And every time I dream about it, I wake up with at least one or two ideas.

All of my ideas come from that notebook. A couple of times I've thought an idea was my own, and tried to start writing about it, but then Silja Saaristo would manage to publish a novel about it first, and then Elias would write something about it, and I'd know I'd been mistaken. I don't have any ideas of my own. Maybe none of us do. All we have are the thousand ideas that we stole from the dead boy.

And that's where I get the ideas for my books.

30

THE GAME ENDED when Martti Winter, the great author, fell asleep in his chair, knocked out by the yellow.

Ella put her feet up on her chair, wrapped her arms around her legs, thought for a moment, and said, "I accept your answer."

They sat in the blueness for five minutes, silent and unmoving. Then the great author shifted in his seat, smacked his lips, and woke up enough to sigh, "And to top it off, I couldn't destroy the notebook. I wrapped it in oilcloth and buried it in the garden. Which may explain why it's come here."

Ella stiffened. "Why what's come here?"

Winter had fallen asleep again.

Ella gathered up four blankets from the neighbouring rooms and covered him with them. She was about to leave when he reached his empty hand towards her, as if it held something fragile and valuable, and whispered, "His name is on the first page. Look. Such lovely, neat handwriting. 'Oskar', it says. 'Oskar Södergran'."

Ella went downstairs into the piano room. She opened the terrace door and was about to step outside. She heard the barks and growls of the pack of dogs on the other side of the wall and decided to stay inside.

She shut the door and pressed her face against the window. Not a single light was burning in the garden.

She wondered if there was anyone in Rabbit Back who could install garden lights at this hour of night. *Sorry, I know it's late, but we need light immediately in Martti Winter's garden, where the statues dance their frozen dances and the trees spread their branches like squids in some historical nightmare—can you come right away?*

While she was wading through the snow in the garden she had been overcome by the feeling that a malevolent creature was lurking nearby.

And somewhere in the garden was the notebook of Oskar Södergran, who died when he was still a boy.

Ella felt herself growing angry at the turn things were taking. Secret members, stolen notebooks, pilfered writing ideas—it was all so ridiculous!

She touched her nose to the window glass, focused on her own reflection, and thought that if she kept this up her research was bound to uncover Laura White's body and a mass grave filled with other bodies and a bomb left over from the war and several buried treasures and a selection of secret tunnels that led to amazing, unknown places.

She tugged the curtains over the window and began looking through the antique bookcase which held all of Martti Winter's works behind a pair of glass doors. There were twenty-four of them. She opened the doors, took out *Mr Butterfly*, and looked at the photo on the jacket flap for a long time.

After a moment's search she found a pen, wrote something in the book, and left the book and the pen on the piano.

When she walked out the front door, the dogs went quiet.

There were dogs everywhere—they had even surrounded the Triumph. Most of them were at the side of the house, right near the wall. They looked like they were keeping an eye on all the doors and windows. They watched her pass with black eyes, ears stiff.

Ella knew one of the dogs. He was her neighbour's old beagle, recognizable from the star-shaped spot on his side. She had often given him a pat.

"Tiplu," she said, "your mama's going to be very worried about you."

The beagle turned his head away.

The other dogs pricked up their ears, alert. A large German Shepherd under a garden light got to its feet and took a couple of steps towards her.

Ella felt not just cross now, but also stupid. That would really complete her evening, to feed herself to a pack of dogs!

She opened the door of her dead father's Triumph, got in the car, and closed the door behind her. The window was nearly frozen over, but she could stop and clean it once she'd got away from Winter's occupying canine army.

Ella Milana had always thought of Martti Winter as a genius.

Now it seemed the ideas in his novels had been stolen from the notebook of a child prodigy. The same shadow had been cast over the work of the other writers in the Society. Even Ingrid Katz might have read the dead boy's notebook before her comrades got to it.

"Shit. It's all shit," she said several times, as Ingrid had taught her the night of Laura White's disappearance.

Ella sat at her desk and thought about what she'd learned and about what would happen when she published the results of her research. She drew a chart on a piece of paper. She had to organize her thoughts.

The revelation was sure to cause a scandal. As Ella understood it, however, it wouldn't diminish the value of the works themselves—they were what they were, whether they were created by the person mentioned on the cover or by somebody else. But it would send a shockwave through the history of literature.

Ella wrote: REVISION OF LITERARY HISTORY. WORKS RETAIN THEIR VALUE. SCANDAL! INCREASED SALES?

The rules of The Game stated: *Secrets revealed during The Game are confidential. They can be used as the raw material for literature, but they cannot be published in any other form or be made known to anyone outside the Society. Any member who knowingly breaches this confidentiality will be punished by permanent expulsion from the Society.*

Ella would have to betray Winter, and the whole Rabbit Back Literature Society, which now included herself. In fact she would throw the writers of the Society into such darkness that they would never get back into the light. The idea theft would inevitably destroy their credibility. The media would rip them to shreds.

With stiff fingers she scratched onto the paper: ME: NO LONGER A PLAYER—INFORMATION SUPPLY CUT OFF! NO SHARE IN WHITE'S INHERITANCE. RELATIONS WITH WRITERS BROKEN. SOCIETY DESTROYED. TRAITOR.

Then something disturbing started to creep in at the edges of Ella's consciousness. She tried to chase the thought away before it became too clear, but her hand started to move across the paper of its own accord, and the following appeared:

HOW DID OSKAR SÖDERGRAN DIE?

Ella blinked. What if someone in the Society was responsible for Oskar Södergran's death?

She clenched her cold fingers and wondered just how much the other children of the Society had hated and envied Oskar Södergran. Enough to steal his ideas, at any rate, and use them to build their own careers, that was clear. But enough to cause his death? Competition strong enough to drive someone to murder?

Ella felt a tingling in her gut.

For her own peace of mind she had to assume that the members of the Society were innocent of the boy's death—at least until she was forced to conclude otherwise.

She looked at what she'd written. It brought tears to her eyes.

What joy is there in research, anyway? someone had once asked in one of her methodology courses. The teaching assistant's answer had made an impression on Ella at the time: *Research brings order to the world. It makes things clearer, helps us to understand things. Could there be any more joy than that? Did you ever put together puzzles as a child? The universe is a puzzle with billions of pieces. Putting it together is society's highest shared responsibility, our right and our joy—and not only that, it is what separates us from the whole rest of creation, with a few possible exceptions.*

Ella buried her face in her hands and let out an exasperated sigh.

In her dream, Ella Milana was climbing the water tower hill.

The cement steps were steep and narrow, so she was going carefully. To fall would be fatal. She wondered whether she would get there in time, whether the green notebook would already be buried in Martti Winter's garden. She had to get there to make notes for her research. She needed to write down everything she could, because anything that wasn't written down would be lost forever.

A red streak on the horizon foretold the approach of sunrise, but Rabbit Back was still in shadow, the people asleep.

She heard a creak and turned around. The steel door of the cement booth was ajar.

She peeked inside. There was a little table in the room. Around it were ten small chairs of different shapes and sizes, truly bizarre little chairs, and Ella couldn't fit into any of them.

There was a book on the table. It wasn't the green notebook, it was a printed novel. The cover said THE RETURN OF EMPEROR RAT, BY LAURA WHITE. UNFINISHED, UNPROOFED COPY.

Ella reached for the book, then jumped when someone behind her said:

It's coming, and she's leaving.

In the corner was a hat rack. On top of it sat a green parrot, eyeing her. Ella started to say something to it, but then there was a loud noise outside.

When she looked out the door, she saw Laura White's body loping down the hillside like a skittish white rabbit.

It's coming, the parrot said.

What is? Ella asked. *What's coming?*

Emperor Rat. It's coming, and she's leaving.

Two days after The Game, Professor Korpimäki called Ella Milana and asked how her information gathering was coming along.

"Very well," Ella exclaimed in a voice oozing with enthusiasm. "Rolling along like a freight train. In fact, I was just on my way to the post office to send you something."

When the call ended, she finished the television show she'd been watching, then went upstairs to her room, dutifully wrote out some descriptions of Laura White and the activities of the Society, and sent them to her professor.

She didn't include the information she'd collected playing The Game. The crumbs she'd gathered chatting with Winter would be enough to thrill him.

Ella had another dream:

She was lying naked in her bed and hundreds of literature professors were standing around her room, Professor Korpimäki among them. He leaned over her, plucked absent-mindedly at her pubic hair, and whispered, *We're very worried. You understand, don't you? We have to have that notebook.*

I understand, Ella said, trying to pull the blanket up and cover herself. The blanket was the size of a handkerchief and filled with notes she'd written in secret that she didn't want the professor to see.

I believe you, really I do, but the others aren't as confident that you're up to the task, the professor said, taking a pistol out of his breast pocket and aiming it at her head, then passing it to her, handle first.

Take this. Don't hesitate to use it if the situation demands it.

Ella woke up, and lay awake the rest of the night.

When morning came, she had come to some kind of compromise.

Of course she could do more research. She could use The Game for good. There was no better tool imaginable for research on the Society. She didn't have to make any final decisions one way or the other. She wouldn't reveal any shocking or sensitive information to her professor just yet. And she wouldn't reveal what she was doing to the other members of the Society.

*

Ella called Martti Winter, started by babbling trivialities about the weather, then burst out with, "We have to talk about the notebook in your garden."

Winter asked Ella in a shocked tone what she knew about the notebook.

Ella explained what he had said when he'd continued to spill in his sleep. "Maybe even as a child you knew instinctively that some things are too valuable to destroy, even to protect the Rabbit Back Literature Society. And now we have to dig it up. If it's the source of all the members' works, it's an extremely valuable literary-historical document."

Winter pointed out that the notebook had been buried for thirty years and must surely have decomposed. Ella reminded him that he'd told her he'd wrapped it in oilcloth. "We should dig it up as soon as possible."

Winter didn't give up. "Some things are better left buried. Ask me again some other time. I have to think about it."

Ella said she would call back tomorrow.

"Tomorrow? Let's see... No, I can't do it tomorrow. Tomorrow I plan to have a little nibble of something and relish the fact that I'm still considered a real author. Ask me in thirty years, or perhaps a little later, preferably a couple of days after my funeral."

The silence lasted an entire minute.

Then Ella said, "Just so you know, Mr Winter, I know who the tenth member of the Society was. I have his name."

"Where did you get this alleged name, since even I don't know what it is?" Winter yelled.

Ella told him she'd got the name the same way she got the memory of the notebook. When he asked her, as she had expected, to tell him the name, she laughed. "Just because the great Martti Winter gave it to me doesn't mean I have to give it back."

"Fine," Winter said. "Now that I think about it, I don't want to know. Please don't tell me. Don't ever tell me or I'll… um… I'll have you killed. I have money, and money can buy a contract killing. Look, nobody's thought about that boy or his notebook in years. And I intend to forget about the whole thing. So please be so kind as never to speak to me of it again."

Ella thought for a moment and said, "What room are you in?" Winter said he was in the piano room.

"There's a book on top of the piano. Open it and tell me what's written on the first page."

"I think I know what's in my own book," Winter said wearily. "What have we here? Why, it's an old photo of me. Then two blank pages. Page four is a list of my works. Impressive. I have been industrious. Page five, the title: *Mr Butterfly*, and the author's name, Martti Winter. *C'est moi*. And then there's something written in pen here—what the devil?…"

"I wrote the dead boy's name under yours," Ella said. "I thought it belonged there."

31

THERE WAS A LONG SILENCE.
Ella thought the call had been cut off. Then Martti
Winter spoke.

"Hey, I have a cherry cake here. And coffee. Come and see
me. But you should go home before ten, for both our sakes. The
Game isn't good for us. We'll just drink some coffee and talk.
Or we could watch *Balanced Accounts*. It's a good show. I have
the whole series on disc."

Ella hung up, went into the living room and turned on the
television.

For the next several days Ella marvelled at the interesting
shows on TV these days. She particularly enjoyed two Finnish
series, *The Last Sixty Years of Our Lives*, and the show Winter had
recommended, *Balanced Accounts*, to which she quickly developed
an addiction.

As she was taking out the garbage one grey morning, Ella
found footprints in the snow. Someone, probably Aura Jokinen,
had been snooping around the house. Whoever it was hadn't
been able to climb the ladder to Ella's room, however, because
Ella had removed the ladder a few days earlier. She had in fact
arranged things so that she could have some time to strategize
before she had to submit to playing The Game again.

In the evenings she locked the doors and closed the drapes,
and didn't answer the telephone for any caller but her professor
or her mother. During the day she went to cafés, flea markets, art

exhibits, kiosks and shops. She sought out conversations with the ordinary people of Rabbit Back that she met, especially if they were old enough to remember things that had happened thirty years ago. Almost all the local people were willing to talk about things, provided the conversation was started in the right way.

"That Petri Schäfer, the director of *Balanced Accounts,* is such a trickster…"

Ella was able to gather some new anecdotes about the Society and about Laura White, which would make her professor happy.

She asked people nonchalantly whether they happened to remember a boy named Oskar Södergran, from the early 1970s. No one did. There were no Södergrans living in Rabbit Back now, and no one remembered anyone by that name ever having lived there.

Ella stopped to tie her shoe near a round wooden booth in the centre of town that served as a board for posting announcements. A sign posted by the Rabbit Back Writers' Association read:

TOIVO HOLM, PRINCIPAL WRITER FOR THE POPULAR
TELEVISION SERIES *BALANCED ACCOUNTS* AND
THE LAST SIXTY YEARS OF OUR LIVES TO SPEAK AT THE
SCHOOL AUDITORIUM ON WRITING FOR TELEVISION

The dates and times were at the bottom. Two lectures had already taken place. The last one was that evening.

When she got home, Ella programmed her video player to record the next episode of *Balanced Accounts* and a couple of other shows and spent a few hours writing down the anecdotes she'd gathered.

That evening she drove to the school in the Triumph, went up to the third floor and stepped into the auditorium, which was buzzing with voices. She would have sat in the back, but the only remaining empty seats were in the front row. The room was stuffy. Someone was explaining to an acquaintance that mould had been found at the school, and the library had been declared off limits, and if they couldn't fix it the whole school would have to be demolished.

Toivo Holm strode onto the stage, noticed Ella and nodded in greeting.

The talk was interesting. It was supposed to end at nine, but Holm kept talking. Ella felt uneasy and glanced around. If anyone else left she would follow in their wake. But Holm's stories of television actors and plot changes were so colourful that no one seemed to mind that the talk was going overtime.

The audience stirred when Holm revealed that he was working on a Finnish version of a popular American series about the sex lives of young women. "Of course, I'll have to study up on the subject extensively before I can write about it," he said.

When the clock on the wall said ten, Toivo Holm hopped off the stage in the middle of a sentence, leaned towards Ella, put his lips to her ear and whispered a challenge.

32

Toivo Holm Spills

ELLA SPILLS FOR FOUR HOURS.
Toivo Holm is interested in her erotic dreams and fantasies
and everything she's ever done that could be called sexual, and
she talks about them as the rules of The Game demand, until
she's left with her mouth hanging open like a netted fish. Holm
looks closely at her and sees that she's been scraped hollow,
emptied out, and he declares himself satisfied with her answer.

Ella takes off the blindfold like she's removing the bandage
from a seeping wound. The light burns her eyes. She feels dizzy
and nauseated.

"You spill well," Holm says, lighting a cigarette. "I got a lot
of useful material for the new series."

They're sitting upstairs at the Rabbit Bar. Holm has had
the room reserved for four days. It's a cramped little nook, the
walls hung with dirty wallpaper. The Hakkarainen Hostel would
have been more pleasant, but, as always, it's full of Japanese
tourists come to look for Laura White's body and admire her
home town.

"Shall we have another round right away, or would you
like to go downstairs and have a beer?" Holm asks, rubbing
his bristled head.

Ella tosses him the blindfold and he ties it over his eyes.

*

Holm fumbles for the ashtray, stubs out his cigarette and asks for her question.

Ella *had* planned a question for Toivo Holm—a strategic, pointed question about Oskar Södergran and the notebook. The game is, after all, supposed to be her tool, to be used for literary historical research, as she is constantly reminding herself.

But she knows that sometimes The Game starts to use the players.

She can't help smiling and asks Holm to tell her about his most shameful sexual experience.

Holm flinches. His posture slightly shifts. He's no longer relaxed and confident, but tense.

As he starts to speak, his voice is small and fearful.

"For a long time I thought of myself as a nice person. Empathetic, sensitive—soft, even. I'd actually been rejected a few times for being too nice. But six years ago

I was engaged to an actress. We were going to be married. I'm sure you remember my first series, The Darkest Turn, *and the woman who played Inka Ilves. It was her. She was at the peak of her popularity at the time, and they still speculate in the press about what happened to her and why you don't see her on television these days.*

I had been planning a television movie about Laura White for a long time and had drawn up various synopses and written a few experimental scenes—some of them realistic and based on fact, and others pure fantasy. But the story didn't seem to open up for me.

At some point I realized that my own beloved actress would, in the right light, look a lot like the young Laura White, especially if her hair were altered a bit.

I had already tentatively sold the project, so I got an agreement that my

fiancée would get the part of Laura White. She was very excited about it when I told her that the director had no objection to giving the lead to one of the country's most sought-after actresses.

Then we started working on the script together. We both had other jobs, but it was fun to work on a project together on the side. I had a chance to spend time at home with her for a change. I had been neglecting her—you know how it is when you're writing. At my suggestion, she went to a hair stylist with a photo of Laura White in her youth and bought white dresses like Laura's—I ordered one of them myself from a dressmaker.

This all suited her perfectly. She had always been a method actor, throwing herself into her roles completely. I described the essence of Laura White to her and she practised her gestures and expressions until she knew them in every detail. She even read all of Laura White's works so she could incorporate them into the role.

The way we worked was that she would always perform whatever I had written so I could find the right words and plot for the story and adjust the whole thing. In the end she knew better than I did what would sound like Laura White and made her own suggestions. Some stories worked, some didn't. The process was tough for both of us, but gradually the script was starting to come together.

At some point the role became as much of an obsession for her as the film was for me. A worse one, perhaps. I knew at some level that she might be getting into the role too deeply, but I didn't interfere because the project was coming along so nicely—we were already planning the shooting schedule.

One evening I found her sitting at the desk. She had memorized pages and pages of one of the Creatureville books and was pretending to write the book herself. When I tried to get her to stop, she became very tense and yelled at me not to disturb her when she was writing; said she had to finish this book, she couldn't keep her publisher and readers waiting.

At that moment she was an exact copy of Laura White, right down to the smallest gesture and intonation, if the man who created the role can make such a claim. It was clear that something wasn't right. I thought I should get her some help. And then I decided to fuck her.

I took hold of her hands and said that they were too warm, that Laura White had cold hands. She didn't resist as I dragged her into the kitchen and made her put her hands in the freezer with the bags of vegetables until they were ice cold. I tore off her white dress—I actually tore the dress in two—and then I fucked her. Fucked. There's no other word for it. Fucked fucked fucked. My God.

She stayed in character the whole time. She tried to push me away with her cold hands and scolded me and tried to explain calmly that it wasn't appropriate to treat a respected children's author that way and that she wasn't even interested in sex because not only her hands but the rest of her was cold as well. Of course she stayed in character—she was experiencing psychosis, for God's sake. And I kept saying "Laura, Laura, Laura" while I fucked her in the mouth and the cunt and in the ass like an animal, and I fucked her for who knows how long and then at some point in all the damned fucking both of us started to bleed. There was such a fucking lot of blood. But I just fucked and fucked and fucked until I finally came.

I lay there puffing, hot and sweaty, and my fiancée got up off the floor and walked, naked, covered in blood and sperm, back into the office and started to try to write with her numb, frozen hands, although they were hanging at her sides like empty mittens.

That's when I finally started to worry. Like a loving, thoughtful mate, I wiped the worst of the mess from her skin and cried and got her dressed and begged her to forgive me, although she didn't understand anything, and I admitted her to a psych ward.

And if you want to know the worst part about it, maybe it's this: even now, if I were completely honest, I would have to admit that it was the best piece of ass I've ever had.

33

AFTER SLEEPING for three days, Ella was awakened by the telephone.

She immediately remembered how The Game had ended. When she told Toivo Holm that she was satisfied with his answer, he collapsed and rolled out of his chair onto the floor, weeping. Ella ran out of the bar and drove home.

Now she was awake and her mother was on the phone explaining that she was having a lovely time at her sister's house and asking how Ella was, and why she sounded so sleepy. She wasn't sleeping in the middle of the day again, was she? Her mother was planning to extend her visit by months and might even end up living there.

"Emmi has such a big, empty house here now that the children have their own lives and families and Tauno's gone, too. And this way you can work on your research in peace."

Ella listened to her mother's explanation and said that as far as she was concerned her mother could stay at Aunt Emmi's house as long as she liked. Ella would be fine. She was a big girl.

A thought occurred to her. "Hey, Mum, does the name Oskar Södergran mean anything to you? A boy about twelve years old or maybe a little older, who used to spend time in Rabbit Back in the 1970s?"

"Hmm... let me think. The name is familiar for some reason... why don't I ask Emmi? She lived in Hare Glen for a while with Tauno. Hold on."

A moment later Emmi came to the phone. "Hello, Ella? Yeah, there was an old woman named Naakkala who lived for a while next door to us, or a little farther away. I think Stiina was her first name. Old as could be, but in the summers she went around on a bicycle and in the winters on a kicksled. And I think I remember that there was a little boy with long hair at her house sometimes. We didn't really know them. Tauno didn't like to get too involved with the neighbours. But he might have been old lady Naakkala's grandson, her oldest son's boy, from Helsinki—or somewhere in the south, anyway. He had the face of an angel, and I think his name might have been Oskar or Osku or something like that."

Ella asked her Aunt Emmi if she remembered anything bad happening to the boy.

Emmi dithered for a moment and then remembered that maybe something nasty had happened to him. "Once when I was on my way to the post office, old lady Naakkala passed me on the way, crying. She babbled something about how Oskar wouldn't be coming to Grandma's house after all, that he was never coming again. He and his mother had been in a car accident. That's all I remember. No, wait. There was one other thing. Your mother says she wants you to put an envelope in the mailbox. She says she left it on the spice rack or someplace. It's an entry to win a year's subscription to *Rabbit Tracks*."

When Ella put down the phone she immediately forgot about the envelope, she was so relieved. Winter and the other Society members may have been thieving magpies and a disgrace to their profession, but at least they weren't guilty of child murder.

Her mood improved. On Monday she called the rectory to ask about Stiina Naakkala's church records. Pastor Karhunen, who answered the phone, thought he remembered the woman. They agreed to meet at the rectory the following day at two.

Ella went into town early. She went to the flea market and then to Mother Snow's Café, where she often went to eavesdrop on conversations and sometimes participate in them.

Although Mother Snow's was almost in the centre of town, it was surrounded by a thick stand of trees criss-crossed with winding footpaths, which made it easy to lose your sense of direction.

The atmosphere in the café was unchanged. There were eleven tables in all. One of them was a table for one with a glass top, roped off between two posts. It was reserved for the exclusive use of Laura White. On the table was an old Creatureville book—a valuable first edition—watched over by both the proprietress and several stone Creatureville characters.

The other ten tables were larger and intended for customers. They were dedicated to the Rabbit Back Literature Society. Each table had the works of a member of the society on it— except for the tenth, which was empty. There was a sign on the wall that read: READING IS NOT REQUIRED BUT IT IS RECOMMENDED.

Martti Winter's table was the one closest to the pastry case. Aura Jokinen's was usually occupied by a crowd of young people, sometimes by older sci-fi fans. Families with children made their way to Ingrid Katz's table, which had a pile of children's books on it and a high chair provided.

The tenth table was set aside for the Society's tenth member, whom Rabbit Back had awaited for so long, with no inkling that the tenth member of the Society had died, his ideas stolen and published secretly.

When Ella, the new tenth member, appeared in the café, old Eleanoora shook her hand, led her to the tenth table, and lamented the fact that there was as yet nothing on it to read.

"But who knows, perhaps soon?" she said with a smile. "You know, I remember how you used to come here for ice cream on Sundays when you were a little girl. Every time you came you would look through those books and even then I thought to myself, I wonder if that girl's going to be a writer. Birgit Ström always said, 'Little Ella might just have what it takes if she ever gets the writing bug.'"

When Ella had come to the café after Laura White's disappearance, Eleanoora had been quiet and serious, bringing her some coffee and a roll and whispering, "Ella Milana, the tenth table is still yours, and it still looks awfully empty."

Ella sat at the bookless table as usual. She drank coffee and read the paper. Now and then she glanced around at the books on the other tables and pondered darkly about how many of them actually belonged to the tenth table, which actually belonged to Oskar Södergran.

The Helsinki paper had once again found some news about Laura White's disappearance, "the tragic riddle of the century". The full-page article discussed police speculation that when spring came and the snow melted, some random wanderer would find the authoress's body, probably in some dell or hollow. The article also reported, however, that "local experts" said that in the past many others had disappeared into Rabbit Wood, never to be found. *What Rabbit Wood takes, Rabbit Wood keeps.* They also interviewed a man who had been part of the search on the night of the disappearance and nearly driven his snowmobile into a ravine.

The section at the bottom of the page was about the tourists arriving in Rabbit Back from all over the world. Dozens of White's admirers had arrived over the winter, particularly from Japan and Germany. There was a picture of two Japanese young people standing at the edge of Rabbit Wood with snowshoes on their feet and packs on their backs. The caption read: TWO BOYS FROM OSAKA INTEND TO FIND LAURA WHITE'S BODY.

Ella had started to tire of the missing author. After all, she was collecting material about her life and works, and the disappearance had nothing to do with it.

She leafed ahead to the culture section. Aura Jokinen smiled at her from the page. The article said that Jokinen's new novel had won a prestigious international sci-fi prize. The caption read: MOTHER AND SCI-FI WRITER ARNE AHLQVIST SEES THINGS DIFFERENTLY.

Ella leafed through the paper and accidentally overheard the conversation of a small group at the Silja Saaristo table. A middle-aged man was turning Saaristo's newest novel over in his hands, saying something about how confused the mystery was in the book, and that he had suddenly stopped sleeping well, how he'd been sleeping poorly for a long time.

A young woman asked if he was having bad dreams. He said, "I'm still only dreaming about that writer. I'm a grown man—I can handle a few nightmares—but my kids are having them, too, waking up the whole house screaming."

An older woman took up the lament and said that she had thrown all of the Creatureville books out of her house in front of the children, to calm them down. "But then the little things had a dream that Laura White's body crawled in the window and put the books back on the shelf and started reading them again. I don't know what to do."

The man spoke in a voice flat with exhaustion. "And then there's the constant Creatureville reruns and documentaries about Laura White you have to put up with. I don't believe they'll ever find her body, even if all of Japan comes to look for it. It's going to lie in the woods and rot."

The young woman said in an unnecessarily loud voice, "Laura White's body isn't anywhere in the woods. It's sneaking around in our dreams."

The group fell silent. Old Eleanoora had a coughing fit.

The silence continued.

The man coughed, got up and went to get more coffee for the women. The women started talking excitedly about the things they'd bought at the flea market.

Ella left the café. It was 1:40 in the afternoon. She stopped on the steps for a moment to button up her black coat and wrap the white scarf she'd bought at the flea market around her neck. She looked at the snowy trees that hid the school and the library. Magpies sat here and there in the shadowy limbs, watching the café.

The rectory was in the old parsonage. Ella was greeted by a small, frail man with a beard that protruded long and thin like a winter-killed creeping vine. He made small talk about the quantity of snow that had blown over the path, asked Ella to wipe her shoes on the mat and wondered how much more snow Our Heavenly Father would grant to Rabbit Back, with it already heaped so high that the rectory's old building superintendent couldn't fight it much longer.

Ella shook the pastor's hand and they went into his office. "Please sit down, Miss."

Pastor Karhunen said he hadn't known old Stiina very well—no one had—but he had met her adult children at her funeral: Iiro, Eino, and Olavi.

"I have a lot of faults," he said, "and the Lord in his mercy forgets them every evening, provided I bear them in mind. Remembering names, however, is one thing I've never had any problem with."

He remembered Olavi Södergran being there with his wife Mirja. A stylish woman in a wheelchair. Her spine had been damaged in a car accident.

"They said that they'd lost their child in the same accident. They were a very impressive and attractive couple. Did I mention that Olavi Södergran was blind? He made a joke over coffee about the blind leading the crippled and she smiled at it—apparently his quip didn't sting in the least."

The pastor offered Ella a chocolate and smiled, thinking of Olavi Södergran's humour.

"The author Laura White was at Stiina's funeral, too, by the way. She came up and kindly shook hands with Olavi and the old woman's other sons and said she had known Stiina a little through Oskar. I talked for a long time with Olavi and his wife about literature and the Lord's mysterious ways. Beneath the humour I could see a certain kind of grief, the kind that can be a particularly hard blow to non-believers. I told them I could send them some passages from the Bible that would provide both beautiful literature and the comfort of God's word, if they wanted me to.

"You're a literary person. If you ask me, there are passages in the Bible that a lover of literature has to appreciate, even if they have no interest in religious matters. The Book of Job, for example. A great mystery, and full of wonderful metaphors. None of this purple prose."

He paused, gazing at her expectantly, and when she promised to make it her business to get to know the Bible on a literary level, he nodded with satisfaction and continued.

Although the Södergrans had said they were agnostic, they had given him their address so that he could send them some biblical selections.

He picked up a slip of paper from the table and handed it to her.

"You said you had some information for the Södergrans about their departed son? I don't have their phone number, unfortunately, but here is their address. This is where they were living six years ago. They might very well still be there."

That evening Ella wrote a letter to Olavi Södergran and his wife Mirja.

She started with polite greetings. She followed with an apology for the manner in which she was reminding them of a tragic incident in their past, but said she believed that what she had to tell them was the kind of information they would want to know, particularly if they were, as she had heard, great lovers of literature.

I am Ella Milana, the most recent and final member of the Rabbit Back Literature Society. I have recently learned that your son Oskar was a member of this same organization before his death. I have conducted some literary historical research within the Society and learned something that I think you, as Oskar's parents, ought to know.

She tried to describe eloquently, without directly blaming anyone, how Oskar's literary ideas lived on in the work of the Society members:

I've been told that the other children of the Society—those who are today the most important names in Finnish literature—had the opportunity, due to circumstances, to read Oskar's notebook after his death, and that it was this very notebook that was largely the inspiration for their most significant literary output.

At the end of the letter she added her own contact information and her desire to meet them and exchange thoughts on their son Oskar and the time he had spent in the Rabbit Back Literature Society. She spent three hours polishing the wording of this request until she had it in a form that, though polite, sensitive and subtle, could not easily be declined.

When she'd finished the letter, she started looking for a stamp. She didn't find one, but as she searched, an envelope fell off the spice rack—the letter her mother had asked her to post. The last unused stamp in the house was stuck to it. The letter was addressed to the offices of *Rabbit Tracks*. Ella used scissors to cut off the stamp and glued it to her letter to the Södergrans. Then she went out and dropped it in the nearest post box.

She felt a deep satisfaction, but she knew that it would quickly fade. Nevertheless, she let herself enjoy the knowledge that she had just put an important piece of the past in its rightful place. It was a small victory in the larger battle against disintegration.

As a child, Ella Milana had thought as a matter of course that there existed somewhere a vast archive where all possible information about the life of the Finnish citizenry was collected.

She had heard of a place called the National Archive, and

looked it up. The encyclopaedia said: *The Finnish National Archive is a central agency of the Ministry of Education that leads and oversees the activities, governance and development of the general archives and acts as the nation's public archive and its associated centre of research.*

Ella had assumed that such a place must have gathered and recorded everything, especially all the people's most valued moments. It seemed only reasonable.

The first time she could remember thinking about it was when she was six years old.

She's at the lake, chasing a beach ball that someone has kicked to her. Her feet sink into the hot sand with each step, but she feels light, almost flies. She breathes in the smell of the lake and feels very clearly and strongly that somewhere, someone is recording all of this on her behalf, so that nothing she sees around her can ever really disappear—not her mother and father, who are laughing, nor the ice cream stand, nor her buoyant joy.

Ella had never believed in Santa Claus, the Easter Bunny, or God; what gave her strength was her belief in this act of recording for all eternity.

Ella dropped her toothbrush in the sink and put her face up against the mirror.

She examined her face so closely that it made her eyes cross. Then she went upstairs—careful not to step on the fifth and fourteenth steps—undressed, turned on the lamp and opened her wardrobe.

There was a full-length mirror fastened to the inside of the door.

Ella had secretly undressed in front of the mirror for years. She had flirted and done calisthenics and examined her appearance critically, admiringly, hornily.

Now the mirror was showing her the features of a grown woman. The same features she had spilled for Martti Winter.

She realized that she hoped Winter would use those features, immortalize them in one of his books so that years from now, readers would recreate an image of her as she was now, over and over.

The thought brightened the eyes of the woman in the mirror.

Finally Ella grew bored and closed the wardrobe.

She started to feel guilty about the stamp. She put on a night-gown, went downstairs and wrote the *Rabbit Tracks* address on a blank envelope. Then she read her mother's contest entry letter.

Since my husband is gone, I feel I'm in a phase of my life where I have both the right and the responsibility to reveal a particular incident so that you no longer need to wonder about it. I hope that for my trouble I will be rewarded with a free subscription to Rabbit Tracks.

I'll let you decide for yourselves in what form you wish to publish this revelation. I request that you not reveal my husband's identity, and refer to him instead as "a certain local individual". I also hope that you inform the person whose car was lost how it all happened, so that he or she can achieve some peace of mind. Please convey my sincere apologies for keeping the truth secret for all these years.

On the June evening when all of this happened, my husband was at a certain house in town at a party also attended by some members of the Rabbit Back Literature Society of his acquaintance, including Laura White herself. (I was at home taking care of our daughter, and was thus unable to attend the party.) My husband came home in the morning very drunk, bleeding from the forehead, and gave me a brief account of the evening, after which, in accordance with his wishes, we never discussed the matter again.

From what I was told, Ms White appeared at the party somewhat tipsy, and at a certain point in the evening she became very excited for some reason. My husband and a non-fiction writer who was also present calmed her down and took her for a walk to clear her mind. Ms White, however, got away from them and ran to the centre of town and spotted a white Renault in front of a grocery store that had already closed for the night. The car was unlocked and the key was in the ignition. Ms White got into the car and started the engine. My husband and the non-fiction author got into the car to try to stop her, but they were unable to prevent Ms White from driving away with the car and unwilling to use force to try to get her to stop the car, instead attempting to talk to her and calm her down.

According to my husband's account, Ms White drove the Renault down a narrow forest road which quickly came to a dead end. Ms White did not stop the car, but continued to drive with miraculous good luck deeper into the woods along narrow ant trails and other routes nature had to offer. I was extremely amazed to hear how far from the road the wrecked car was when it was recently found, and can unfortunately offer no other explanation than Ms White's extraordinary driving skill, combined with a series of fortunate accidents.

In the end, however, Ms White's luck gave out and the Renault hit a tree. My husband's head was injured in the collision. My husband and the two women abandoned the vehicle and returned in a state of confusion to the road, and to their respective homes.

Sincerely,

Marjatta Milana
31 Garden Road
58625 Rabbit Back

34

E LLA LAY in her old room, in a bed that was too short for her, and wiggled her toes. She closed her eyes tight and waited in vain for sleep. She had been lying there for two hours already, thinking about the letter.

"For heaven's sake, Mum," she whispered in the darkness. "You and your free *Rabbit Tracks* subscription…"

The fifth and fourteenth steps of the staircase creaked when stepped on.

Someone stepped on the fifth step.

Ella opened her eyes.

Then the fourteenth step creaked.

When the door to her room started to open, Ella was standing on the hinge side of it, her back to the wall. She held her breath, a heavy vase hoisted over her head.

Her arms started to ache. The vase trembled, but she couldn't put it down yet.

A shadow slipped into the room and stole over to the bed.

Ella roared and flung the vase at the intruder.

It shattered on the floor.

The shadow jumped, crashed into the desk and fell, pulling the items on the desktop with it. Ella hit the wall three times before she found the light switch.

A pink form clambered to its feet behind the desk—a small,

slightly plump woman in a pink snowsuit. A grin spread over her hamster face.

There had been an article about Aura Jokinen in the Helsinki paper when she won a prize that read: *Aura Jokinen, alias Arne Ahlqvist, is one of the most significant sci-fi writers at present, a winner of international awards and a respected visionary whose works are sought after as far away as Hollywood.*

Now she was standing in Ella Milana's room brushing bits of broken vase off her feet and rubbing her hands together.

"Hi," she said. "Nice room. Phew! You really scared me there. If you hadn't missed me, you know, you would have been able to tell everyone what really is in my head. So many people have asked about it, ha ha…"

They looked each other in the eye. Ella acted before she knew what she was doing.

"Aura Jokinen, I challenge you to The Game."

Jokinen smiled.

"Well that's a pretty picture. I go to all this trouble to pick your lock and nearly get my head broken, and then you challenge me? Shame on you, Ella Milana."

Ella said that the rules didn't prohibit the ambusher from being ambushed, and besides, it was always better to challenge than to be challenged.

Jokinen admitted that she was correct, but added that she hadn't come for The Game, she'd come for an entirely different reason. Suddenly serious, she urged Ella to sit down. What she had to say wouldn't be at all pleasant to hear.

Without waiting for a reaction, Jokinen whispered, "I came to warn you, Ella. And to betray the other eight members of the Society while I'm at it, so this isn't easy."

Ella blinked.

Jokinen smiled and brushed her hair out of her eyes with a thumb.

"Little Ella, we all know you want that notebook. You see, Martti called all of us and warned us about what you've been up to. I hear you've used The Game to find out the secrets of the Society. And you plan to dig things up that are better left buried."

Aura Jokinen's eyes filled with tears that flowed in salty rivulets down her cheeks. She shuffled over to sit on the edge of the bed, crossed her arms in front of her and started speaking, as if to herself.

"Oh, Ella. Oh, oh, oh. If only you had understood in time that the notebook belongs more to you than to literary history. It's always been a private Society matter, and it will stay that way as long as it stays within the Society."

Ella felt weak. She crouched down and rubbed her temples.

"A notebook stolen from a dead child is a private Society matter? You don't all have the right to steal, and hide what you've stolen and then declare it a private matter. The notebook belongs to literary studies research and to the dead boy's parents."

"Right. But listen—that's not the opinion of the Society."

Ella said it wasn't for the Society to decide, and that even though the Society was guilty of the theft, the members had been children at the time, and besides, it all happened a long time ago, over thirty years ago. "You have nothing to fear. Except..."

A shadow passed over Jokinen's eyes, and Ella stopped mid-sentence.

"We may have nothing to fear but the loss of our reputations," Jokinen said, "but you do have something to fear. There's a plan to murder you tonight. Whether it will be carried out remains to be seen."

Ella opened her mouth, but couldn't get a word out. She looked at the little woman sitting on her bed, searching for a sign that this was some kind of bizarre joke.

"You needn't be afraid of me," Jokinen said. "I'm here to rescue you. I'm the only one who wants you to still be alive in the morning. The other members are terribly nervous."

Jokinen glanced at the clock on the wall. "Is that the correct time? You ought to know that in forty minutes, at two-twenty, four members of the Society will come into this house and…"

She swallowed and grabbed hold of her chin, unable to go on.

Ella opened her mouth but Jokinen raised a hand and said she didn't intend to tell her which four planned to murder her.

"I'm between a rock and a hard place here. Murderer or traitor, those are my choices. I don't want to be a murderer, but the Society plans to silence you. For good. Click. Snuff you out. Pow."

Ella's legs went numb.

"So they're on their way to take my life so I won't reveal the secret," Ella said. "Why are you against it?"

Jokinen explained.

"Aside from Ingrid, I'm the only member who didn't go to the water tower that night. I would have gone—I'm no saint—but I fell asleep, and when I woke up it was morning and Martti had already taken the notebook away."

She took out a handkerchief and a small mirror and tidied her dishevelled face.

"I've always used my own ideas in my books, so I have nothing to fear," she said with a smile. "But I do think the whole thing should be kept secret. Let sleeping dogs lie. I'm with the others on that." Her gaze sharpened. "If it comes to murder, I can't condone that. But if I had made it to the water tower on time, I might very well be with the others tonight."

Ella tried to make sense of the situation. "That's quite a story," she began with feigned nonchalance. "Let's assume I believe you…"

Jokinen jumped to her feet with surprising agility, leaped across the room, grabbed Ella by the sides of her mouth, spread them in a clown smile, and whispered, "Ella, little one, you must know by now what kind of a bunch this little literary club is. Fine, talented writers, yes, great contributors to our culture, indisputably. Long live the Rabbit Back school of literature!"

Ella's mouth was starting to hurt. Jokinen flashed her a tight smile, let go of her lips, then grabbed her temples, her eyes glittering.

"That literary history of yours probably doesn't mention that a lot of us older writers have a history of trouble in the head. Ding dong. Laura White succeeded in mixing our little heads up pretty well all those years we went to her school for writers. She knew where literature comes from, all right."

"What do you mean?"

Jokinen let out a laugh and almost shouted. "Everybody knows that no healthy person would take up writing novels. Healthy people do healthy things. All this darned hoopla and hot air about literature—what is it really but mental derangement run through a printing press? And when you've written as many stories about murders and acts of desperation as we have, it doesn't take much skewing to get you to thinking you might be up to all kinds of things, should the need ever arise.

It's remarkable how much easier it is to do something if you've written believably about it.

"So now four fixtures of the literary firmament are on their way here," Jokinen sighed, touching her cheek with trembling fingers. "You want to know how they've prepared for their visit? At this point they've finished off a generous dose of good whisky and equipped themselves with two baseball bats, two metres of wire, a roll of duct tape, and a sufficiently large garbage sack. I provided the duct tape. I got it from my kids' hobby box. They told me to bring it. It's to keep you from making too much noise when they strangle you with the wire and beat you with the baseball bats."

Ella crouched in the middle of the floor, no longer listening to what Jokinen was saying. She was analysing the situation she'd somehow ended up in.

One possible definition of murder would be "an illegal activity that causes its target to cease to exist". One of the many murders committed annually was about to happen in Rabbit Back, and its target was Ella Milana.

Like everybody, Ella lived inside herself. That's why she was apt to think of herself as an exceptional case when it came to statistical facts. She understood in theory that she could be the victim of a violent crime just like anyone else, but it hadn't occurred to her that her literary-historical research could put her at risk of being murdered.

Murder was a criminological, ethical and physiological phenomenon. The Society had failed ethics thirty years ago, when all of this began. Murder in the physiological sense was a simple, mechanical process, a breaking of a body so thorough that the body ceased to live. Old people and little children and housewives did it; why not writers who felt threatened?

Sci-fi writer Aura Jokinen turned out the lights and Ella's reality was broken to pieces. The pieces shifted: the new reality was for the most part like the old one, but in this reality Ella Milana couldn't go back to sleep because in a moment her murderers would arrive with tape, wire and baseball bats.

Ella's heart beat three times. Then she realized that she felt like she'd just been born—born into a reality where she *really could* die.

Like all newborns, Ella filled her lungs with air and wailed. This gave Aura Jokinen, who was peering out the window, a terrible fright.

Ella sputtered out her first words in this new reality. "Duct tape! Duct tape! Shit. How did this happen?"

She looked at Aura Jokinen. She couldn't remember ever having felt this helpless. Jokinen looked at her, picked up a pile of clothes from the back of the chair, threw them at her and told her to get dressed quickly.

"I have a feeling they're out there. I saw something moving in the woods. We have to go."

They ran from the house to Jokinen's old Volvo.

Jokinen backed the car up onto the road and hit the gas so hard she knocked the mailboxes over.

"Can you see anything?" she asked.

She shifted gears and the car sprang forward.

"I don't think so," Ella answered. "I don't know. There might be someone hiding there."

"They wouldn't stand in plain sight." She was barely able to keep the car on the road. "We've been ambushing each other for thirty years. It gives you quite an adrenaline rush to sneak up on somebody, unheard and unseen. Oy yoy. Let's play, my friend. Let's spill so long that we're drained empty, cold and empty. You can really develop an addiction to the Nosferatu game. You might stop playing for a while, but only for a while."

"Unheard and unseen," Ella said quietly. "I've tried it a couple of times. But you weren't unheard today. I heard you."

"The stairs," Jokinen said with a sigh. "When we were planning your murder at Martti's house, Ingrid Katz said the stairs were quiet. Shoddy fieldwork. By the way, did you get the book plague under control at your house? Ingrid mentioned that you were having a problem with it. It got into the kids' room at our house when I got a book from Ingrid and the kids stuck it on the shelf. The Bram Stoker classic, don't you know. It changed remarkably. But in the end it had to be burned. So did the children's books that were infected. Kukka Kaalinen got mixed up with Pippi Longstocking…"

Ella asked if Ingrid Katz was really in on the murder. It was hard to imagine the librarian approving the order to kill.

Aura Jokinen's curls shook with laughter. "It was Ingrid who first suggested it. They all wanted to rub you out. And I didn't object out loud when I realized how united they were. I thought if I did, I wouldn't get away alive to warn you."

Ella felt like throwing up. "What about Martti Winter? Did he…?"

Jokinen nodded. "Kill your darlings. That's the first rule of a writer. Martti does like you, but you could spoil everything. Literature is forever, but people are fleeting butterflies. Put her in a jar. That's what he said when he voted to murder you. It wasn't easy for him, though."

Jokinen glanced at Ella and smiled. "Shall we put on some music? It might take our minds off unpleasant things."

She turned on the radio. The car filled with a lecture on Dostoevsky, and Ella recognized Professor Korpimäki's voice. She changed the station and found some international pop.

They drove about a hundred metres along the tree-lined road. Ella noticed they'd come to Hare Glen.

She closed her eyes and tried to think. The woman in pink at the wheel couldn't be taking her to Martti Winter's house, could she? What if this was a trick? It was possible. But what could she do?

Then Jokinen turned off the engine. Ella opened her eyes. Laura White's house loomed in the darkness.

"What are we doing here?" Ella asked.

"Not much. But we'll be safe here for a little while," Jokinen said. "It won't occur to them to look for us here. And we can play The Game you challenged me to."

"The Game can wait," Ella said. "I'd rather concentrate on staying alive."

"Nyet. If we don't play The Game sometime tonight, we'll no longer be members of the Society. Rules are rules. It's a shame no one thought to add a rule specifically forbidding members of the Society from murdering each other."

"Killing people is forbidden by law," Ella said.

"That may well be. But breaking the rules of The Game voids your membership in the Society. If we end up outside the Society, we can never get back in. We'll lose everything."

"Being a member doesn't seem that important to me," Ella said. "In fact, at the moment I wish I'd never..."

Jokinen patted her and flashed a bright smile. "Yes, yes, I'm sure you feel bad right now. But you don't give up membership in the Society just like that. These things happen, even in the best societies. Let's go inside. The lady of the house isn't home, of course, but we are her heirs, after all—provided we remain in the Society and play The Game."

They walked towards the front door. The snow was knee deep. The façade was closed up and dark.

When she was on her way to the party here Ella had been bubbling with excitement. She had admired the large house, thought of it like an ocean liner in an old movie, full of festivity, light, life and possibility, full of interesting people and clever conversation. Now it felt like a mausoleum.

A couple of nights earlier she'd had a dream. Laura White's house was completely filled with black water. All of the missing authoress's furniture was drifting around on the current. Ella was swimming among the floating chairs, buffet tables and dishes, looking for the exit.

A bed floated into view. On it sat Laura White's pale body, tapping on a typewriter.

When she woke up, Ella imagined she could still hear the typewriter. Then she realized that the sound was coming from the plumbing.

They went up the snowy steps. The front door was locked. Aura Jokinen took out a coil of thick wire.

"To pick the lock," she said. "We can get in the side door, if the locks haven't been changed."

Jokinen picked at the lock for a minute, grinned and tugged the door open.

They stomped the snow off their feet and walked through the house. They didn't turn on the lights because they would have been visible across the valley, all the way to where Martti Winter's house stood, besieged by dogs.

Aura Jokinen led the way with a pocket flashlight. The light bounced off dusty furniture, paintings and empty bookshelves.

They stopped at the foot of the staircase where Laura White had disappeared. There was dust on the stairs, and small footprints visible in the dust. Jokinen examined the tracks. "One of the women from the Society, I should think. I haven't been here since the party."

They went up the stairs. "I'll show you the room where Laura White wrote. She was sitting in there the night of the party, while her guests waited. Here it is!"

Jokinen opened a door, revealing a darkened room. She turned on the light—Laura White's office had no windows.

The room was surprisingly small. The walls were hung with dozens of paintings. Each was by a different artist, and every one was of Laura White.

"She was an inspiration to artists," Jokinen said. "Do you know much about art? A few of these are well-known names. Laura didn't like photographs. She said she wanted to be properly seen before she became an image. She felt that the quick, dead eye of a camera was too ghostly."

On the desk was an old typewriter. There was paper in it, with writing on it.

A little bird leaped in Ella's breast. There were three lines written on the paper.

The first two said:

THE RETURN OF EMPEROR RAT
BY LAURA WHITE

On the third line were two words:

I saw

"An unusual beginning," Aura Jokinen said, sitting down in a rococo chair.

Ella thought she understood what Jokinen meant. None of the Creatureville books used the first person.

"I came here twice that evening," Jokinen said. "The first time was a couple of hours before the disappearing act. I thought I'd remind the authoress about when the party was starting and who the guests were. Then I saw those words. I came back again half an hour later, after everything ended in chaos. I had to come and see if she'd finished that sentence. She'd tried her best, but for some reason that next word was an insurmountable obstacle."

Ella looked at the paintings. In some of them, Laura White was in her twenties, in some she was clearly older. There were nudes among them, too. You could tell from the brushstrokes that the painters would have liked to touch her, lie down with her. But the expression on her face was withdrawn, guarded, and Ella didn't think that any of the artists would have dared to try.

She would have to come here again and take photos of them. Aura Jokinen continued. "I knocked on the door and came in without asking. I walked right up behind her as she was writing. I saw what she had written and I asked her what exactly she had seen.

"She jumped up so fast that the chair fell over and nearly frightened me to death. I said I was sorry but the party had begun and she stood there looking pale and sick and said she would be down soon. She was sweating terribly. She smelled like illness. I knew she wasn't well, but she said she would be down momentarily and asked me to go back to the party and make sure that the new girl felt welcome."

Jokinen got up, turned out the lights and opened the door.

"Let's go, Ella. I have a headache. This place still has the same strange smell it had that night. I remember I thought I could smell Laura's cold sweat."

Ella sniffed the air. There was a whiff of something, faint but perceptible—something sour, stale and damp.

She walked quickly out of the room.

Ella descended the same stairs that Laura White had been descending the moment before the snow storm.

She looked down at where she had been waiting to meet the authoress and marvelled at how insignificant this experience was. She had imagined she would feel something special, something affirming about walking up those stairs and looking down at the drawing room from the same place where Laura White had stood. But the stairs were very ordinary stairs, and the house was just a dark house. She wasn't thinking about the mystery of Laura White, she was just focused on not stumbling in the dark and falling on her head. She would have to come back here to do some literary research.

Of course, as a member of the Society, she could come back here—provided she avoided being murdered.

There was dust everywhere, but the house was otherwise clean. The aftermath of the storm had been cleared away. The furniture had been put right, the broken windows replaced, the floors swept.

Then Aura Jokinen started to wonder out loud about the missing books. The house had been full of books before, hadn't it? There used to be a shelf full there, and another one over there, and now they were empty. They started looking for books. The dark, bookless rooms seemed to go on forever.

Finally they came to a room made of nothing but windows. Even the ceiling was a window. During the daytime it was no doubt a cradle of light, but now it seemed crushed under the weight of the winter night.

One of the large windows was ajar. There were almost-fresh footprints in the snow just outside. A little farther off was a flat, pitch-black hole. Jokinen shone the flashlight through the window and into the hole. At the bottom was charred paper and the remains of book covers.

"Ingrid has been here," she said. "Of course. She's still carrying on her holy war against the book plague. That woman is a complete obsessive, by the way—off the charts."

They stared a little longer at the place where Laura White's amazing library had been burned to ashes.

Then Jokinen sighed, turned from the window and started to speak in the rote style of a museum guide. As she spoke, she walked slowly around the room, her pink snow suit rustling.

"This, then, is the room where we read stories out loud. You know, there's never been a single person as interested in my thoughts as Laura White was. Not my parents, not one of my friends or lovers. Laura had a burning need to understand what we thought and felt and did."

Ella looked at the curly-haired woman with a slight feeling of amusement. The books she wrote had a photo of a man inside the cover. Ella had heard that it was a photo of Jokinen's grandfather, who'd once sold encyclopaedias door to door.

There were eleven chairs ranged around the darkened floor. Ten of them were in a half circle. One chair had a higher back and more ornamental carving than the others. Aura Jokinen sat down in the half circle and stared at the chair—the one that Laura White had sat in.

With her gaze fiercely fixed on the chair, speaking as if from beyond time, she said, "My parents always said I ought to be nice and quiet when adults were talking. They talked constantly, about the obligations of a social democracy and cash flow and the German Democratic Republic, while I sat in the corner.

"But Laura White listened to my every thought. She would even ask me questions until she was sure she understood what was really on my mind. It was intoxicating.

"I thought she must love us very much and think of us as very important people. I decided that I would be eternally grateful and faithful to her and do everything I could to be worthy of her respect."

Ella stood farther back and looked at Jokinen in profile. The chair under Jokinen creaked when she moved.

Ella's gaze wandered over the chairs. In the thick darkness it was easy to imagine the children in them and in the most important chair the woman Jokinen was talking about. Her words were as light as snowflakes, but they were forming an ever-heavier load.

"Later on I realized that the whole time she was teaching us, she was actually studying us. She was interested in us, but to her we were little bugs under a magnifying glass. She taught us to play The Game and see inside each other and write down what we found. And once she had us figured out, she put every one of us in her Creatureville books." Jokinen laughed. "You probably didn't know that, even though you studied literature. Martti was so proud and beautiful as a child that it made your heart ache, and of course he thought he was very important. When Laura White got to know him thoroughly, he showed up in her books as Bobo Clickclack. Before that Bobo was just a name, a shadow, a sort of empty husk. If Martti had realized what she'd done he probably would have fallen apart. He always used to laugh at Bobo Clickclack and say that Bobo was without a doubt the stupidest, most disgusting character in the whole series. Poor Martti. He never understood how Laura had come up with such a horrible character."

Ella chose a chair and sat down—she had a right to her own chair in this room. "Which character are you, then?"

They both looked at Laura White's chair.

"Yeah…" Jokinen said. "When I realized that Laura was putting replicas of us in her books, I tried to hide my true personality. I started to take on new personas, a different me from one day to the next. I piled different emotions around myself until even I wasn't sure what I really thought or felt. But Laura eventually broke my code."

She turned to look at Ella across the dark room, a sly smile on her face. "Why don't you guess? You've studied the books. Which Creatureville character best represents world-famous science-fiction writer Arne C. Ahlqvist, alias housewife Aura Jokinen?"

Ella looked at her for a long time. Jokinen aimed the beam of the flashlight at her own face so that Ella could see her changing expressions. Powerful, conflicting emotions passed over her face.

"There's one character in the books who could fit your profile," Ella said at last. "Who tries to hide, to appear to be something other than what it is. A character who makes up new names for familiar places and things, tries to make the familiar seem strange and the strange familiar, to make other people as bewildered as itself."

"Yes?"

Ella took a breath and said, "You're the Odd Critter, also known as Baron Bewilder."

Jokinen clapped her hands and nodded. Ella gave her a dubious look. Jokinen got up, went to stand next to Laura White's chair and continued her presentation.

"When I realized that Laura White was studying us, I decided I would study Laura White. All the others adored her—behold the pride of Rabbit Back! I tried to practise looking at her more closely, looking in a different way. I wanted to find out exactly who Laura White was. *What* she was."

Jokinen's hands shook as she pointed at her own head and said, "I've been collecting observations of Laura White for thirty years. It's all up here. That's why, I'm sorry to say, my head is more than a little cluttered. It's like my kids' room. And messy rooms get on my nerves. They make me really angry." She sighed. "I'm not saying that Laura wasn't a wonderful teacher.

But the main goal wasn't to teach, it was to learn. She taught us one particularly important thing that I used as a weapon against her. She said that a writer should know how to think about everything there is to think about, even when everyone else is thinking only about the possible, or the probable. That was damn good advice.

"It's been my guiding thought whenever I contemplate Laura's essential nature. And everything I've written and published over the years—all of my prize-winning novels and acclaimed short stories, all that vaunted Hollywood adaptation crap—it's all been my way of preparing myself for understanding what I was about to discover."

She grinned at Ella now, and sat down in Laura White's chair. She took the scarf off her head and placed it on her knees, took a bottle of yellow out of her pocket, and said, "Of course, all of this mental preparation has taken its toll. Once you start wondering about things, you end up wondering about your own turds. Take the children, for instance. I have children. At least, we call them 'children', but what are they really? What do they mean? They came into the world from between my legs and at first they lived off a fluid that started oozing out of my breasts. Now they live in my house and perform endless rituals they call 'playing'. They use words that are strange to me. When they look at me I can never be sure what's going on behind their eyes. They might as well be aliens from another planet."

Because of the open window it was cold in the room. Ella rubbed her thighs. Aura Jokinen laughed out loud, threw her head back and let out such a cloud of steam that it looked like her guts were on fire.

"I think I feel something for them, and if the need arose I

would probably even die for them, rescue them from a fire or something. But when you really think about it, isn't that love just a hereditary, biologically determined reaction, part of my electrochemical makeup? If too much or too little of something was excreted, would that love disappear, just like that, *poof*? Would my children start to look like vermin to me, like little beasts? Is motherhood just based on the fact that chemicals from my organs drug me into imagining that taking care of my children is the most important thing in life? In the end, they'll move away and become strangers to me, which is what they basically are."

She looked as if she were waiting for an answer. Ella said she wouldn't know anything about it.

"It's a matter of surrendering to the obvious," Jokinen said. "It's frightening, but also liberating. Once you learn to wonder about things that are considered normal, you can keep a cool head, even when something less normal crosses your path."

The two of them sat quietly in Laura White's cold, dark, windowed room and looked at each other in the pale moonlight. The flashlight lay on the floor, its batteries fading. Jokinen's thought structures wrapped around them in a spiral that both fascinated and frightened Ella.

"I want to ask a favour of you," Jokinen said. "I brought you to this place because this is where Laura White lived her life, and where the Rabbit Back Literature Society was created and developed. The reason I brought you here particularly is that you have research training, and at this point I need your help."

Ella lifted her hand and touched her lips with her fingertips. She noticed that her muscles were clenched. She said nervously, "Well, it's fortunate for both of us that you saved my life tonight."

The sci-fi author nodded and continued with a smile, "I want you to ask me an all-encompassing question about Laura White's inherent nature, and make sure that I spill until you're sure you've received a complete answer. Use Rule 21 freely if you need to. Otherwise I'm sure I won't be able to get it out. I've tried, but I couldn't do it. Something inside me always fights it, in spite of all my preparation. And after that…"

"Yes?"

"After that, I'll ask you what an unbiased, intelligent young researcher can make of it."

Ella got up, walked slowly over to Jokinen and stood behind her with her hands resting on Jokinen's shoulders.

"We should play The Game all the way through on your terms?" Ella said. "And I should be glad to do it because you rescued me and betrayed your old comrades for my sake?"

"If that's how you want to think of it," Jokinen said humbly.

Ella watched the cloud of breath in the dimness. She smiled, leaned over, pressed her lips to Jokinen's ear and whispered, "Help! Help! The fierce and dreaded Emperor Rat is after me and will be here any minute!"

Jokinen turned to look at her. Ella grabbed her by the nose and squeezed until she gave a squeal.

"When I look at you now," Ella whispered, "I really can see the Odd Critter, alias Baron Bewilder, in the flesh. Tell me the truth now, and I won't rip your nose off, and I'll do what you ask. Did the Society really decide to murder me tonight?"

She gave Jokinen's nose another twist and looked into her eyes from five centimetres away. The corners of Jokinen's mouth turned upward and revealed her trick.

"I'm sorry, sweetheart," Jokinen whispered through her blocked nose.

Ella let go of Jokinen's bloody nose and wiped her hand on her pink snow suit.

"What about the meeting? The one where you decided to murder me because of the notebook?"

"There was no meeting," Jokinen laughed, gingerly feeling her nose. "We can't stand each other. There's no way in hell anything could make us get together for another meeting. I managed to challenge Ingrid, and Martti, too, after endless surveillance, with those damn dogs trying to bite me. I got them to spill everything they'd talked about with you."

Ella slapped her on the back of the head. Jokinen gave a yelp and said, "It was filtered information, of course, which there's generally no point in collecting. But it did make this whole thing seem believable."

She looked Ella in the eye and said she wanted to play The Game all the way through with her and find out Laura White's inherent nature.

"I could have just challenged you in the normal way. But I'm writing an escape story. I thought I would research how a person really behaves in a situation like that. But there's another, more important reason I did it. I'm sorry for the shock I gave you, of course, but you must admit that it's helped you understand something you absolutely have to understand."

"Which is?"

Jokinen smiled.

"That anything at all can happen at any moment. There—I've got the blindfold on, and I've taken the yellow. Let The Game begin."

35

Arne C. Ahlqvist Spills

"YOU AND MY FATHER knew each other," Ella says. "You were with Laura White in that Renault they found in the woods."

Aura Jokinen's curls swung nervously. "Don't start asking about your father. Hell, I can tell you about your father and that drive after The Game, free of charge, with as many details as you like. Ask me about Laura White."

Ella coughs.

"What?" Jokinen says. "I didn't hear what you said."

"I didn't say anything yet."

"Oh. Why not? The Game has started. I've got the rag over my eyes and the yellow in my belly. I'm hellbent and ready. Ask me a basic question about Laura White."

Ella doesn't answer, she's gathering her thoughts first. Jokinen huffs and cracks her knuckles.

"I had a dream a couple of nights ago," Ella finally says. "When I was a kid, about ten years old, I got a jigsaw puzzle as a present from my father. On the box there was a picture of the finished puzzle. It was a picture of the inhabitants of Creatureville—Bobo Clickclack, Dampish, Crusty Bark, Mother Snow and the rest, in the middle of a forest. I had a dream about that puzzle."

Jokinen tilted her head. "So?"

"In the dream, though," Ella continued, "the pieces were different from what the picture on the box led you to expect. I started putting the puzzle together, and it was forming the wrong picture. In one corner you could see a hand—white, and obviously dead—and I knew that it was from Laura White's body. And the Creatureville characters that had been smiling on the box were frightened now. They were looking at something behind the trees. I knew that if I followed the direction of their eyes, I would find Emperor Rat when I finished the puzzle."

Ella is silent. She doesn't remember any more and Aura Jokinen doesn't say anything. She sits hunched over in Laura White's chair with the blindfold on, completely still. Through the window Ella can see the moon and the garden bathed in moonlight. Farther off she can dimly see the tangled undergrowth of Hare Glen, which was once, they say, a very beautiful place.

A noise of dogs drifts over the valley. Ella guesses the sound is coming from Martti Winter's house. Maybe they're barking at the large man as he peeps out the window, or maybe they're barking at the moon as it clatters along its invisible tracks.

"Why don't you ask me a question?" Aura Jokinen says irritably. "Unless another interesting dream has occurred to you that you want to tell me about. We have to play The Game. Otherwise neither of us will be a member of the Society anymore. I'm sorry for being impatient, but I have a hell of a headache. My blood pressure keeps going up, and I left my medicine at home. And it's damned cold in here. And I'm as ready as a trembling virgin. My head is splitting, so please will you play it all out of me and tell me what the hell you think it means?"

Jokinen's face is pale, tense and sweaty. She holds her trembling hands to her temples as if her head really were about to split in two from the pressure of her thoughts. Her blonde curly hair sticks out between her fingers as if she were pulling on it.

Ella takes pity on her and asks her question.

"What do I need to know if I want to get a clear idea of the true nature of Laura White?"

Ella waits for a flood of words, but Jokinen doesn't seem to know what to say.

A minute passes.

Laura White's chair creaks nervously as the sci-fi writer rocks herself back and forth.

Ella thinks about the house around them. She thinks about the walls and floors, the joists, the unlit stairway and the dozens of rooms. The house around them is empty now, but she can feel the Society's past hiding just around a corner, almost palpable.

Ella blows on her fingers and rubs her hands together. Outside the windows the stars swing slowly into new positions.

Aura Jokinen sweeps back her curls, sighs gently and starts to speak, at first with care and concentration, then more quickly:

"The story that Laura White always told goes like this: Laura White wrote the Creatureville books, founded the Rabbit Back Literature Society, and trained nine children to be successful authors. It's a very good story, of the deeds of an esteemed and beloved authoress. But when you look for answers to the question of who or what Laura White really is, you find all kinds of peculiar little

things that are hard to fit into any reasonable story. So you forget about them, because that's what people generally do with things like that. People can't stand it if a thing doesn't fit into any mould or conform to a ready pattern. Some things just can't be fully explained.

For years I've been collecting these banal peculiarities, all the while living the story that everyone tells, the story that's been built around us. I studied literature in the Society, then I wrote books, because that had become my nature and it was expected of me. And then when the time came I had sex and I had children and served as their mother. That fit into the larger story we were living, too. And I took great care to learn to see things as they really are, without any filters or forced patterns. It's left its trace on everything I've ever done. On my books, too. A review of one of my books once said: "Arne Ahlqvist has once again whipped up some delicious gingerbread, but thrown away the recipe book—" Ha ha...

I'll tell you the story now—sorry, I mean I'll spill some things that are as much a part of a portrait of Laura White as anything else that's known about her.

You already know about the book thing. It's bizarre as hell. I've never completely understood exactly what it is. I just know that many of Laura White's books turn volatile somehow. They start to change. And the same thing has happened to the books in the Rabbit Back library, to Ingrid's delight. Laura said it was bacteria, but I don't know. It could just as well have something to do with quantum mechanics. I've written lots of stories about that, just so I could learn to understand it as a phenomenon. Or maybe the books are haunted. I don't know. But one thing I do know is that sometimes reality shrivels up and blisters around Laura White, almost as if she isn't really completely suited to the reality she's trying to fit into.

The things I'm talking about, there are so many of them... once, for instance, when I was about nine or ten, I happened to go into Laura White's room while she was sleeping. She was amazingly beautiful lying there on her bed, like something out of a painting or a fairy tale. She was wearing a white summer dress and the window was open, and it was autumn outside.

I knew I ought to leave, but I sat down quietly on the bed and watched her while she slept. I even secretly sniffed her hair and her skin and her breath, and they were full of the smell of dying autumn flowers and fallen leaves. A sad smell, and I thought, I love Laura White so much, much more than I love my own mother.

Then I heard something. Laura was saying something to me. Whispering. Her lips were moving. But she wasn't saying anything—a bee crawled out from between her lips: that's what the noise was.

It was confusing. I was startled, and I don't remember much of what happened after that. I just remember that the bee buzzed around the room and then suddenly it was on my face and it stung me on the cheek and it hurt awfully.

I ran out of the house and went home. I remember that my cheek was throbbing and I was crying. The next time I saw Laura White she said, "Oh, my, Something must have stung poor Aura's face," and I just said, "Yes, a bee stung me in the meadow."

I've never told anyone about this until now.

Of course it could have been partly a dream. You can't completely trust a child's perceptions. I'm sure that's what you're thinking. That's what I'd like to think, too. It would give me a way to comprehend these aberrations.

But bizarre little things like that happened again and again, and no one ever took any notice of them. How can you tell someone about these things? How do you go up to someone and say, "Laura White was just walking in the rain, and she sneezed, and for half a second I could see right through her?" There were lots of things like that—not really frightening. The worst things, the things that really weren't according to the recipe, were still to come.

Oh yeah, before I get to that, I ought to mention something you should pay special attention to when you form your theory about Laura White's nature. There's an event connected with her childhood that... well, maybe if you get the chance you should talk to this retired doctor—his name is

Jansson and he knows more about the incident than I do. I don't know if the two of you were introduced at the party, but he was there. Do you remember him? A thin, white-bearded gentleman, quite elderly? Anyway, he was the doctor who treated Laura White when she had the accident, when she was a child. What happened was that…

Ella grows nervous.

Aura Jokinen is still speaking, or at least trying to speak, but Ella can't make out what she's saying now. Her words start to slur, then fragment into mere babblings.

Jokinen sniffs a couple of times, tries to sit up straight, opens her mouth wide, leans to one side, then slumps onto the floor.

Ella jumps out of her chair, bends over Jokinen, and takes the blindfold off. She can see a helpless look in Jokinen's eyes, and a flaccid shapelessness on one side of her face.

"It's OK, my friend," Ella whispers, stroking her hair. Drool runs out of one side of Jokinen's mouth. "I'm sure this is reason enough to leave off playing The Game for now. I'm sure you'll be all right. You probably just tried to spill too many big things all at once."

Ella calls the emergency number and tells them that a middle-aged woman has suffered a stroke in front of Laura White's house.

Then she drags Jokinen outside so they won't have to explain, and won't be blamed for the break-in.

They wait on the porch for the ambulance, Ella holding Aura Jokinen in her arms. Jokinen's left eye is closed, but the right one is staring at her intently.

Her mouth keeps opening, as if she were still trying with all her might to spill.

36

PROFESSOR KORPIMÄKI called the next morning, wished Ella a good day, and, without waiting for a response, started to comment on the coffee klatch stories she'd sent him.

"Very interesting. Very interesting indeed. Those are just the kind of anecdotes that let you see Laura White's work and the work of the writers in the Society in a whole new, more exciting light. I've already incorporated several of them into my lectures. I hardly need to tell you that the lecture hall's filled to the rafters these days. Laura White always draws them in. But what about your earlier finds? Have you dug up anything new?"

"Definitely," Ella said. "I'm finding new stuff all the time. But…"

She raked her fingers through her hair and tried to gather her thoughts. She'd been up most of the night.

"Yes?" her professor said expectantly.

"Um, d'you think we'd have any use for… um, what should I call it… inappropriate material?"

The professor whistled. "Do you mean material related to Ms White's sexuality? Have you come across any revelations? Or scandals?"

"I'm talking about ghost stories," Ella said, and immediately thought she ought to have used more academic terminology. "Yesterday one of my informants had an attack of illness during an interview. Probably a stroke. Before it happened, she told me an anecdote about Laura White that... um... had many of the characteristics of a miracle narrative or ghost story."

The complete silence on the other end of the phone chilled her. She could hear the professor breathing. This was what she had been afraid would happen—even attempting to work non-standard puzzle pieces into official literary history could destroy her research career before it started.

"Well, we're trying to form as complete a picture of Laura White as we can in order to get a deeper understanding of her oeuvre," the professor said thoughtfully.

Ella could hear a ballpoint pen scratching on paper on the other end of the line. He was writing something down.

"We'll have to see. Part of the research has to address Laura White as a person, so we should look at her personality and human relationships. Your anecdote may serve nicely as material for that aspect of it. Another part should relate her life story, from childhood to her disappearance, as comprehensively as possible. We have some general facts, but we definitely need to get more details, so keep that in mind as you gather information." He coughed and continued. "The third, most important part is the analysis and interpretation of Laura White's literary output. Your thesis will serve as a wonderful starting point for that, not necessarily for the project in its entirety, but as one possible direction to take. Naturally, it's appropriate to include biographical particulars in relation to her work. You may find something valuable in it."

He clicked his ballpoint pen.

"We must remember, though, as we look at all of this personal information, that the most important thing is what Laura White wrote. We should, of course, gather all the information

we can about her life as well, by all means. It's our duty to literary history. But when you look at the big picture, Laura White's
life isn't terribly important. In the end, from a literary point of
view, it hardly matters what the person who wrote the books
did, or thought, or felt, although such things naturally arouse
our human curiosity."

The scratching of his pen ceased for a moment.

"As far as these 'ghost stories' you mention," he said, "perhaps
they could be attached as a small footnote to the biographical
section."

After talking to her professor Ella drank some coffee, looked
up a couple of things on her phone, then called the other eight
writers.

Although the members of the Society didn't enjoy each
other's company, long friendship weighs heavily, and every
one of them agreed to go the next day to the university
central hospital to visit Aura Jokinen—particularly since Ella
told every one of them that all of the others had already
agreed.

Ingrid Katz, who Ella called first, put a stop to her idea of
renting a minibus.

"Just getting everybody to agree to come is an achievement.
You ought to get a medal. But don't overdo it. It takes a few
hours to get there. Let's do this: We'll reserve seven taxis to
pick us up in front of the library at ten o'clock. We can meet
there. You, Martti and I can go in one cab. The others can
each have their own."

The following day dawned mild and partly cloudy. The
members of the Society arrived in front of the library and

exchanged polite, distant greetings. No one came closer than two metres to another except for Ella, Ingrid and Martti Winter, who stood together trying to look unconcerned.

"The snow will start to melt soon," Ella said.

The three of them turned momentarily to marvel at the shrinking snowdrifts.

"Yes, it will," Ingrid said.

"We'll see," Martti Winter said. "The ground's frozen so hard in my garden that I doubt it will melt all summer."

Ella and Winter looked at each other.

"Would you like some liquorice?" Ingrid said, bending over her bag.

They ate liquorice, and then the taxis came and the members of the Rabbit Back Literature Society got in.

Three hours later, Ingrid Katz was conferring with the nurses.

"I understand—the patient shouldn't be needlessly disturbed and she's scheduled for more surgery and only family is allowed to visit. Do you understand that we were once an extremely close-knit group? Good friends. Family, even, literarily speaking. Believe me, Aura Jokinen, alias Arne C. Ahlqvist, would definitely want the authors Winter, Saaristo, Seläntö, Kangasniemi, Oksala, Holm, Kariniemi, Katz and Ella Milana here at her bedside. It can only be good for her recovery that we've come to visit her. We came straight here. We got here even before her blood relatives showed up."

Naturally all of the nurses knew who Laura White was and were to some degree aware of the nine members of the Society. In fact, two of them proved to be fans of Martti Winter's work, and a third confessed that she enjoyed Silja Saaristo's mysteries and had once bought one of Ingrid's books as a Christmas gift for her children.

"You mean one of our patients is a writer, too?" one of the nurses said. "You don't say. I've never met a writer, and suddenly the hospital's full of them. Show me one of their books in the hospital library and I'll be more interested. What did you say your name was?"

It was eventually agreed that each of them could visit Jokinen's room separately and spend a maximum of one minute each.

Silja Saaristo insisted on going first, because she had an urgent need to use the ladies' room.

"I'm going to wet myself soon, and I want to get this out of the way. There's something so depressing about friends dying. And that hospital smell. Ugh."

Within six minutes every one of the old members of the Society had gone in, and now it was Ella's turn. She walked into the room, which at the moment contained only Aura Jokinen. Jokinen lay in bed with dark circles under her eyes, a bandage around her head and intravenous drips in her arm.

The nurse had prepared them by saying that even if the patient were conscious she might be confused.

"We'll continue The Game where we left off," Ella said. "As soon as you're ready to start prowling again. I asked the others and they said that of course you can postpone The Game when something like this happens. But until then, try not to think about large, complicated things. I guess they're getting a chance to look inside a sci-fi writer's head after all. I just hope they fix your head well enough that you can start writing about this reality instead of writing about everything else."

Jokinen smiled, raised one eyebrow and murmured something.

Ella bent closer and breathed in the sharp smell that wafted from the bed and the patient lying in it. "What did you say?"

"Jansson," Jokinen whispered, pointing to the door. "Just here. Went to the cafeteria. Ask about Laura."

Ella stepped into the cafeteria.

People came and went. The clatter of dishes was swallowed up by the sound of conversation that flowed over everything. Ella walked slowly along the wall. She was looking for a table with a man who fit Doctor Jansson's description—a thin, elderly gentleman with white hair.

The Society authors had taken over seven tables in various parts of the room.

Ingrid Katz and Martti Winter were sharing a table. The long deli counter was behind them. Ingrid bent her thin neck to drink her coffee. In the harsh light of the cafeteria she looked old and stressed.

Martti Winter was eating a large chocolate doughnut. On his plate was more food: a ham sandwich, a chocolate bar and two large pastries. He was dressed in a white suit. A chocolate stain on his silk tie was visible from a distance.

Ingrid noticed Ella and beckoned her to their table. Ella parried the invitation with a gesture the intricacies of which made Ingrid smile in bafflement. She continued her circuit of the room. Nervous looks were thrown at her, as if she were a leopard searching for suitable prey.

She thought wistfully of the photograph on Martti Winter's wall of himself and Ingrid as children. Then she came up with an idea for a camera that didn't just record people in a momentary flash, but captured their entire chronological existence. *Could you turn a little so that your childhood is in the picture? Right now your middle age is obscuring it…*

A mural of a gleaming mountain landscape inhabited with people and sheep was painted on the cafeteria's farthest wall. Ella looked for a long time at a white-bearded, stylishly dressed older man sitting among the sheep.

Her lack of sleep was apparently starting to affect her vision; the mural seemed to swim and buckle before her eyes.

The old man moved, took a drink of his coffee. It was only then that she realized he wasn't part of the painting.

She got herself some coffee and a biscuit. As she approached Doctor Jansson's table with her tray, she did remember seeing him at Laura White's party. He had been standing at the foot of the stairs right next to her when Ms White had started down the stairs.

"Doctor Jansson?"

"Oh, hello," the old man said with a smile. "The lovely Miss Milana, of the Rabbit Back Literature Society. I remember you well. We unfortunately didn't have a chance to introduce ourselves at that ill-fated gathering, but you were pointed out to me. Please sit down, if such humble company suits you."

Ella put her coffee on the table and sat down next to him.

"I hope you won't take offence if I say this at the very beginning of our acquaintance," Doctor Jansson said, leaning towards her, "but you have unusually gracefully formed lips, if you ask this retired physician and art lover. Nature has its own whims and missteps, which in my profession one sees all too often. But your lips are evidence of nature's gifts."

Ella thanked him for the compliment, wiping her mouth and smiling awkwardly.

THE RABBIT BACK LITERATURE SOCIETY

The doctor let his attention wander over the bright hospital cafeteria and Ella followed his gaze. The server behind the counter was refilling the pastry case, which Martti Winter had emptied significantly. A little farther off, Winter could be seen watching the activity at the counter, no doubt pondering whether to purchase anything else to nibble on. Ingrid Katz sat with her chin resting on her knuckles, explaining something to him.

"It seems the whole Literature Society is here," the doctor said. "One is lying upstairs with an IV in her arm and the rest are here in the cafeteria. Do they still not speak to each other?"

"Not really," Ella said.

Doctor Jansson shrugged sadly. "Well, it's been that way for years. It's not something an old man like me can understand, people remaining strangers to each other when they used to be so close. They did everything together for years—vacations and parties and studying their writing. Some of them even dated. Perhaps all they need is to get up from behind their keyboards. You never know."

"It's good that they came to see Aura, though," Ella said. "I was with her the other day when she had her stroke. We, um, met to discuss some things, now that I'm a member of the Society."

The doctor nodded. "Yes, I heard."

"We talked about an incident that happened to Laura White when she was a child."

As she tossed this bait to the doctor, she lifted her coffee to her lips to hide her face.

Doctor Jansson looked at Ella with watery eyes and raised his bushy eyebrows. "It's good that Aura remembers that incident," he said. "Very good. I'm glad. It was an extraordinary thing, and a heartening example of what rehabilitation can do. It's not surprising that people don't talk about it here…"

Doctor Jansson's demeanour changed as the memories revolved in his mind—he stroked his beard, tapped the table with a long index finger and started to speak:

"What a case that was! A ten-year-old girl who was angry

at her parents over some small thing and ran off into the woods, naked for all practical purposes, wearing nothing but a thin nightgown. She had a bad habit of running away in a temper, out of the house, wherever her feet took her. She had a blind trust that her mother and father would always catch her before she got too far away.

It's night, there's a quiet snow falling, the ground's been frozen for some time. It doesn't occur to her parents to call anyone for help at this point. They run after her and think they'll catch up to her in a moment, like they always have before.

They're right behind her for a long time, and many times they almost catch up with her, but this time she's faster than usual, or perhaps her parents are getting slower—in any case things go wrong and they finally realize to their horror that they've lost her completely. A nearly naked child, lost in the woods at night in freezing weather that's growing colder.

A couple of hours go by as they search desperately. The mother is hysterical, gives up the search and goes to alert the police, the family doctor and the ambulance. They both cherish a hope that she's gone home on her own and is sitting by the fire warming herself.

That's when her father finds her footprints and follows them to a small pond. He looks into the clear ice and sees his daughter underneath it. Farther off there's a hole in the ice where she's fallen in. He understands the situation immediately—she's fallen through the hole in the ice and can't find her way out again.

He yells at the top of his lungs—the neighbours hear him from a kilometre away—and starts hacking at the ice with his flashlight. When he's got her out of the pond he runs with the lifeless girl in his arms for fifteen minutes to get her home. The ambulance is already there and they rush her to the hospital. But her heart has already stopped, she's not breathing, her body seems cold and dead—too much time has passed.

Somehow, as if through a miracle, they manage to revive her—she starts to breathe and her heart starts up again.

It's clear that the best they can hope for is that she'll spend the rest of her life in an institution. That's what their own doctor tells them. I'm ashamed to say that this short-sighted, foolish pronouncement can be attributed to me. God have mercy on me.

Of course, the facts supported my prognosis. The girl's brain was badly damaged. She could no longer speak, eat, walk or do anything else. She'd regressed to the state of a newborn baby. For a long time she didn't respond to anything, and then, when she did begin to respond, she didn't even recognize her own parents. Her mind was truly a blank slate.

Well, against the warnings from the hospital and the pessimism of their doctor, her parents bring her straight home, travel to Switzerland and hire an army of specialists to rehabilitate her.

And a miracle happens. It takes time, but in the end she learns everything all over again and recovers. It's truly an old-fashioned survival story. The White family leave Rabbit Back with a helpless, brain-damaged ten-year-old, and return six years later with an intelligent, civilized young lady.

You could perceive only a few small signs of her previous condition. One of them was that she could never remember anything about the accident or her life before it happened, except for one small memory.

Some time much later the girl, who at that point was already a woman, mentioned to me that she remembered seeing something on the night she drowned, the night that she died for a while. She wouldn't say anything more. But she asked me a lot of questions about how exactly the human brain works and what kinds of hallucinations a person might have when the brain is deprived of oxygen.

Another trace of the accident was that she didn't want to touch the piano anymore, although before she had been a gifted student. It was no doubt due in part to the coldness and numbness of her fingers—she never fully regained her circulation.

Aside from the way it began, this story isn't such a bleak one. In place of music, she took up other interests, and her talents found different ways to blossom. Can you imagine? Three years later this young woman who should have been a mere phantom of her former self published her first children's book, which was, of course, Creatureville.

Her proud family invited their pessimistic old doctor to dinner and presented him with a copy of the book, inscribed by her. It read: "For Doctor Jansson from his friend Laura. We both strive to understand what makes a person tick."

Doctor Jansson's hands were trembling as he took a handkerchief from his pocket and wiped his eyes.

"That book is in a place of honour on my shelf, and in my capacity as a doctor I've ordered myself to look at it every day—once in the morning and once in the evening. This prescription has helped me to keep my ego from overreaching, which it has a tendency to do. That book has helped me remind myself daily that though we humans have learning and wisdom and imagine we know everything—imagine ourselves gods—events will take their own course, in spite of divinities such as ourselves and our little ideas and assumptions. We thought we'd lost Laura forever, and we got her back again. Why? Because anything can happen—even the kinds of things that we can't predict or understand. For that same reason, we have to accept that Laura finally did leave us the way she did, tragically and unexpectedly."

The old man stared into the distance. Then his furrowed face quivered and a smile spread over it.

"Tragically and unexpectedly, I say, but in actuality it was a beautiful thing. *Poof*, she's gone, and in her place is white, wildly dancing snow! You know, Ella, it's just like Mother Snow says in Laura's last book:

Dear creatures, sometimes we are allowed to experience wondrous things and go places we couldn't reach even in dreams. Only someone who hasn't learned anything from it all can think that they'll be able to hold on to what they've found forever.

EPILOGUE

37

Ella Milana stands with her back to the bed. Her clothes fall to the floor.

The dim room smells like dark chocolate. Ella ties the blindfold over her eyes, turns, gropes her way to the bed and reaches both hands out in front of her.

He takes hold of them, and a small yelp escapes her.

Afterwards she draws another X on her calendar and smiles.

The whole thing was hard at first.

The first time, she got caught under him and nearly smothered, her side crushed. The second time, she sprained an ankle and almost broke her nose. Their third time it ended with him making an ill-advised movement and getting an attack of lumbago and starting to yell out loud, unable to stop. Ella called a doctor who came and pumped him full of three syringes of painkillers.

The fourth time ended with both of them laughing uncontrollably.

The fifth time went better. Neither was noticeably injured and they both had an orgasm—they were finally starting to find a way to fit their bodies together.

Ella and Martti Winter never talked about their relationship, and they didn't comment on each other's actions—words can be razor sharp when it comes to tender matters of the flesh.

The only exception was an ode that he wrote to her—to her nipples, to be precise. At first she thought it a ridiculous idea, but when she heard the poem she ran out of the room with tears in her eyes.

Things you don't talk about aren't completely real. After the fifth time, as Ella is rinsing herself in the bathroom, she tries to recount the experience in her mind. She wants to find something in it to shape into a memory.

It isn't easy. She doesn't remember the act at all, except for a surreal general impression and an idea that formed in her mind at the final moment: she was a little crawfish swirling in the eddies of the sea, slamming herself again and again against something large and powerful.

Ella Milana returns to the bedroom. The bathrobe she's wearing is much too big for her. She lets it slide off onto the floor, steps out of the pile of fabric, and starts putting her own clothes on.

He looks at the outline of her body in the dimness.

"What?" Ella asks.

"Ella Milana," he says, "May is half over, and the weather report promises a warm, sunny day tomorrow. It's time we went for a picnic. Let's have one out in the garden. I'll make the food."

"Oh," Ella says happily. "Can I bring anything?"

Winter is breathing heavily. Ella turns to look at him.

When he finally answers, his voice is scooped hollow.

"Bring a shovel."

38

T HE DOGS haven't gone anywhere.
Ella Milana and Martti Winter counted all the dogs gathered around the house on April Fool's Day. They got as far as thirty-eight.

Every now and then someone appears at the house to pick up their pet and take it home. Within a few days, the creature runs away and comes back to Winter's house again. The *Rabbit Tracks* dog psychologist A. Louniala has been flooded with questions from weary dog owners. The dog column has tripled in length.

When Ella gets out of the car on the day of the picnic she realizes it's been a long time since she's paid any attention to the dogs. She's started to think of them as a normal part of Winter's front garden. The dogs, for their part, haven't shown any interest in her comings and goings lately. When she opens the back of the Triumph, however, and takes out a shovel, the dogs prick up their ears and the atmosphere turns tense.

The hair on the back of Ella's neck stands up.

To get to the front steps she has to pass a large Great Dane.

She gets nervous, of course, and stumbles, and the shovel falls to the ground with a clang.

The Great Dane shows its teeth and lets out a deep growl.

The snarl continues as she goes into the house and pushes the door shut behind her.

*

For the picnic they take along a picnic basket, a blanket and the iron shovel.

Ella and Winter go out to the garden. When they've found a pleasant spot under an apple tree, they spread the blanket out on the grass and sit down to drink some coffee and eat some chocolate cookies.

They smile at each other with shared understanding.

They might be about to rewrite the history of Finnish literature. They'll probably destroy the Rabbit Back Literature Society in the process. But first they intend to enjoy their picnic. It's a beautiful day.

They have a long, meandering conversation about the chocolate cookies. Winter ordered them especially from Rabbit Market, as well as the cream puffs.

Their relationship is founded on an agreement that they will only talk about unimportant things. Over the spring they've kept their physical experiments, banter and laughing paramount.

Summer has started outside the walls, but inside the garden there are still wintry spots—there's even some ice still at the base of a few of the statues. This Thursday, however, is a sunny one, in honour of which Ella is wearing a short skirt and a red summer blouse with white polka dots.

She feels a little chilled.

Her blouse amuses Martti Winter, who makes some discourteous comments about it that cause Ella to laugh out loud.

Winter is wearing a brown suit, more sporty in cut than usual. He calls it his "sauntering suit". It has a tie embroidered with gold thread, which is now hanging over a limb of the apple tree, where Ella perfunctorily placed it.

They sit on the blanket and eat their picnic lunch.

The shovel is leaning against the tree behind them. It isn't yet time to pay any mind to it.

Ella is still researching the history of Laura White and the Rabbit Back Literature Society. That's what she's being paid to do, after all.

Martti Winter tells her brief anecdotes about the authoress during their afternoon coffee conversations. Since the information spilled in The Game can only be used as literary raw material, their coffee chats keep Professor Korpimäki satisfied without breaking the rules of The Game.

Ella plays The Game with all the members of the Society except for Winter.

In addition to her research, she's begun writing a novel. She's already written ten pages and filled numerous journals with notes. No one knows about this, not even Martti Winter.

The developing novel is based on Laura White's story—or rather, on the nine different stories Ella has gathered from the things that have been spilled to her.

Some of the stories are more usable than others.

Two weeks ago, Ella finished The Game she'd started with Aura Jokinen. The still-recovering sci-fi writer did her best to spill, but it was difficult to make out what she was saying. Her thoughts were fragmented and vague, and many things remained unclear, which she herself understood all too well. *"I'm sorry, friend, but my mind isn't quite working. Or my speech."*

Ella felt sorry for her, but she knew when she started The Game that Jokinen's view of Laura White would be unsuitable for her purposes. She doesn't want to write science fiction, and she isn't thrilled with the idea of a supernatural horror story, either. She intends to write a proper psychological novel, respectful of the realistic tradition of Finnish literature.

Ella has acquired some useful material from The Games she's played over the past few weeks with Helinä Oksala, Elias Kangasniemi and Oona Kariniemi. Two days ago she finally got to play with Anna-Maija Seläntö. Seläntö came to Rabbit Back to speak to an amateur writing club and got it into her head to go out for a late dinner, to the delight of Ella, who was stalking her in the Triumph.

Ella's been thinking she'll use Seläntö's succinct point of view about Laura White's nature as a starting point for her book. A novel about "a schizophrenic personality trying to heal itself by pumping out children's books and making the children who read them see the monsters" is much more likely to be taken seriously than one about the ghost that's sprung up in Aura Jokinen's suffering mind.

Ella is made of slender stuff, but she casts a surprisingly large shadow over Winter.

She's standing behind him. She got up a moment ago to stretch her legs, and now she has the shovel in her hand. Winter glances at the rusty shovel and continues to eat his cookies.

Ella notices him looking at the letter lying unopened on the blanket. It came four days ago. The sender's name is on the envelope: *Mirja Södergran*. Ella showed it to him as soon as it came and said that they should open it together—once they dug up the dead boy's notebook.

"We had the mythological mapper come over three days ago," Ella says.

She's chatting idly, as if she doesn't know that the shovel

she's nonchalantly holding has become a scalpel with which to excise the Rabbit Back Literature Society from literary history.

"My mother entered a raffle last year, I guess, and she won a free mapping. It got overlooked last autumn for some reason, and the mapper showed up the other day to do it. You know me—I would have sent her to bother the neighbours, but Mum was at the house and she said that when you win something you ought to accept your prize. So the mapper went out to our garden with a sleeping bag and slept for a couple of hours under the berry bushes."

"Did you get a good report?" Winter asked, giving her such a mournful look that she felt guilty.

She forced herself to smile and showed him the document the mapper had written for them:

MYTHOLOGICAL MAPPING CERTIFICATE

Location: The Milanas' Garden, Rabbit Back

A complete mythological mapping of the above-mentioned location was performed by an accredited mapper, and the following mythological creatures were detected.

After this introductory statement there was a form with a long list of possible mythological creatures. The mapper had detected two different types in the Milanas' garden:

8 house elves or elves of other buildings (barns, playhouses, sheds, etc.)
3 gnomes

Additional information about creatures or other beings detected:

Notes—The elves (or house spirits) on this land are particularly cranky, because they are in a struggle with an invading elf. This may cause occasional disturbances for the house's inhabitants. The situation can be mitigated by leaving milk and bread under the large stone behind the currant bushes in the evening and absolutely avoiding the garden after the sun has set.

Ella remembers the other mythological mapping—the one the mapper wrote for Martti Winter, warning him not to show it to anyone. She looks at him and guesses that he's thinking about the same thing.

Ella thinks about the ground under her feet.

The names and order of the layers of earth that she learned in school pass through her mind. She can see the soil, the stones and moraine. She can smell the little animals burrowing in their dens. She can hear the moles, ants, beetles and centipedes scratching in their tunnels.

She closes her eyes and feels the quiet, deeply nested mysteriousness of the earth.

She starts to feel dizzy.

She opens her eyes and glances at the sky, where the fluffy parade of clouds continues its noiseless march. Martti Winter looks in the same direction and mutters something about "flaming, vengeful eyes" and a "retreating enemy". Ella looks at him worriedly—it takes her a moment to realize he's reciting poetry.

As the sun disappears behind a blanket of clouds, the air cools and the shadows pour their darkness over the whole garden.

They look at the darkness of the sky until the sun bursts through and shines on their faces again.

Martti Winter turns to Ella and says they might as well get started—now is as good a time as any.

Ella nods, then immediately shakes her head. She opens her mouth to say something clever, but nothing appropriate comes to mind. She stands there, blinking like a mute, simple-minded child.

Martti Winter's eyes are murky. He smiles patiently and takes the shovel out of her hands. Then he walks away and wades through the raspberry bushes holding the shovel, which looks very tiny in the grasp of such a large man.

Ella hurries after him. This is her project, after all, she reminds herself; this corrective surgery on literary history is a fulfilment of her wishes.

Winter tramps a path for her through the rattling underbrush, wider than is necessary. The thorns on the berry bushes neverthe-less scratch her legs and catch on her skirt—she's apparently too clumsy for a trek through nature. She tries to avoid the thorny branches and Winter leaves her behind, and just then she turns her head and notices a figure looking at her from the bushes.

Ella stiffens and puts her hand over her mouth so she won't yell.

The sun cuts out a silhouette of the figure on her retina.

She can't make it out very well even when she squints, but when she takes a couple of sideways steps, the sun is hidden behind a tree trunk and she can see it better.

It's standing near an apple tree and two maples, in the most inconspicuous of places: a naked wood nymph.

It's carved out of dark wood. Its surface skilfully mimics the forms of living flesh. No wonder her hurried eye was fooled.

Ella steps closer and sees that the nymph's wooden features are badly worn. Her delicate lips, the thin edges of her nostrils, and the nipples on her small breasts have nearly disappeared, but a memory of them is still perceptible. Her slender hands are cracked, pressed against her body as if she were trying to stop them from decaying completely.

A melancholy expression plays across the nymph's face. Ella carefully touches the smooth wood of her cheek, then hurries after Winter.

As she walks past the nymph her skin tingles. She can't help turning to look behind her.

Now she can see the figure from the back. It's bark-covered wood, with dry branches growing out of it. From this angle the illusion is lost. There's no woman at all—just an old, broken stump quietly decaying in a garden.

Ella reaches Winter. He's stopped near the wall under a large maple tree. She asks if they're in the right spot—is this where little Martti Winter hid the dead boy's notebook?

Winter starts to dig.

Ella stands a little ways off. Winter swings the shovel in a dangerous-looking manner. Dirt patters over Ella's shoes. The deepening hole fascinates her and she doesn't notice at first that the pack of dogs has broken into a pandemonium of howls and a cold gust of wind is rushing through the garden, whipping up leaves, rattling branches and settling around them in a whirlwind.

Ingrid Katz wrinkles her brow at a noise in the library foyer.

She snorts and leans over the check-out desk.

Aura Jokinen is rolling towards her in an electric wheelchair that needs to be oiled. Beside her walks a thin man dressed in black with a frizzy mane of hair and lots of jewellery.

Ingrid guesses that the leather-coated man is a member of an organization that worships the works of Arne C. Ahlqvist and their paranoid-schizophrenic vision of reality. The club holds regular Arne C. Ahlqvist discussion groups. Sometimes they come to her house to interview her for their newspaper, to deliver the assorted prizes she is invariably awarded and to ask for autographs.

"He came to do an article on Arne C. Ahlqvist," Jokinen explains after greeting Ingrid. "And to bring me a prize, for the seventh time."

Jokinen's mumblings are hard to understand, though she tries to speak clearly. She says that she dropped in to ask if the library has a new book that isn't yet in the bookstore.

"Let me guess," Ingrid Katz says. "The book you're looking for is *The Return of Emperor Rat,* by Laura White."

Aura Jokinen nods and nervously fingers the wheelchair controls.

Ingrid Katz sighs. "You're only the tenth person to ask about it since the library opened half an hour ago. I called the bookstore—it's the same story there. People asking for a book that they don't have for the simple reason that it doesn't exist."

Aura Jokinen shakes her head, drools a little down her front, and says, "I'm sure I heard, or maybe read somewhere, that it had been published. I heard the publisher found it…"

"They didn't," Ingrid Katz says. "Someone must have dreamed it and talked about it and at some point the dream became a news item. Trust me—I just called Laura White's publisher and he, at least, doesn't seem to have found any such manuscript."

Over the next hour the phone rings five times. Library patrons asking to reserve *The Return of Emperor Rat* and wanting to know how many people were already on the waiting list.

Finally Ingrid makes a decision. She leaves the check-out desk in the care of the new library assistant and goes into the back room. She takes the key from around her neck, opens the top drawer of the desk, and takes out the package wrapped in Christmas paper—the one containing the infected copy of *Creatureville*.

She unwraps the package.

What she sees makes her feel dizzy and sweaty, although she isn't really surprised.

The cover says:

LAURA WHITE
THE RETURN OF EMPEROR RAT

The cover illustration is of the familiar Creatureville characters and the dreaded Emperor Rat, whose name is of course mentioned in many Creatureville books, but who has never before actually appeared in them.

On the left side of the picture are all the Creatureville characters. They look shocked. Their features are grotesquely distorted with fear; Bobo Clickclack's mouth is snapped open and the Odd Critter is holding its head in both paws. On the right side, Emperor Rat is holding on to Mother Snow, pulling her away from the others—not angrily, as you might expect,

THE RABBIT BACK LITERATURE SOCIETY

but more like they're old friends, if Ingrid is reading their expressions correctly.

Ingrid tries to still her trembling hands as she opens the book and looks at the first few pages.

The Return of Emperor Rat seems like a perfectly ordinary book, with publication information, a title page—the only thing that amiss is that it's a book that has never been written or printed.

Also, there's only one page of actual text—only one sentence, in fact:

CHAPTER ONE

I saw the girl coming over the ice, and her shadow fell over me.

Ingrid Katz reads the sentence many times.

Then she wraps the book up again. It will have to be destroyed, of course. It's as volatile as can be, and will spread the book plague. Tomorrow, at the very latest, she'll drive to the cabin and heat the sauna with library discards.

But first she'll show the book to Martti. And if that fish-lipped girl is hanging around, she can see it, too, since she's so interested in everything to do with Laura White.

And that way Ingrid can check to make sure Martti is all right. She's been having bad dreams lately, dreams that his house is surrounded and the dogs get in and eat him.

The hole is half a metre deep now.

The work advances slowly. Martti Winter is panting and sweating in his suit. Ella offers to take the shovel, but he shakes his head.

The gusts of wind increase. Ella's skirt flaps and flutters. Her legs are cold. The branches are thrashing with a wooden sound that whirls around within the walls like an invisible beast, while outside the walls the dogs continue their commotion. Ella rubs her arms and shifts her weight from one foot to the other. The garden feels dimmer and colder than it was a moment ago, although the sun is still shining in the sky.

The ground is hard and full of roots that have to be hacked away.

Then come the bees.

They rise out of the earth a little way off, circle the maple in a dark cloud, and come to swarm around them.

Martti Winter grimaces and stops digging.

"Dash it," he says, fastening his gaze on the bees.

He hands the shovel to Ella.

Ella starts to dig.

Winter brushes bees from his shoulders, lures them away from Ella and the hole. The bees arrange themselves in attack formation around the large man—an easy target.

One of them stings him on the wrist, another on the back of the neck. He roars with each sting, spinning around with surprising agility and slashing at them with a stick like it was a sword.

Ella feels weaker than she expected. The shovel is too heavy for her and the ground too hard. But she doesn't give up.

Finally something that looks like fabric comes into view.

The shovel falls from her hands.

A musky smell of earth rises to her nostrils.

She reaches towards the bundle of fabric, but doesn't touch it—not yet.

With the discovery quivering on her lips, she turns around

and summons Winter, who seems—oh, no—to be even more harassed by the thick swarm of bees.

Just then a long shadow moves among the apple trees. It bends towards Martti Winter until it's touching his feet.

The bees increase their altitude and veer away.

The dogs howl.

Winter looks at his legs in bewilderment.

"Cold," he whispers.

He flops onto his back in the weeds and mud.

The dogs' racket grows, members of the pack stoking each other's fury. They dash back and forth on the other side of the wall, leaping against the stones in frustration.

Ella covers her ears and leans over. Sweat is running down Winter's broad forehead, which is now as white as marble. He's having difficulty breathing. His pupils are steadily widening—not a good sign.

Ella first pats, then slaps him on the cheeks.

He takes a breath, gestures with a limp hand towards something behind the trees, and gasps, "It's over there. Can you see it? It touched me. Cold as the devil."

Ella turns to look.

Among the trees and spring plants is a blur of something. She can't see it clearly, but she feels a coldness radiating from it. It's a piece of dark winter night, a gaping hole in the fabric of the day.

The phantom.

Its shadow stretches as far as Winter's feet. His massive body is shaken with the power of some internal earthquake. Foam trickles from between his pale lips.

Ella pants in quick breaths.

She stretches out her hand.

She must be trying to touch him. Or maybe she just wants to know what a phantom's shadow feels like.

She stretches out her hand, and the shadow hits her skin.

Her teeth knock together as her body stiffens to a steely tenseness that reaches to every muscle. She makes a feeble sound, and falls.

No names, no memories, no future. Just an empty vessel with the cold of a winter night coiled inside it. Ella collects herself. She gathers her thoughts and feelings like seashells on a deserted beach, searching out her nerve pathways, wiring commands to her muscles.

She is able to rise, but then the earth wrenches her back and her chin slams against the ground.

The tears begin to freeze in her eyes.

She can't seem to direct her own gaze anymore—her eyes stare straight at the phantom. It's moving across the grass, headed towards Winter.

This is what tore up the bird last winter.

Now it's here.

Ingrid Katz bicycles to Martti Winter's house with the Christmas package strapped to the rear rack.

Luckily, there are no dogs in the front garden. They're gathered next to the wall surrounding the back garden, making a racket like it was the last day on earth, their last shred of sense vanished. They must have flushed out a rabbit or a cat, or perhaps Martti's grilling sausages in the back garden and the dogs are complaining of empty stomachs.

Ingrid hurries up the steps, takes out the spare key and opens the door.

She doesn't go directly inside. She holds the door open with her foot long enough to put the key back in her purse. If Martti sees it in her hand he might demand that she give it back.

Something heavy knocks against her side. She falls and tumbles down the stairs. Her tailbone hurts. Her ribs tingle. She screams. Something is pressing down on her chest.

She thinks she's been knocked down by Winter's door, but when she opens her eyes she sees a black snout above her belonging to a large German Shepherd. The dog's front paws are holding her against the ground.

The dog looks off to the side as if unaware that it's holding her down. Its breath stinks. Ingrid feels like throwing up.

When she tries to wriggle free there's a rumble of thunder within the dog and she loses her desire to resist its authority.

She forces herself to breathe. There's no hurry. She can wait for the dog to tire of her and go and do something else. She has a patient nature. The dog clearly doesn't intend to bite her face off, provided she doesn't do anything to make it angry.

Ingrid manages to calm herself. She's a little nervous about what's happening at this moment behind the German Shepherd. At the moment, it's a bit difficult to see anything very well—the dog won't let her—but Ingrid's dreams unfortunately seem to be coming true.

The front door is open.

A parade of dogs is scrambling into Martti Winter's house.

Ella wakes up to the sound of dogs barking.

She's lying on her side on the ground. She sees a beetle

wriggling over her hand. The grass tickles her lips. Her head seems to have changed into an enormously large, heavy iceberg with her teeth chattering inside, but she gathers all her strength and manages to look in the direction the noise is coming from.

Dogs are streaming out of the terrace door into the garden.

She sees large dogs and small dogs, retrievers, collies and pugs, terriers, Great Danes, German Shepherds and spaniels, Belgian Shepherds, greyhounds and mutts.

The garden is full of dogs, and more keep coming. They bound through the trees, statues, and garden lights, an invasion covered in fur. They're not barking now. A fierce war cry rises from their throats, a mixture of growls and howls and various small sounds as they rush with their mouths open towards Ella and Winter.

Ella closes her eyes and lets the cold lull her into oblivion.

A second passes, then perhaps a small eternity. Ella's eyes blink open for a moment—a flash of yellow fangs, red mouths and slobber splashing through the air.

She wraps herself in darkness and breathes in the thick dog smell. The canine army streams over her in a heavy mass of fur. She crouches on her knees and covers her face with her hands as dozens of paws scratch and thud over her.

Somewhere very near the dogs sink their teeth into something and start ripping it to pieces. Ella's consciousness and all the world is pierced by an inhuman cry.

Ella realizes that she's relatively unscathed.

Her feet and hands are cold, stiff as wood and hurting, but when she examines herself she can see that she's not bleeding. The dogs didn't bite her. They just streamed over her and fell upon their enemy.

She crawls farther away from the ripping, snarling pack.

She sighs.

She wipes snot from her face, vomits and pisses her pants. She's alive.

Then she freezes. She's all right, but what about Martti? She turns her trembling head towards the pack of dogs, looking for him. All she can see are hairy paws, leaping rumps and tails.

And a spatter of red.

A cheery dog food commercial starts to churn mockingly through her mind—a woman with a small dog opens a can of "new, more nutritious, and best of all, tastier" dog food. Then she notices dogs running at her from all directions.

"Our best friends certainly know what they want for dinner!" she says.

39

T HE RAGING, snarling commotion doesn't stay put.
The victim at its centre tries to get away. The pack of
dogs shows no mercy, moving with its prey, not letting the biting
circle break for even a second.

Ella can't see anything through her tears. It's all covered by
flowing salt water. She sinks to her knees, her hands behind her
neck, and sways back and forth.

"Dash it," someone says, quite nearby.

Ella wipes her eyes and blinks.

The mêlée continues in a new place now, the dogs growling
and howling. In the spot where they were a moment ago lies
Martti Winter's stout, unmoving body, looking like a beached
whale. He sits up, takes out a white handkerchief, puts it over
his face and expels the contents of his nose into it.

"I thought they'd never leave," he mutters. He plucks hairs
from his clothing and sneezes.

"I think you're allergic to dogs," Ella whispers.

She stares at him and then turns to look at the dogs, who
continue as raucously as before, battling the thing the mapper
called the phantom. They sniffed it out long ago, but it wasn't
until today, after a year of anticipation, that they finally got the
opportunity to do what their instincts demanded.

The furry battlefield moves around the garden like a whirlwind, bounding and barking.

A grey spaniel is left lying on the ground, its side ripped open. Then a small German Shepherd puppy breaks off from the pack, turns around once and slumps limply onto the ground.

Over the next minute the dog army loses more blood into the garden soil. Ella sees eight dogs die in all. Others are left lying wounded, yelping quietly.

They cast dark glances at Ella and Winter.

The dogs refuse to surrender. When one is wounded or killed, the others fight that much more doggedly.

Then, just as the battle is at its most ferocious, the noise ceases totally unexpectedly and the garden is filled with a bewildered silence.

The dogs back away from the circle and start to disperse, glancing around them.

Ingrid Katz appears on the terrace.

"There you are, " she shouts. "I've been looking all over the house for you. Or rather, looking for your mournful remains. I was already planning a pretty funeral for you, and you're out here smelling the flowers. You have a lot of nerve."

Then she looks regretful and says, "Martti, I made a bit of a mistake. The dogs that were in the front garden got in the house. One of them came and… I don't know where they are, but I think…"

She suddenly stops speaking. The German Shepherd lopes past her unconcerned and goes into the house, followed by two small mixed-breed dogs. Then the Shepherd stops, turns around and looks at her expectantly.

Martti Winter wipes his nose and shouts to Ingrid to call a

veterinarian. "Tell them there are injured dogs here. And could you let those dogs out? They want to go home."

Ingrid looks flabbergasted. Martti Winter impatiently waves her back into the house. He'll explain everything later. For now she should just do as he asks.

Ella and Winter walk deeper into the garden.

The day is still beautiful. Dead and wounded dogs are lying here and there. The vet can help the living, they can bury the dead in the garden in a formal ceremony (Winter is moved at this idea and his voice breaks), but first they should finish what they've started.

When they get to the hole, they take out the oilcloth bundle and lay it on the grass, kneel beside it and carefully unwrap the notebook.

They exchange a look. Winter nods, and Ella begins to examine the book. She turns it over in her hands. It smells like old potatoes. The cover is faded almost to grey. All in all it seems to be in one piece.

"Just as I remember it," Winter says, bending over to touch the cover. "My dream book… Well, go ahead and open it. You'll see his name on the first page, in a beautiful, intelligent hand."

Ella opens the notebook.

On the first page there is indeed written, in ornate lettering:

Oskar Södergran

"And on the next page," Winter says, "his notes begin. Turn the page and you'll find all the incredible, marvellous ideas that Oskar thought of and the Rabbit Back Literature Society stole. For thirty years I've dreamed up my own books from the contents of this one."

Ella turns the page. They look at it for a long time without speaking.

"Turn to the next page," Winter says at last.

Ella obeys.

"The next one."

After a few pages, Winter tears the book from her hands and starts flipping through it. They turn page after page, tense, not daring even to look at each other, until they reach the end of the book.

"Dash it," Winter whispers.

Aside from Oskar Södergran's name, not a single word is written in the notebook.

The pages are, however, filled with writing.

At first, the eye can almost make out ancient runes, or magical diagrams of some kind. But when you look more closely, you see that they're just abstract patterns drawn in intricate detail.

It makes Ella think of an address book that you doodle in during long phone conversations—all of the marks obviously took a lot of time and effort, but with no hint of an idea or a purpose.

Martti Winter presses his fingertips against his face and says, "This notebook contained a thousand story ideas. A thousand ideas, just as we suspected. That's how I remember it."

Ella gets up and fetches the letter from the picnic blanket. "It's time we looked at what Oskar's mother has to say," she says, and starts to read the letter aloud.

Dear Miss Milana,

Thank you for your letter! It was wonderful to hear that our poor Oskar made such a big impression on his comrades before his untimely death. He was very proud to receive that notebook, and was always making his own strange little marks in it. He threw quite a fit when he noticed he'd forgotten it at Laura White's house on his final visit there. If his book ended up in the hands of the young writers of the Rabbit Back Literature Society and was some sort of inspiration to them, I can only say that I'm happy to know that there was some small good in his tragic accident. If you do happen to find the notebook, could you possibly send it to me? I wrote Oskar's name on the first page, and the book would have great sentimental value for me.

I understand, of course, if the members of the Society have something else planned for the notebook, but perhaps I could at least see it if I happen to visit Rabbit Back, or if one of you is in our area?

I was saddened to read in the paper about the events at Ms White's house. She had a heart of gold, always looking after Oskar when he was staying with his grandma in Rabbit Back. It was sweet of you to refer to him as the "tenth member" of the Literature Society, and I believe with all my heart that it meant a great deal to him to be with children his own age, although he couldn't communicate with them in the normal manner.

My husband and I always admired Ms White and thought of her very warmly. Although she was a famous author, when I met her on the street with Oskar and my mother, she took time to chat with a humble old woman, and when she heard about Oskar's condition (which nowadays would be called autism), she invited our beautiful but otherwise very challenged child to spend time at her house with the other children who came there regularly.

Of course, we didn't know at the time that those children would become the most important names in Finnish literature. If we had, we would hardly have dared to send our Oskar, who couldn't read or write, among such illustrious company.

Both I and my husband, who has passed away, were avid readers, and because of my husband's visual impairment, I read the classics aloud to him whenever I could. There is a funny anecdote that my mother once told me she'd heard from Laura White: apparently our normally quiet son would often quote long passages from books I'd read aloud by writers such as Melville, Waltari and Proust when he was at her house, which greatly impressed Ms White.

Oskar may have been disabled in many ways, and of course he didn't understand the things he was quoting, but he was granted special gifts like these. If they brought joy to others, that's one more thing for me to be grateful for.

Sincerely,

Mirja Södergran, mother of Oskar

Rabbit Back Mythological Heritage Society

Certificate of
Mythological
Mapping

....
Location (client name and address)

A complete mythological mapping of the above-mentioned location was performed by an accredited mapper, and the following mythological creatures were detected.

REPORT OF RESIDENT MYTHOLOGICAL BEINGS

_____ deceased beings
_____ earth elves
_____ house elves or elves of
other buildings (barn,
playhouse, shed, etc.)
_____ milk or fertility spirits
_____ wood elves
_____ wood nymphs
_____ water nixies
_____ water nymphs
_____ gnomes
_____ gnome animals
type: _____
_____ treasure elves
_____ other mythological
creatures
type: _____
_____ lack of mythological
creatures detected (see
additional information)

Additional information about creatures or other items reported:
....
....
....
....
....
....

I affirm that I saw the
above-mentioned creatures
in a dream

....
Time and location

....
Mapper's signature